BLUE, GRAY &
CRIMSON

BLUE, GRAY & CRIMSON

A STORY OF CIVILIAN COURAGE AT GETTYSBURG

SARAH KAY BIERLE

GAZETTE665

Gazette665
www.Gazette665.com

ISBN-13: 978-0-9862020-0-1
LCCN: 2015909078

Distributed by Itasca Books

Book Design by Emily Keenan

Original Artwork "Up At First Light" by Cheryl Schoenberger, 2015. Used with permission. For additional works of fine art, please visit: cherylschoenberger.fineartstudioonline.com

All Scripture quotations are taken from the The Holy Bible, New King James Version. Copyright 1979, 1980, 1982, Thomas Nelson, Inc.

Printed in the United States of America

To my friend and pen-pal,
Mrs. Stavinoha,
who always believed I could write a book

To my Mom,
who listened to all my ideas,
taught me to study,
and let me be a writer

Foreword

What a genuine pleasure it is to write the foreword for this literary work by Sarah Kay Bierle. I want to thank you, Sarah, for letting me have this opportunity.

Long before Sarah's birth, I had the responsibility of educating Sarah's mother, Susan, in my fifth grade classroom. Little did I know or realize at that time, this teacher/student relationship would grow and prosper into a decades' long friendship. Often at the end of a school year the children in one's class depart, and a teacher is left wondering what the future holds for them. Perhaps one is fortunate enough to run into a former student around town or at a special event, but Susan was not content with accidental meetings. She arranged to faithfully come back to her old elementary school to visit with me each fall on the occasion of my birthday. Susan continued to do so through her high school and college years, and I looked forward to such visits giving me the opportunity to catch up with her life experiences.

It wasn't too many years later that Susan, now as a young married woman, came back to visit with a beautiful, young child accompanying her: Sarah – the first born of three in the marriage of Susan and Shawn. The annual visits took on a totally new dimension with the addition of the children. It was soon evident that Sarah was very much in the mold of her mother, full of enthusiasm for learning all she possibly could each and every day. And these two were a marvelous team as Susan faithfully oversaw the home education of Sarah.

During these homeschooling years, Sarah developed a love of learning and a real affinity for music, first learning piano and then devoting her musical talents to the harp. Though she worked hard in all her studies, music, reading, history, and writing became her favorite subjects.

Susan nurtured Sarah's love of American history during these formative years of education and allowed Sarah to explore the era which fascinated her the most: the mid-nineteenth century and the American Civil War. Working in a collaborative fashion as a mother/daughter team these two have been involved in living history activities throughout Southern California, and now they portray members of an actual family from Civil War era Winchester, Virginia. Sarah has created a blog (www. Gazette665.com) to present relevant information about re-enactments and other facets of history that intrigue her. Her motivation to share what she has learned, especially about civilians and the care of injured Civil War soldiers in both armies, has lead quite naturally to the creation of this literary work.

The protagonist in this writing, Betsy Westmore, actually took form in Sarah's young mind over a decade ago. When Sarah was about nine years of age, she crafted a story involving this fictional young woman during the pivotal battle of Gettysburg. Young Sarah asked me to read her original story, and I encouraged her to continue studying Civil War history and the Battle of Gettysburg. In 2008, Sarah had the opportunity to visit Gettysburg battlefield, and I was excited for her to have this special experience. During more recent years, she has studied/consulted numerous primary sources regarding this battle in Pennsylvania, the treatment of the combatants in its aftermath, and the experiences of Gettysburg civilians.

Sarah has woven a narrative that includes all members of the Westmore family as they watch with great apprehension the coming together of the two great armies of the Civil War near their small community of Gettysburg. The resulting battle creates the need to care for the wounded soldiers, which totally involves the Westmores and their family home.

So I invite you now to read and ponder *Blue, Gray, & Crimson: A Story of Civilian Courage at Gettysburg* by my special friend, Sarah Kay Bierle...

Ted McCord

Ouray, Colorado
February 2015

Chapter 1

The rays of the late June sun burned, causing fourteen-year-old Betsy Westmore to pause in her work and wipe away the sweat under the brim of her straw hat. She straightened from her slightly hunched position and gazed down the long garden rows. Since looking at the work would not accomplish it, she parted the large leaves again, searching for the long green beans ready to be harvested. Handful after handful dropped into the basket at her side as she steadily worked down the row.

Betsy faintly heard the lilting melody her mother sang as she and Rachel, Betsy's eleven-year-old sister, gathered household linens off the clothesline on the other side of the small clapboard house. Betsy had volunteered to work in the garden this afternoon rather than fold the clean sheets and tablecloths. She liked the smell of the rich Pennsylvania soil and the delight of harvesting the vegetables which would be the family's food supply throughout the winter.

However, it seemed hard to focus on the task at hand. Although warm, the day was beautiful, and the road passing by the Westmore farm beckoned with a promise of adventure. That road, the Baltimore Pike, went northwest for about a mile into the nearby town of Gettysburg. There were simple pleasures in town, like ice cream at one of the confectioner's shops, but there were also cool shady groves along the road where it would be nice to relax and enjoy the beauty of the land. Wild raspberry patches could be found, and cool Rock Creek wound through the woodlands bordering the farm fields. Picnics, wading in the shallows of the creek, or berry picking with friends were activities to anticipate when the work was finished.

Although Betsy thought of the pleasant countryside, she was content to work, desiring to help her parents as much as she could. Before leaving for military service, her older brother, Philip, had made her promise to be brave, act responsibly as the oldest child at home, and look after her younger siblings, Rachel and James. She smiled sadly, missing Philip, but hoping he would approve of her efforts.

It had been almost a year since nineteen-year-old Philip Westmore had left home, enlisting in Company B of the 138th Pennsylvania Infantry Regiment with other men and boys from the town and surrounding countryside. He had marched off in a blue wool uniform that barely fit his tall, lanky frame. The bands played, Union flags waved, and the scene had blurred in Betsy's eyes, but she had quickly wiped away the tears. Philip had made her promise not to cry, and promises to her older brother seemed like sacred things.

The war had taken Philip from home, forcing written letters to try to fill the void left behind. For two years, war had raged in America. Southern states had left the Union and formed what they called a separate nation. The northern states and President Lincoln opposed this secession and fought to restore the unity of the country. Although there had been panics in town that Confederate raiders were coming, the war was far away from Gettysburg and its country farms.

Pennsylvania seemed peaceful, though Betsy had heard rumors marching faster than the armies invading the state. Fourteen days earlier, on June 12, 1863, the governor had issued a proclamation calling for emergency militia to defend the state against General Robert E. Lee's Confederate army. Yet, even now, with a Rebel army scattered throughout Pennsylvania, it seemed unlikely the Westmores and their neighbors would ever see the gray-clad enemy. Betsy remembered Father's confident response to the children's fearful questioning. "Why would the Confederates want to come to Gettysburg? And, even if they came, why would they come to our farm?" She had felt calmed by his reasoning. Compared to the capital and large cities, Gettysburg was an insignificant town, surrounded by farms, ridges, and wooded hills.

Glancing at the sun, Betsy estimated it was about half-past three. Almost finished, she thought, looking down the garden row again. She would complete her task in good time and be ready to help Mother prepare supper. A songbird chirped merrily as it hopped along the low picket fence surrounding the garden; laughing at the bird's antics, Betsy plucked a few more of the green beans.

She was about to toss them into the basket when a shot echoed in the quiet land. Startled, she glanced around. Nothing. Shrugging, she dropped the beans and murmured, "Probably just a farmer shooting a wild animal near his chicken coop. It sounded far away." More shots sounded rapidly, one after another. A farmer would not shoot a pesky fox six times. A little alarmed, Betsy stood up, brushed the dirt from her light blue work dress and calico apron, and looked for danger. The house obscured the view of the road toward town, the direction the shots seemed to be coming from. Just to be safe, she decided to find Father and see what he thought was happening.

Before Betsy reached the garden gate, Rachel ran from the house. Her calico sunbonnet had slid off her head, and her two light brown braids flew behind her. "Betsy," she called, her brown eyes wide with fright, "Rebels are coming down the road!"

"Oh, surely that's impossible," Betsy replied, trying to calm her sister's fear.

"No. They're really coming. Mother and I saw them," Rachel insisted anxiously. "Mother says go to the barn and stay with Father. She's going to hide the silver."

More shots and a wild, screeching yell resounded. Betsy dropped the basket, ran through the gate, grabbed Rachel's hand, and sprinted toward the barn, pulling her sister along beside her. Beyond the house, she saw the road to Gettysburg. Four horsemen galloped toward the

Westmore farm, occasionally shooting their pistols into the air and yelling like fiends. She ran faster, her heart pounding. What were the Rebels doing here? What would they want?

The barn, with its stone foundation and wooden structure, stood like a safe stronghold. Seeing Father standing by the small door, Betsy felt reassured. He shielded his eyes and looked at the approaching horsemen, frowning in surprise. James, Betsy's eight-year-old brother, peered out from the doorway, asking excitedly, "What is it, Father? Is it the circus come to town again?"

"No, son," Father calmly said. "It's Confederate cavalry. They've actually come to Gettysburg."

"What will they do?" Betsy asked. "Will they shoot us?" She put her arms protectively around Rachel, who was trembling.

"I don't think they'll shoot us," Father responded. "But I don't know what they want. The rumors I've heard say they want valuables and horses."

"You won't let them take our horses, will you?" James shouted, alarmed at the thought of losing his favorite animals.

"Be quiet, James," Father said firmly. "Do not cause unnecessary trouble. Rachel, where's your mother?"

"In the house. She's hiding some things, and then she said she'll come here."

The noisy band of horsemen turned off the road and cantered on the wagon path around the house toward the barn. The dust from the horses' hooves swirled, dirtying the still-hanging laundry. One of the riders jerked his horse to a stop at the back door of the house and hammered on it with the butt of his pistol while the other three crossed the short distance between the house and the barn, reining in front of Father and the children. These dusty Confederate raiders had patched uniforms, worn saddles, and tired horses, but the fierce expression on the men's faces made Betsy shiver. Rachel inched behind her older sister. James scowled from the doorway.

"Afternoon, folks," one of the soldiers said in a gruff Southern accent. "I think y'all might have some things that'd be useful to us or to Gen'l Early whose brigade's up in yer town."

"And what, precisely, are you looking for?" Father replied, his arms folded across his chest.

"Ha! That's a good one," the leader laughed to his companions. "By lookin' at us, I'd thought you'd know we need us some new horses, cool water, and a good dinner."

"Well, I'm sure we can get you some water and maybe even a good meal, but most of the farmers around here have sent their horses away for safety." Father spoke with polite firmness.

"Open up yer barn there," the Rebel leader ordered, suspiciously eyeing the closed doors, "and prove that you've sent yers away, then, mister."

Reluctantly, Father unfastened the latch on the big barn doors, and three of the Rebels rode inside, whooping delightedly when they saw two strong farm horses standing placidly in their stalls. James and Father followed them inside. The fourth Rebel eyed the girls; Betsy shifted uncomfortably, unsure what to do.

Mother, carrying a bucket of water and some tin cups, came across the yard, looking as calm as if she was going to visit neighbors. Her brown calico dress hung straight, and her dark hair was smoothed neatly back. She exhibited no rush or panic in her movements; only the lack of a smile betrayed her nervousness. Betsy stood a little straighter, trying to copy her mother's composed attitude. Philip had told her to be brave, and she would not show the Rebels she was afraid.

Mother went near the fourth soldier, who had dismounted, and said, "Here's the water you requested."

"Good to know that banging on a door can get what I want around here. I'll have a drink in a minute. Right now, I've got to collect me my dinner."

The girls moved to Mother's side and held her hands. They noticed the soldier was unfastening some large sacks from the back of his saddle. "What are you doing?" Mother asked in a puzzled tone.

"Gonna take yer chickens. They'll make good eatin' tonight, ma'am," he replied, grinning antagonistically.

"Oh," Rachel quavered. She liked the chickens and treated them almost like pets.

He strode to the chicken coop beside the barn and went inside. The hens' cackling protest was the only sound as the other raiders rode from the barn, leading the Westmores' two black horses, Abby and Mary. Father followed them slowly, holding onto James's shoulder to keep him from doing anything rash.

Betsy blinked angrily, determined not to cry. It wasn't right! The Confederates weren't supposed to come to Gettysburg, and now, here they were: stealing most of the animals.

"Hey, Trooper Mart, where are ye?" the leader called, seeing the empty saddle of the fourth raider's horse.

"Here ye are," Mart cried triumphantly, emerging from the chicken coop with flopping, clucking sacks. "Pan fried chicken alright fer supper, sir?"

"Mighty fine. Here. Let me hold those for ye while ye mount up. Oh, and folks, how 'bout if some of ye hand us some of the cold water."

"I'll throw it on them," James muttered, kicking dust. Father shushed him. Mother stepped forward and handed a full tin cup to the leader.

"Well, don't just stand there gapin', girls," the chicken-thief called. Rachel was too frightened to move. Although upset, Betsy followed her parents' unresisting example and obeyed, handing him a full cup of water.

"Yeah, wouldn't mind livin' in Pennsylvania, myself. Good horses and chickens are free fer the takin'," he chortled. Betsy's face burned with anger, but she looked down and did not respond.

The leader mockingly thanked the family and then

signaled his companions to ride off. The chicken thief tossed his tin cup at Betsy's feet, spurred his horse, and rode away with the others. Laughing and singing "Dixie" in their out-of-tune voices, they departed, leading the faithful farm horses and carrying two sacks of chickens.

Rachel sat down on a straw pile and started crying. Mother pressed her lips together, put her arm around Father, and leaned her head on his shoulder. With a tense, unreadable expression, Father stared at the departing horsemen and possessions. "I hate Confederates," James announced, stomping the ground. "They're mean. They took Father's and my horses."

Watching the noisy foursome trot back up the pike toward town, Betsy felt her world was not quite as secure as it had been a quarter of an hour before. She looked at the feathers fluttering from the open coop door and at the empty cup at her feet, and her mind echoed James's sentiments.

Chapter 2

Be brave, Betsy thought, smoothing the gingham cloth over the dining room table and stepping through the open doorway into the kitchen to gather eating utensils and five china plates from the dish cabinet. She wanted to forget the raid and pretend it never happened, but reality tugged at her heart. If the Confederates came once, couldn't they come again? Who knew what they might do the next time they came? The afternoon's events made Betsy realize the vulnerability of her location in the world.

In the kitchen, the aroma of fresh cornbread united with the smell of frying fish, creating a delicious scent. The dull chopping sound of Rachel's knife beat a steady cadence as she cut some of the green beans. She glanced apprehensively out the kitchen window toward the barn and shuddered. "Mother, do you think Philip has seen Confederates like those we saw?" Rachel questioned hesitantly.

"I don't think so," Mother replied, replacing a jar of dried herbs on the kitchen shelf with a thump. She returned to the cook stove, directly across the room from Rachel, where she was pan frying some fish Father and James had caught in Rock Creek early that morning.

She added, "From his letters, Philip's regiment has been guarding locations. They haven't been in battles."

"But if those Rebels saw Philip, they could hurt him," Betsy said seriously. "Maybe they didn't hurt us because we're civilians, but they could hurt Philip."

An oppressive silence descended on the kitchen; the events of the afternoon replaced the usually cheerful atmosphere with concern and apprehension. As Betsy filled the washbasin on the medium-sized wooden table between the stove and the window worktable, she regretted her comment.

"That's true," Mother admitted, responding to her oldest daughter's statement. "But thank God Philip hasn't been in danger thus far." She wiped her hands on her apron with a gesture of finality, as if pushing away the dangerous thoughts. "Betsy, please run down to the cellar and bring up some butter. Then, you may cut the cornbread."

Betsy carefully raised the large trap door in the kitchen floor to the right of the stove and went down the steep stairs into the underground chamber. When she was little, Betsy had been terrified to go into the cellar alone, fearing a monster would grab her, but now she knew there were no giant beasts in the cellar. The large underground room contained bins for potatoes, carrots, and other vegetables; small barrels of other supplies stood in the far corners where the light did not illuminate. The shelves, normally lined with preserved fruits, vegetables, or jams, were mostly empty. Summer was the season to eat the fresh foods from the garden or fields and begin preserving them for the winter months.

As she emerged from the cellar bringing a small crock of butter, Father and James came in, the former carrying two pails of fresh milk. The meal preparations were finished quickly, and the family gathered at the dining table, ready to begin their evening meal. Father sat at the head of the table, facing the open sitting room door, and Mother sat at the opposite end. The girls sat to Father's left; James sat across from Rachel, next to Mother.

A cool breeze drifted through the open dining room window, and Betsy glanced toward the Baltimore Pike. No one was coming right now. Good. She knew for a long time she would be alert for coming raiders. Security, even at home, was threatened.

Rachel nudged her, and Betsy reached out to hold hands and bowed her head. Father's low voice prayed solemnly. "Heavenly Father, we thank You for the provision of this food and for the safety You gave us this afternoon. I ask that You help those Confederate men to understand that stealing is wrong. And I ask that You give us grace to forgive them. In Jesus's name, Amen."

When the food had been silently passed around the table and the plates were filled, James said, "You know, I've been thinking…" He paused to take a bite of fish.

"Yes?" Mother prompted when he finished chewing.

"Well," James began, "it's too bad Philip isn't here. If he'd been here this afternoon, he'd have had his rifle, and he could've shot those Rebels, and we'd still have our horses and chickens."

Father cleared his throat. "James, that's enough. Even if Philip had been here, it wouldn't be wise for one man to start a fight, and, if the regiment was here, there would have been a battle before the Confederates got into town."

"A battle would've been a fine thing!" James exclaimed, gesturing with his fork.

"Battles are not 'fine things,' as you call them," Father said solemnly.

"Oh, but soldiers fight in battles. They do brave things. They could've defended the town, and then the raiders would never have got down here. If the war lasts 'til I'm old enough, can't I enlist? I want to be a soldier. I really want to be a cavalryman and have a horse. What do you think, Father? Would that be alright?"

Father laid down his knife and looked patiently at James. "You're eight years old, Son. If the war is still being fought in ten years, we'll think about your idea. We've discussed war and soldiers before. I'm going to remind you that you have not seen war. You don't know what it is."

"Philip does. I'll ask him when he gets home," James murmured. "He'll tell me about glorious cavalry charges with courageous soldiers and fiery steeds, or infantry marching into battle with their flags, or artillery firing loud shots."

Betsy, Rachel, and James looked up to Philip, not just because he was taller than them, but because he was a good example, an attentive listener, and always ready for innocent fun after completing chores. It was hard with him away; he wrote frequently to everyone, but words on paper did not fill the void his absence produced. Words couldn't replace his laugh, his thoughtful actions, or his confident attitude; they could not substitute his good humor during a water fight in Rock Creek, his industrious work in the fields, or his patient help with arithmetic sums for school. Betsy even longed for him to tease her or tell her to leave him alone when he was trying to read – things she had not liked before. Although the children copied their parents' example of pride in Philip's service for their nation, there was always the knowledge that he wasn't there.

"Do you think our army will come here, Father?" Rachel asked hopefully. "They could drive away those bad Confederates."

"I don't know. The newspapers and the rumors in town cannot decide where the two armies actually are, but I don't think the entire Union army is going to come here to chase off some raiders inconveniencing the civilians."

"Oh," Rachel said, looking down. "I was thinking the army would come, and then I wouldn't be scared anymore."

"Put your trust in God, Daughter, not in an army. Armies can be defeated, but God is the same yesterday, today, tomorrow, and for all eternity." He finished the last bite of fish on his plate, and said cheerfully, "That was a delicious meal, Martha. Thank you. Now, children, I want you to help your mother with the dishes, and then we'll have our time of scripture reading."

"Do I have to help the girls?" James asked, disdainfully wrinkling his nose.

"Yes. They've worked hard to put this meal on the table, and I'm sure you can help them clean up. I'm going to haul some buckets of water and bring in extra firewood so breakfast can be cooked in the morning."

Mother washed the dishes; James and Rachel dried the plates and utensils, racing each other to see who could do the job most efficiently. Betsy shook out the tablecloth and folded it neatly before sweeping the floor and checking the oil in the lamps. Father brought in the water and wood and carried out the dishwater. In a quarter of an hour, the chores were completed.

Chapter 3

Twilight filled the sitting room, but the oil lamps banished the shadows to the corners of the room. Mother sat in a comfortable rocking chair in front of the tall bookcase that was filled with practical and beautiful books. The books were one of Mother's treasures; she had been a schoolteacher before she met and married Mr. Henry Westmore. She always enjoyed an interesting story and taught her children to appreciate good literature. Tonight, Mother seemed tense, but her expression was calm, and she busily knit a stocking for a soldier far from home. Her smooth brown hair was pulled into a low bun, and her dark brown eyes darted from the work in her lap to Father, who was adjusting his reading spectacles.

Father's work-calloused hands opened the family Bible. He moved quickly through the beginning pages, where the names of generations of Westmores of Gettysburg were written, until he found the passage he wanted. The lamplight illuminated Father's strong features, his determined, squared jaw, short sideburns, and blue eyes. He appeared stern and unapproachable, except for his warm smile which softened his whole face and conveyed friendliness and understanding. Father usually had a cheerful expression radiating from his eyes or the corners of his mouth, but tonight he looked grim, like a solemn king ready to pass gentle judgment.

The children waited silently for Father to begin. Betsy and Rachel sat near a small table and lamp, sewing shirtsleeves. James sprawled cross-legged on the braided rug, strategizing an imaginary battle with pebbles he had collected from the creek.

"Children," Father began, "this afternoon and during dinner, I heard some of you using various descriptive words when speaking about the Confederate raiders, and at least one of you expressed that you hated them." He looked at James. "What the Confederates did wasn't right. They took things that were not theirs. Unfortunately, this is what happens in war. War is one of the ultimate expressions of man's sinfulness."

"They really deserve everlasting punishment, don't they?" James exclaimed angrily.

"Don't we all?" Father asked pointedly. "Aren't we all sinners in God's eyes, saved only by His grace received through faith? No, children, we shouldn't hate them. We're told in Luke, chapter six, to do good and pray for those who wrong us."

Betsy blushed guiltily. She knew she should forgive those raiders, but it seemed so hard. They had taken the horses, the source of transportation and power for farm fieldwork. They had taken the chickens, a food source. Her conscience nagged her.

Father continued. "I want us to avoid unkind words and thoughts. I know it may be hard, but we must try to forgive them. If you've been thinking hateful thoughts, I want you to ask the Lord to forgive you. Alright?"

Betsy momentarily considered bargaining with God – if the Confederates would never come back, she'd forgive them. She shook her head; negotiation was not obedience or trust. Betsy bent her head over her work and closed her eyes, whispering under her breath, "Please, Lord, help me forgive them. Please forgive me for hating them this afternoon. But please, I humbly ask, don't ever let them come here again." The guilty feeling lifted, and she contentedly listened while Father read two chapters from the Book of Ephesians.

After Father finished, Mother said, "I think we should work on our recitations tonight. Who would like to go first?"

"I will!" James responded, hopping to a kneeling position. He was very enthusiastic about his verse, especially since Philip had suggested it in a letter. "Second Timothy, chapter two, verse three: 'You therefore must endure hardship as a good soldier of Jesus Christ.' "

"Very good," Father said. "You'll need to choose a new verse to work on. Maybe you could do that tomorrow. Rachel, will you recite as far as you can in your passage?"

Nodding, Rachel waited until Father found the place in the Bible, then she began in her soft, clear voice. "Psalm Twenty-three, the shepherd's psalm: 'The Lord is my shepherd; I shall not want…' " Reverently, she recited the attributes of God's care for His people, and only stumbled slightly in the last two verses. "I'll keep working on the ending," she said apologetically after Father helped her finish.

"I think I've finished learning my psalm," Betsy said eagerly. Father turned a couple of pages, nodding for her to begin. "Psalm Forty-six," she said firmly, ready to recite the poetry of providence and protection.

> "God is our refuge and strength,
> A very present help in trouble.
> Therefore we will not fear,
> Even though the earth be removed,
> And though the mountains be carried into the midst of the sea;
> Though its waters roar and be troubled,
> Though the mountains shake with its swelling.
> There is a river whose streams shall make glad the city of God,
> The holy place of the tabernacle of the Most High.
> God is in the midst of her, she shall not be moved;
> God shall help her, just at the break of dawn.
> The nations raged, the kingdoms were moved;
> He uttered His voice, the earth melted.
> The Lord of hosts is with us;
> The God of Jacob is our refuge.
> Come, behold the works of the Lord,
> Who has made desolations in the earth.
> He makes wars cease to the end of the earth;

He breaks the bow and cuts the spear in two;
He burns the chariot in the fire.
Be still and know that I am God;
I will be exalted among the nations,
I will be exalted in the earth!
The Lord of hosts is with us;
The God of Jacob is our refuge."

"Nicely done, Daughter. You remembered every line perfectly."

Betsy smiled, pleased that her efforts had finally reached the standard of excellence. "Father," she asked, "why do you and Mother want us to memorize so many verses? Couldn't we just read them in the Bible?"

"There may be a time or situation when you cannot stop and search for a passage in scripture," Father explained. "Memorizing portions of God's Word prepares your mind and heart to recall His truth when you need encouragement or an answer 'for the hope that is in you.' Learning scripture will help you praise God in joyous times and give you strength in life's challenges. It isn't mindless memory work."

Betsy nodded understandingly, and Father said to Mother, "Shall we sing a hymn?"

Smiling, Mother agreed. James's hand waved wildly to gain her attention. "Yes?"

"Can we sing *Stand Up for Jesus*? It's a good song about brave soldiers, you know."

"Alright." Mother hummed for a moment and then

started while Betsy and Rachel chimed in their alto and soprano voices, and Father's bass added yet another musical dimension. James warbled loudly, but out of tune, occasionally making up lyrics when he could not remember.

> *"Stand up, stand up for Jesus, Ye soldiers of the cross*
> *Lift high His royal banner, It must not suffer loss;*
> *From victory unto victory, His army shall He lead,*
> *Till every foe is vanquished, And Christ is Lord indeed..."*

They sang the four stanzas of the hymn, and, as the notes of an "Amen" faded smoothly, the clock struck half-past eight, the chime making the final music of the evening. "Bedtime," Mother announced, putting away her knitting and preparing to light the lamps to be taken upstairs.

The shadowy night melted away like fears during songs as Betsy and Rachel carried lighted lamps to the bedrooms upstairs. Betsy carried her lamp down the hall into the second front bedroom and placed it carefully on the bedside table.

"Thanks for carrying the lamp for me," James said, leaning on the bedpost and watching her adjust the wick. "When do you think Mother'll think I'm big enough to carry it by myself?" Betsy only shrugged, so he chattered on, his voice becoming serious. "You know, I used to always wish I could have a room all to myself. I always thought Philip hogged the covers and snored too loudly, but now I'd be happy to let him have all the covers and snore so loud it would wake me every night, 'cause then he'd be home." He ended in a whisper.

"We all miss him, James," Betsy said, giving him a hug.

"But," and his face brightened, "he's a soldier with a blue coat and gold buttons with eagles on them. I wish I had a button like that."

"Well, I think you should get ready for bed. Don't forget to blow out the lamp, alright?"

"I won't. G'night."

"Good-night," Betsy replied, closing the door behind her and entering the bedroom that she and Rachel shared.

She pulled out the hairpins which secured her braided bun and dropped them in the small dish on the dressing table. Clothes hung neatly on a row of pegs, and Betsy slipped on her long nightgown. She blew out the lamp and flopped onto the mattress beside Rachel, who pulled the hand-sewn quilt over them to keep away the cool air.

Betsy was almost asleep when Rachel's soft voice murmured, "Do you think those Confederates will come back tomorrow?"

"I don't know," Betsy said hesitantly. She did not want to frighten Rachel, and she could not find the right words to describe the feeling, but, for the first time in her life, she felt really afraid. It had always seemed home was forever safe and untouchable by frightening incidents. The events of the afternoon revealed that home was not always a safe refuge when danger threatened the homeland.

Chapter 4

Betsy opened her eyes, startled. It was just a dream, at least that is what she hoped. Sliding out of bed and lifting the curtain on the window revealed the empty road. She breathed a sigh of relief. No Confederate raiders. The soft morning light indicated it was time to be up and getting ready for the day's work.

Rachel moaned. "Do I have to get up?"

"Oh, yes. Good morning, dearest Sister," Betsy said cheerfully.

"Fine ladies never have to get up early. I wonder what that'd be like."

"You're not a fine lady. Besides, who'd want to lie abed and miss the cool morning air and those happily singing birds?" Betsy responded sharply. She had little patience with her sister's daydreams of a wealthy lifestyle.

Betsy poured water from the pitcher into the washbasin, washed her face, and then turned toward the small oak vanity table and mirror which Grandfather Westmore had made years ago. She sat down in front of the table and brushed her dark brown hair, parted it, and plaited it into a single long braid. Carefully, she twisted the braid into a knot at the base of her neck and poked hair pins into the coil to hold it in place. She put on her stockings and shoes next; it would be fun to go barefoot all the time in the summer, but that wasn't proper for a young lady, especially when the Westmores could afford shoes. Glancing in the mirror, she noticed Rachel still lounging in bed. "Come on, get up," she scolded. "Mother expects us downstairs, and I need help with my stays."

"Again?"

"Well, I haven't yet mastered the stays' laces in the back." The corded stays were like a soft corset, but were not intended to be pulled tightly; they helped with good posture and provided comfortable modesty. Slowly, Rachel climbed from bed and began tightening the laces until the stays fit comfortably over the chemise and drawers.

"Thanks," Betsy said as she pulled two petticoats over her head. Fashionable ladies might wear hooped skirts, but that was not practical on the farm. Sometimes, though, Betsy wished she could try on a hoop, just to see what it was like. She fastened the wooden buttons on her light blue bodice and slid the outer skirt over her head, asking Rachel to clasp it in the back.

"Your collar's crooked," Rachel commented and then smoothed the white linen around the bodice neckline. "There, now won't you help me with my skirt?"

"Do you want me to do your hair?" Betsy asked.

"No, thank you. I can manage it today, though won't you do it tomorrow since we'll be going to church, and I'll want to look very nice?"

"Sure. Just think, next year you'll be twelve and can start wearing your hair in a bun."

"I'll look very grown up, won't I?" Rachel responded gleefully, resting her cheek on her hand and making a flirtatious face in the mirror.

Betsy smoothed the white bed sheets and spread the log cabin quilt neatly. She had finished this first quilt last year and was delighted with the different pastel calico fabrics she had collected or exchanged with friends. Light calicos – whites, creams, or yellows – made half of each log cabin square while a variety of muted pastels formed the other side. Mother said someday it would be beautiful in the guest-room of Betsy's house when she got married. Betsy smiled innocently; she had to grow up first before she thought about such things too seriously.

"I'm going down to help Mother with breakfast," she told Rachel, who was attempting to twist her hair into a fashionable style. "Stop dawdling and braid your hair neatly."

The girls' bedroom was one of four, opening into the upstairs hallway. James's room, or "the boys' room," was to the left, and across the hall were Father and Mother's room and the guest-room. Two windows, one at each end of the hall, let in light. Under the far window stood a large chest, almost spanning the width of the hall and storing extra quilts until the winter months necessitated their use. The wooden stairs led the way to the lower level.

The last stair squawked loudly, announcing Betsy's arrival into the downstairs hallway which led toward the front door of the house. Halfway down the hallway were doors from the sitting room to the right and the parlor to the left. Betsy stepped directly into the sitting room through an open doorway across from the stairs; two more steps would take her through another doorway into the dining room and the kitchen beyond to the right.

She paused in the sitting room and went to straighten the large braided rug in front of the fireplace. The fireplace and chimney, located along the western wall, were not used during the summer months. Against the wall across from the fireplace was the bookcase; Mother's rocking chair was in front of the shelf, and Father's comfortable chair stood guard close beside it. Small tables and a couple of wooden chairs were placed around the room. A desk was in one corner, equipped with paper, pens, and ink for letter writing. The windows, one facing the pike and the other toward the west, were framed with pretty curtains.

Betsy went through the dining room and into the kitchen where she cheerfully greeted Mother. The preparations for breakfast included setting the table, carefully watching the bread as it toasted, and cooking the eggs.

"I guess this will be the last of the fresh eggs for a while," Mother commented. "I wonder if any of our neighbors have chickens left after the raid. Maybe we could trade for eggs or purchase new poultry from them. Until we get more chickens, I suppose we won't be able to do much baking."

"And imagine how upset Philip would be," Betsy commented. "Remember how many eggs he could eat for breakfast?"

"Yes, I imagine the hardtack he writes about is not as filling," Mother answered, smiling. "As for our chickens… I'll be charitable and hope the Confederates had a good dinner." Betsy shrugged, not anxious to discuss the events of yesterday and hoping to banish it to the forgotten past.

Rachel appeared, her hair neatly braided into two side braids. She smiled and said, "Good morning, Mother. Is James with Father in the barn?" Before Mother could answer, three taps echoed on the kitchen wall above the stove. "I guess not," Rachel murmured, replying to her own question. Every morning, James knocked on the wall separating the kitchen and the stairway. It was an old trick he had learned from Philip; the boys claimed it was a secret code to Mother, a signal to remind her of their love.

"Good morning!" James exclaimed, dashing into the kitchen. He skidded to a stop, nearly running into Betsy, who was carrying a pitcher of fresh milk to the dining room. "I'm pretty sure that the Union troops are coming today, and those wretched – I mean, um – Confederates will have to leave. Sorry, didn't mean to call them names," he explained apologetically to Father, who had come in and heard the comment.

After breakfast, the girls helped with the household chores and then went outside. James joined Mother and the girls in the garden. Pulling weeds, harvesting ripe vegetables, and repairing the rabbits' hole under the fence were tasks that Mother assigned. The day was overcast, and, though Betsy watched the road as best she could with the house blocking the view, no gray-clad troops appeared. Despite James's announcements, no Union soldiers came either. Betsy wondered what the Confederates had done in town and if they had left the area. Had the Gettysburg residents known about the coming raid, or were they surprised like the Westmores?

Mother and the children finished the garden work by mid-morning and sat down under one of the fruit trees in the orchard. Father joined them there. "The west field will be ready to cut and harvest next week," he said. "I'll speak with some of our neighbors at church tomorrow to see if I can arrange to borrow their horses and ask them to help with the harvesting. Some of them were going to send their horses away when they heard the Confederates were coming. Of course, I will repay our neighbors by helping when their fields are ready. I think Thursday of next week would be a good day for cutting the grain. Is that a convenient day for you, Martha?"

"That should be fine. I'm glad the crop will be good this year," Mother answered joyfully.

"Yes, God is good. Children, did I ever tell you about what happened to the crops seventeen years ago?"

"No, I don't think so," Betsy replied for all of them.

"There was a locust plague," Father explained. "Grasshoppers invaded and ate every green thing in the countryside. The fields were destroyed. All the crops were lost which was a hardship for many families. The creeks got contaminated when hundreds of grasshoppers fell in and drowned. It was an invasion. Some of the older farmers predicted that there would not be an invasion and destruction like it for another seventeen years. Thus far, there have been no grasshoppers this season, and the weather has been uncommonly overcast and somewhat cool. I think the crops will be fine this year."

"Was it like the locust plague in Egypt when Moses was arguing with Pharaoh?" Rachel asked.

"Well, I don't know for certain," Father said teasingly. "I'm not old enough to have lived way back then, but it certainly seemed very much like what I think the Egyptian locust plague must have been like."

"I wish I'd been here to see all those grasshoppers," James said with a mischievous glint in his eye.

"I'd enough trouble keeping two-year-old Philip from eating them," Mother laughed. "And Charles was born that year. I remember, Henry, we were worried about how to make ends meet."

"Charles?" James questioned. Betsy poked him and shook her head.

"You remember," Mother said softly. "We've told you about Charles. He was your older brother, but he died in 1856, when you were only a year old, James."

"Why did he die?" James asked.

"It was a childhood disease. None of our home remedies helped, and there was nothing the doctor could do either," Mother answered quietly while her eyes filled with tears. Betsy looked at the surrounding hills, trying to forget those sad days.

Finally, Father cleared his throat and said, "Look, some of those cherries are ripe and ready to be picked. Unless you have other plans, Martha, how about if we work here in the orchard?"

The orchard included two cherry trees, a peach tree, a plum tree, and a couple of apple trees planted in a row southeast of the garden. The girls got baskets, and Mother put away the garden tools while Father went to retrieve a short ladder with James tagging along.

It was fun to stand on the ladder and pluck the early harvest of cherries from the branches. The children took turns climbing up to pick the fruit while Father thinned the green peaches on the nearby tree.

"Can we bake a pie?" Rachel asked as they carried the baskets to the house.

"Yes," Mother replied, smiling.

"I'm glad we don't have to go to school right now."

"Well, you wouldn't go on Saturday, silly," Betsy mockingly replied.

"Don't call me 'silly.' I'm not!" Rachel retorted.

"Girls, that's enough. It's not kind to argue and call names. As for school, you aren't attending classes at the country school because the board couldn't find a teacher for a summer term, but I think we will work on lessons here at home."

"Do we have to?" Rachel asked reluctantly.

"Yes. In the afternoons when it gets warm, you children will work on your studies. We'll plan to start after the

Fourth of July. Is that a fair compromise?"

"Oh, yes, Mother. When is Fourth of July?"

"On the fourth day of the month of July," Mother teased. "But I suppose you mean what day? Saturday, a week from today."

"Will we go into town or have a picnic with our friends?" Betsy asked eagerly.

"I don't know yet. We'll have to ask Father if he has any plans and talk to our friends."

They cooked a hearty dinner, typically eating their large meal at mid-day. Last evening had been an exception because the men got back late from their morning fishing trip. During the meal, Betsy asked Father about the Fourth of July.

"I'm thinking a picnic might be nice. Mr. Spangler and Mr. Wolf both mentioned to me that they were happy to have folks picnic at the pretty spots on their properties. What do you think, Martha?"

"I'm partial to going to the lovely meadow near Wolf's Hill. We've been to Spangler's Spring earlier this year. Maybe the Thorns and some of our other friends from town might like to meet us there."

"Could we get some firecrackers?" James requested. "And could we invite Gates Fahnestock and Charles McCurdy to join us?" Those boys were his special friends.

"We'll see what the Fahnestock and McCurdy families are planning. Yes, I think we'll get some firecrackers, but you must promise not to annoy your sisters with them."

"You mean I can't set off a firecracker behind Rachel and see her jump a hundred feet into the air, like I did last year?"

"James Westmore!" Mother exclaimed. "No, that's not the right thing to do. You know Rachel doesn't like loud noises. Do you recall your punishment for that unkind act?" Nodding regretfully, James promised to "be good."

After the meal and kitchen chores, Mother agreed to the children's request to play hide-n-seek, on the condition the girls would come into the house later to help with the sewing. The children determined the game's boundaries: they could hide in the barn, barnyard, garden, or orchard, but not the house, the fields, or the woods. The seeker had to stay by the well, which was between the house and the barn, keep their eyes closed, and count to one hundred.

Laughter burst like a ray of sunshine as they forgot their apprehension of returning Rebel raiders. Betsy had felt the threatening cloud of war dissipate throughout the peaceful morning. Now, only Philip and his creative hiding places could have made the fun better.

They played a few rounds of the game and were just beginning again when Mr. Nathaniel Lightner came striding from the house toward the barn. "Good afternoon, Mr. Lightner," Betsy called pleasantly.

"Good day to you, children," he replied, but without his usual smile. "Your mother told me your father is in the barn, is that correct?"

"Yes, sir."

"Thank you. I'll speak to him there."

"Aww...I guess the Lightner children didn't come," James lamented. "It'd be fun to have more people to look for. I mean, I always know where my sisters hide." Mr. and Mrs. Lightner and their six children lived a little northwest of the Westmores on the other side of the Baltimore Pike, and the children enjoyed playing together when they could.

"You won't find me so easily this time," Betsy promised. "Now, start counting."

The girls hurried off as James shouted numbers. Betsy ran into the barn and glanced around. Father and Mr. Lightner must be in the paddock, she thought happily; she didn't want to eavesdrop. Betsy slipped behind the open door of the dusty feed room and waited.

James called that he was coming and, through the crack in the door hinge, she saw him enter the barn and climb up into the loft. Suddenly, a figure stood near the doorway, and Mr. Lightner's voice said, "Of course, I'd be happy to loan you my team next week, but I actually came to tell you the Rebels are gone. They took what they wanted in the town, burned the railroad bridge over Rock Creek, but they're gone. Marching north toward York. I don't think they'll be back."

Betsy breathed a sigh of relief. That news was reassuring. No more reason to fearfully watch the Baltimore Pike. "Thank you, God," she murmured.

"No one in town was injured, I hope?" Father asked.

"Not in town. But James McAllister was over at my

place this morning, all fired up angry and rightfully so, I guess. You knew George Sandoe?"

"Slightly acquainted. He seems like a good young man. He had joined the emergency cavalry troop, right?"

"Yes," Mr. Lightner said solemnly. "According to McAllister, he was fleeing like the rest of his unit, and he was pursued by some Rebels. Those Confederates were shooting at him, but Sandoe wasn't returning fire. One of the shots hit Sandoe, and he fell from his horse. Dead. McAllister saw it, and he was madder than a bear. Went out and read those Rebels the riot act about shooting a man in the back when he was not even returning their shots."

Betsy pressed her hand against the solid wood wall behind her. No! The dark cloud descended, just when she thought it had lifted. The community had been touched by war.

Chapter 5

The next day, standing outside the church after the service concluded, Betsy realized how disruptive the Confederate raid had been. Everyone had a tale about the shocking events on Friday. Father and Mother talked with some of their acquaintances while the children waited politely.

Beside her, Rachel gave an undertone commentary on ladies' fashions as she noted the dresses of the town women. Betsy self-consciously tugged on the too-short sleeves of her light brown Sunday dress and straightened her straw bonnet, trimmed with brown ribbon and pretty dried flowers. By her comments, Rachel indicated she could not wait to exchange her pale green frock, hemmed mid-calf in girlish fashion, and little straw hat trimmed with green ribbon for the long, full skirts worn by young ladies.

Wearied by the fashion monolog, Betsy looked around for James. She sighed. He was drawing in the dirt and explaining a military strategy to his friend, Gates Fahnestock. The knees of his trousers would be filthy, already his white shirt was smudged, and his coat had been carelessly unbuttoned.

"Greetings, Miss Westmore," called a girlish voice, and, turning, Betsy saw Miss Tillie Pierce and her family. The girls were about the same age and had met at social events in town. Mr. Pierce, Tillie's father, owned the butcher shop, and the family lived in a nice brick townhouse along Baltimore Street. Tillie said something to her mother, who nodded, and Tillie crossed the dirt street quickly. "Good day, Betsy and Rachel. I was so worried about you all. Did the Confederates go to your farm?" Betsy explained what had happened.

"Wasn't it awful?" Tillie exclaimed. "I mean, I never thought the Confederates would actually come to Gettysburg, and then they were here. I had to run home from school. Oh, did I tell you that I'm now attending the school for young ladies on West High Street?"

"No, I didn't know that," Betsy replied. "Did the Confederates take your horse?" she asked, remembering how much Tillie admired a beautiful horse the Pierce family owned.

"Yes. We begged them not to, but they did anyway. Then – it really was too provoking – they rode the poor animal up and down the street in front of our house until it was nearly lame. And there wasn't anything we could do about it. Weren't those soldiers the dirtiest men you ever saw? One of them was so covered in dust that he blended into the road when he was sitting on our doorstep."

"Well, I'm glad they have gone away."

"So am I. Did you ever think there could be such excitement in our town?"

"No," Betsy responded. "I hope the Confederates won't come back." Tillie nodded solemnly, and Betsy resolutely changed the subject. "What is your family doing on the Fourth of July? Will I see you at a picnic?"

"I think so."

Rachel said, "Betsy's going to help me piece a quilt of my own. Do you think we could trade some fabric pieces like you did with my sister?"

"Of course, that would be fun," Tillie agreed. "Can you bring what you have to the Fourth of July events, and I'll do the same? Mother has some really pretty fabric left over from a dress, and you'd like the pattern."

"Thank you," Rachel said, very pleased.

"Do you think your mother will be able to send some canned fruits or vegetables for the soldiers?" Tillie asked. "My mother was wondering if she would." Mrs. Pierce helped to organize the efforts of the Gettysburg's Ladies' Union Relief Society, collecting food, clothing, bandages, and other items to send to the army.

"Probably," Betsy replied. "I'll ask her, and I'm sure she'll let Mrs. Pierce know."

"Alright. I need to go home now, but I'm so glad I saw you today."

The friends said farewell, and Betsy turned to see where James had gone. He was sitting on the edge of the sidewalk, chatting with one of his chums. A few minutes later, the boy's father called to him, and he scampered away while James came to tell his sisters the news.

"Guess what? Charles McCurdy says that he watched from his front porch when all the Rebels came to town.

He said he wasn't scared. Anyway, he also went walking 'round town, and he heard that the general – I think his name was Early – wanted to get a lot of money. The town leaders said they didn't have that much money, but the soldiers could get things in the stores. So Charles was walking by Mr. Winter's Candy Store, and there was this long line of soldiers outside the store, and some of them were banging on the door. Well, Mr. Winter had to come out and open the shop, and then the soldiers got lots of candy. They paid for it in Confederate money, but Charles says that's worthless, so I guess they got it for free. I sure wish I'd been in town because Charles said that, as he sat there, this friendly-looking cavalry guy came out, and his hat was full of candy. Heaping full of yummy candy..." James paused dreamily.

"What happened?" Betsy asked, amused.

"He gave some of that candy to Charles! I sure wish I'd been in town."

"Children," Father called, "come along. We're going home." They strolled slowly down Baltimore Street, which led into the Baltimore Pike, greeting acquaintances as they went. Father and Mother walked together and discussed what they had heard from their friends.

"Poor Mrs. Buehler," Mother said, "she was all alone and quite frightened. I guess the Confederates made more noise in town than they did out at our place. Mr. Buehler barely got away with the mail. She's glad he escaped because she feared they'd capture him since he's the postmaster."

"I heard that Hugh Scott just made it out of town. He took the telegraph equipment which greatly disappointed the raiders," Father commented. "The storekeepers wisely sent away most of their stock weeks ago when the invasion rumors started. There wasn't much for the Confederates to take, and, of course, the reserve in the bank had also been shipped out."

"Some of the ladies said there had been so many false alarms that they did not believe the Confederates were actually coming until they were in town."

"Yes, but I did hear some of the townsmen went out early this week and tried to block the Cashtown Pass by cutting trees across the road. Joseph Broadhead helped with that." Father paused and raised his hat to greet the family standing in the shade of one of the large trees. "Mrs. Thorn, Mr. and Mrs. Masser, children."

"Good day, Westmores," Mrs. Thorn replied, her speech clear, but with a German accent. "It's good to see you all." Mr. and Mrs. Masser smiled their greeting; they were Elizabeth Thorn's parents and lived with the Thorn family in the cemetery gatehouse.

"Look, Mama," shouted seven-year-old Frederick Thorn. He pointed to the rising ground of Cemetery Hill. "Horses and soldiers!"

For a moment, Betsy could hardly breathe. Not again! Another raid was the last thing they needed. Rachel clutched Betsy's hand and hid her face. The adults exchanged worried glances. Then James shouted jubilantly, "Look at the flag!" Betsy shaded her eyes and smiled broadly. The glorious stars and stripes had never looked so beautiful. Union troops meant safety.

As the blue-clad cavalry came down the street, townspeople rushed out with fresh water and friendly words. The Westmores and the Thorns watched from the shady sidewalk as they rode by, the horses' hoof-beats echoing on the hard-packed dirt road. The sight of hundreds of proud, confident troops guaranteed protection. James and Frederick jumped up and down, waving in excitement, and five-year-old George Thorn asked his mama, "Is Papa coming home?"

"No, dearest," Mrs. Thorn said sadly. "Your Papa doesn't ride a horse. He's in the infantry and has to march everywhere." She shifted a wriggly two year old in her arms.

"Let me hold John," Mrs. Masser said to her daughter, taking the little one and speaking softly to him as he toyed with the ribbons of her bonnet.

"Thank you, Mama," Mrs. Thorn sighed.

"You have heard from Mr. Thorn recently?" Mother asked as they watched the long lines of friendly horsemen. Mr. Peter Thorn was a corporal in Company B of the 138th Pennsylvania. He was in the same company as Philip.

"No. Do you hear from your son?" Mrs. Thorn inquired.

"Not recently. We heard rumors that the 87th was involved in some fighting in northern Virginia, but nothing from Philip."

"The 87th Pennsylvania? Isn't that the regiment the Skelly boys and the Shields enlisted with?" Mother nodded.

"Oh dear, all these men and boys away from home, and we are left behind to worry about them and take care of the little ones," Mrs. Thorn remarked, resting her hand protectively on her abdomen.

"Are you and your baby doing well?" Mother asked.

"Yes. Tired…and frightened when the raiders were here. They actually rode into the cemetery shooting their pistols, and then they wanted water and food. I saw the horses they took from your farm. I am so sorry."

"What regiments are these?" Father called to an officer riding close to the sidewalk.

"We're the 5th and 6th Michigan Cavalry, sir," the man shouted back.

"We hope you'll be here to stay a while."

"Yeah. The ladies a few houses down the street told us about those Rebs. Don't know how long we'll stay, but the gray monsters won't come fooling here with us in town."

"We're safe," Rachel whispered. "The Confederates won't come back."

Betsy sighed and relaxed. When she looked up or down the road, she could see the Union horsemen, and the sight was reassuring. She would not have to watch the Baltimore Pike for enemy raiders anymore! They were safe; the raid on Friday would be forgotten, and life would continue as before.

"Aren't those horses beautiful?" James mused.

"Uh-huh," Frederick nodded. He shared James's military infatuation. "I'd like to ride that black one there. What about you?"

"I'd take the chestnut coming our way, if I had a choice."

The dust, which had swirled up from the road, settled as the last horsemen passed the group. "I think we should go home now," Father said.

"Oh, but, Father, the cavalry's here. Can't we stay, and I can see the horses and talk to the soldiers?" James pleaded.

Betsy frowned. She might have liked to see the horses, but wandering around town with a few hundred strangers did not sound appealing or safe.

"No," Father said decidedly. "The soldiers are here to protect the town. We shouldn't distract them from their duty."

Frederick made a similar appeal to his mother and grandfather, but received the same answer. The families started walking back together. Before the war, Mr. Peter Thorn had been the caretaker of Evergreen Cemetery, and his family lived in the dwelling rooms of the gatehouse. Now, while he was away, the family still lived there, and Mrs. Thorn and her father did their best to keep the cemetery in order and attend to the occasional burial duties.

"Mr. Westmore," Mrs. Thorn said as they went through the outskirts of town and began the ascent of Cemetery Hill along the Baltimore Pike, "one of the fences around the cemetery is falling into disrepair. I'm really sorry to trouble you with this request, but I was hoping maybe you could help us repair it? My father cannot do it alone, and, though I don't mind hard work, I think it wouldn't be the best for the baby."

Father nodded. "Of course. I'm sure Mr. Masser and I can fix the fence in a few hours of work. Do you have the new posts or rails?"

"Yes. It's just a couple of sections and probably less than a half-day's work for two men."

"Alright. Well, the almanac predicts rain tomorrow, but shall we plan on Tuesday, if the weather permits?"

They agreed, then Mrs. Thorn said pleasantly, "Mrs. Westmore, won't you and the children come to visit? Mother and I don't have as many visitors as usual. Everyone is preoccupied with war rumors."

"Yes! Oh, please say yes, Mrs. Westmore," Frederick coaxed. "Then James and me can play together all day."

"I think it would be nice," Mother replied, accepting her friend's invitation. "Shall I bring something for the noon-meal?"

Betsy and Rachel smiled at each other. They liked to go visiting, and Mrs. Thorn was a good friend. She had come to America from Germany, and sometimes they could persuade her to tell stories about her former homeland. One day, Mrs. Masser had let the girls examine some beautiful linens she had brought from Europe and, in her broken English, had told them about the traditional embroidery decorating the tablecloths and napkins. And, of course, there was two-year-old John to watch and amuse. He was too small to frolic with his brothers and James, so the girls enjoyed playing with him in the house while the ladies chatted.

Betsy's fears drifted away, and comforting reassurance settled as she looked back at the town and saw the clusters of blue-uniformed soldiers on guard. The Union troops had come. The Confederates were gone. There were plans to visit, to harvest some of the crops, and to celebrate the holiday next week. The chickens and horses were gone, and stories about the adventures of Friday still circulated, but, on the whole, the normal routine was reestablished.

Chapter 6

The almanac was correct: Monday was rainy. After breakfast and morning chores, the children went to the barn to help Father organize the feed and equipment rooms. As they worked, Betsy and Rachel hummed cheerfully, James chattered, and Father answered questions.

"Those Union cavalrymen were very brave, don't you think?" James started.

"They just rode through town. How was that 'very brave'?" Betsy asked, looking up from the box of bent nails, screws, and broken hinges she was sorting.

"I mean they looked brave. Didn't you feel the glory of war when they rode by? And those horses were perfect. I sure wish I could go to town today and see them. Do you think they'll be there tomorrow? Could Frederick and I go see them, Father?"

Father put a stack of wooden crates in the corner, then answered, "I don't know if they'll still be there. No, you and Frederick may not go into town by yourselves."

"Not even if we promised to find Dan Skelly or Albertus McCreary to go with us?" James responded hopefully, mentioning two teenage boys in town.

"No. Dan Skelly works at the Fahnestock Store, and I'm sure Mr. McCreary has tasks for his son."

"Oh, well. Too bad Philip's not here." Though disappointed, it was not long before James started talking again. He leaned on an empty barrel and watched Father mend a harness. "Father, do you think we'll ever get some horses again?"

"Probably, Lord willing. We'll need them for field work. Maybe another farmer will want to sell his team."

"I've got a good idea! I could go ask the cavalrymen if they have any lame horses," James advocated brightly.

"No," Father replied absently, examining the torn leather.

"It was an idea. Just not a good one? I'll bet cavalry horses are the best in the world because they have to be really brave to gallop around during a battle. They never spook."

"To say they 'never spook' is wrong, son," Father responded. "I'm sure those horses have learned to trust their riders and not panic during battles."

"Maybe I could ask the cavalrymen how their horses are trained?" James suggested hopefully.

"James, we're not going to make a special trip into town for you to talk with soldiers, and you're not allowed to go by yourself. Begging or pestering isn't going to change my mind. Now," Father instructed, "go up to the loft and bring down that small crate of leather scraps we've been tripping over the last few weeks. I need a piece to fix this rein, and then we can store the box down here."

James scampered off. "Wow," Betsy sighed dramatically, "it's quiet down here."

Smiling, Father shook his head. "Now, Betsy, he does have big ideas and good questions. However, I hope someday he'll realize the world doesn't revolve around soldiers and horses."

Crash!

Rachel jumped in surprised alarm. "What was that?"

Betsy glanced out the open door to see scraps of leather scattered on the floor of the barn. The doorframe blocked part of the view, but she could see two legs waving in the air, and then the rest of James appeared as he dropped down from a low beam. She stifled her laughter at her brother's antics.

"James Westmore!" Father called. "What are you doing?"

"Well…um. I thought it'd be the quickest way down."

"You broke the storage box and fortunately not your leg. You should've used the ladder. Pick up the leather and the pieces of the box. You can sit next to me, nail the box back together, and not say anything while you accomplish the task," Father said sternly.

After a quarter of an hour, James said, "Father, I'm finished. I'm sorry about tossing the box down and not using the ladder." Father accepted his apology.

When the work was finished, the children gathered, watching Father stitch the leather in place. "What would've happened if James broke his leg?" Rachel asked curiously, twisting the ends of her braids.

"Either the doctor or I would've had to set it. A very good reason to not break a limb."

"Have you ever done that before? I mean, set a broken bone?" Betsy wondered.

"Yes. Twice," Father admitted. "The first time my father had an accident here on the farm, and I helped the doctor. The second time my cousin fell off one of those big rocks down at Devil's Den."

"Why's the big rock pile south of town called Devil's Den?" James questioned.

"Oh, that's an old legend. Way back in the 1700's when the first settlers came to this area, there was some sort of beast's lair in those rocks. Some folks say it was a ferocious bear, others claim it was an enormous black snake. Whatever the animal, it terrorized the surrounding land, eating farm animals, scaring people, and being a general nuisance. Since it always retreated to those big rocks, somebody came up with the colorful name of 'Devil's Den' for the boulders."

"Does the mean animal live there now?" Rachel asked timidly.

"No. There's probably snakes, raccoons, and maybe some foxes down there, but no bears or monster snakes." He tied the final knot in the stitching and hung up the harness on a peg. "Alright, someone can bring those couple of poles and stakes lying on the ground and stand them up here by the workbench. Then, I think we're finished."

"Is this what you'd use to splint a limb?" Rachel wondered, holding up a large pole.

"No. That's too big. These would be about right." He showed her two stakes, thick enough to not bend, but small enough to not be cumbersome.

"You're not planning on breaking anything, are you?" Betsy teased.

At dinnertime, Mother said the girls were going to help her with some sewing in the afternoon. "My dress?" Betsy asked hopefully, anxious to have her new Sunday best.

"Not yet," Mother responded. "We need to finish a couple of shirts for Philip and one for James. Then we'll start on your new dress."

The pretty parlor was a peaceful place to sew. Nicely carved chairs with beautiful cushions stood near a round table where the girls worked while, at a nearby square table, Mother leaned over the pattern she was cutting out of plaid fabric. Betsy liked sewing; it was nice to sit still and rest, even if her hands were busy. The seams lengthened, the hems shortened, and button holes crafted as sung melodies kept time for their busy fingers.

"Mother," Betsy asked, pausing to snip the end of a loose thread, "do you think it was good that Philip enlisted?"

Mother considered for a moment, then replied. "It is hard for a mother to call something good that puts a child in danger, but I think it was the right thing. He felt very strongly that it was his duty, and it would have been wrong for me to selfishly hold him back."

"I wonder if all mothers and sisters feel the same when their boys leave," Rachel said sadly.

"I suppose they do," Mother replied.

Later, as she folded the half-finished shirts, Betsy lingered at the cutting table. The fabric for her new dress lay there – dark brick red with a tiny pattern of cream-colored flowers scattered across it. She and Mother had gone to several dry goods stores before finding this perfect material at Mr. Schick's store on Baltimore Street. Betsy re-wrapped the calico in a piece of brown paper to keep it clean and glanced at a couple of sketches in a copy of *Godey's Ladies Magazine*; she still had to decide what style of day dress she wanted…something practical and pretty since this would be her Sunday dress for several years.

Rachel leaned on the table, gazing longingly at the sketches of elaborate hooped gowns crafted of delicate fabrics and trimmed with lace. "I wish I had a beautiful dress like that," she murmured.

"Oh, Rachel, your clothes are pretty. Besides, do you know how dirty a dress like that would get on a farm?"

"Well, if I had a dress like that, I wouldn't live on a farm. I wouldn't have to work hard. Imagine just sitting around, drinking tea all day." Wishfully, Rachel smiled.

"You should be content where God placed you," Betsy responded severely. "You have a good family."

"Except my sister always tells me what to do."

"I do not!"

"I'm not going to argue with you. It wouldn't be lady-like," Rachel replied, lifting her chin and speaking loftily.

"Oh, you…someday you're going to appreciate what you have and stop dreaming and wishing for things you don't."

"I want to be a fine lady and wear a beautiful dress. What's wrong with that?" Rachel protested. "Fine ladies in beautiful dresses never have any trouble," she finished dreamily.

Betsy was annoyed at her sister's lack of contentment and responsibility and walked away.

That evening, as Mother and Rachel prepared some food to take to the Thorns' home and Father and James scoured a newspaper for equestrian ads, Betsy sat down at the small desk in the sitting room and turned up the wick of the lighted lamp. She wrote letters to Philip often; it made her feel closer to her older brother, and telling him the news of the week helped her feel less lonely. She thought for a while and then moved the metal pen quickly across the paper, pausing only to dip it in the inkbottle or to listen to dictations of the family's news.

June 29, 1863
Dear Philip,

I trust this letter will find you well and safe. We are all in good health and the crops are growing well. Father plans to harvest the west field on Thursday.

There have been <u>frightful times</u> here in Gettysburg. Three days ago, some Rebel horsemen came. They took all the chickens and the two horses which is a great hardship. I thought they were rude. Rachel was scared, and James was angry.

Supposedly, the Confederates have gone to York. We do not know where our army is, but two Michigan cavalry regiments arrived in town yesterday. We feel safe again.

I'm going to ask you something, and I won't tell if you say your answers are secret. Does being scared make a person a coward? Do you hate the Rebels? Father says that we must obey the Bible and love our enemies. I don't hate the Confederates, but it seems too hard to love them when they were so mean. Yet, I know Father is right.

James wants me to tell you that he has grown a whole inch since you left. Rachel says she will write to you soon. Father and Mother send their love. We are all keeping you in our prayers.

Has your food improved? We will send some berry jam after we have canned it. Will that improve the hardtack? Have you learned to march better? We are making you a couple of new shirts. Mother wants to know if you need anything else.

I am nearly out of paper. I miss you, but I remember what I promised.

Your sister,
Betsy Westmore

Carefully, she sanded the paper to dry the ink, then folded and addressed it. It seemed odd to write to her brother at a strange address: 138th Pennsylvania Regiment, Company B. She wondered where he was and what he was doing tonight. She wanted him to come home and tell her the armies would stay far away.

Chapter 7

"Are we ready to go?" Father asked, looking into the kitchen where Mother and the girls were packing a basket of food.

"Almost," Mother responded, tying the ribbons of her bonnet. Betsy settled the vegetable and gravy pie into the basket, and Rachel smoothed a calico cloth over the bowl of fresh cherries.

When they were ready, Father locked the door, and they started on their walk up the Baltimore Pike; it was less than a mile to the cemetery and gatehouse. Father carried his shovel, and James toted a bag with some other tools in it. Betsy and Rachel agreed to take turns carrying the food basket. Mother carried another basket with her sewing tucked inside.

Though it was still early in the morning, the day was already quite warm, and the overcast clouds increased the humidity. Little birds chirped and sang merrily, fluttering between the rail fences or tree branches. Neighbors called greetings from their fields, gardens, or front porches. Wildflowers blossomed along the road, and Rachel gathered some to make a pretty bouquet for their friends. They passed the heavily wooded slopes of Culp's Hill on their right; the trees were dense, but the undergrowth had been cleared, allowing passersby to see deep into the groves where boulders sat like resting sentinels. The scenery was peaceful, and it seemed nothing could mar the beauty of the place and day.

The tree line swept back from the pike, and the meadow between Culp's and Cemetery Hill could be seen. Rising above the meadow stood Cemetery Hill with its gatehouse guarding the entrance to the resting place of Gettysburg's deceased. It was a little climb to the gatehouse where they found Frederick Thorn watching for their arrival.

Frederick and George greeted James and decided to play in the small front yard. Mrs. Thorn and her parents came to the gate and warmly welcomed the Westmores. The men industriously went to evaluate their task, and the women went into the home.

They entered the north side of the building and went into the pretty parlor. "Won't you take off your bonnets and make yourselves at home?" Mrs. Thorn said with a smile. "I'm so glad you could come and visit today." She untied her green checked apron and smoothed her dark gold dress.

"Thank you. It's good to see you, too," Mother answered. "Would you like us to take the food into the kitchen?"

"Oh, no, I'll do that," Mrs. Masser said in her heavy German accent. "I have to go down and finish something, then I'll join you." The kitchen was in the cellar, below the parlor.

The gatehouse was a unique structure. The dwelling rooms were on two sides with an arched outdoor passageway and gate separating the living areas from each other. The Thorn family lived in the rooms on the north side, and Mr. and Mrs. Masser lived in the south side, though they shared the kitchen and common rooms.

John squealed and toddled over to Betsy carrying his red ball, which he handed to her. "Thank you," she said. "Do you want me to roll it on the ground for you?" He nodded, anxious to play. Betsy sat down on the wood floor, and Rachel helped John. They rolled the ball back and forth, amusing the little one.

"Don't let him tire you, girls," Mrs. Thorn called from her rocking chair where she worked on some knitting.

When John lost interest in the ball, they played with the little rocking horse and the spinning top. Then he decided to enthrone himself on his mother's lap and sat quietly while she chatted with Mother.

"The Michigan cavalry left yesterday," Mrs. Thorn said. "I'm not sure that's a good thing. At night, I can see campfires on the ridges far west of town – near the Cashtown Pass – and I'm sure some of the Confederate army is out there."

Betsy and Rachel looked at each other in alarm. The enemy troops were that close? What would they do if the army came? Betsy felt apprehension. Or was it fear? She feared the unknown. What might happen to them that could not be prevented? Could she keep her promise if war came close to home? She silently prayed, "Dear God, please keep the Rebels far away from here and don't let anything bad happen. Please send someone to keep us safe."

Mrs. Thorn was still conversing with Mother. "Yes, Captain John Myers, our neighbor, thinks we should look for Confederate spies."

"Spies?" Mother questioned. "And what are we supposed to do if we should happen to find one?"

"I don't know," Mrs. Thorn admitted, laughing nervously. "Tell him, I guess. It's not a woman's duty to arrest spies. Did you know he fought in the War of 1812? I hear Mr. John Burns, who works at Kendlehart shoe store, was also a soldier in that war."

"1812?" Mrs. Masser questioned. "That was long before you were born, Daughter. And forty-two years before we came to America."

"Yes," Mrs. Thorn said thoughtfully, "but they were fighting to keep this land free so people like us could come here and have a better life."

"Were you sad to leave Germany, Mrs. Thorn?" Rachel asked.

"At the time, yes. You see, I...well, I had an understanding with a young man, and I wasn't very happy about leaving him behind."

"Was it Mr. Thorn?"

"No. I met Mr. Thorn, who was also a German immigrant, when my parents and I came to Gettysburg. I liked Peter Thorn, my parents liked him, and, after a

nice courtship, we decided to get married. I never thought
I'd see the other young man again. I had a new life in
America, and I decided not to wait and see if he would
ever come. So Mr. Thorn and I married in 1855. The next
year he got a good job as caretaker of the cemetery, which
I liked much better than his previous job at the mine on
High Street. We were very happy."

"Did you ever see the young man from Germany
again?" Betsy asked. "I mean, if you don't mind my
question, ma'am."

"No, I don't mind. Yes. He did come to America, and
he found me. It was shortly after Frederick was born that
he arrived, and he asked me to go away with him. But I
couldn't. It wouldn't have been right, and, besides, I had
a kind husband and a little baby. I'd made a new life for
myself, and I had to stay." She blushed and looked shy.
"And I realized I loved Peter Thorn more than any other
person on earth."

Rachel sighed happily. "That's a nice story."

"Mama, Mama," Frederick shouted from outside.

Mrs. Thorn glanced at Mother and rolled her eyes.
"Why can't they come to where I am? Why do they have
to yell?"

"Mama, Captain Myers is here. He wants to tell you
something."

"Invite him to come in," she instructed.

"No, he says he can't stay."

They stepped outside, and Captain Myers came to

share his news. He took off his hat and ran a hand through his gray-white hair. "Morning, ladies. Just wanted to tell you that we've captured a spy this morning."

"Really?" Mother said, raising her eyebrows.

"Yes, ma'am. I was in town and saw this fellow asking some schoolchildren strange questions. How many cavalry had been in town, where the Union army was – things like that. Well, I found a Union trooper who'd somehow been left behind, and he caught the fellow. The sheriff found papers in the fellow's boots, proving he was a spy, and the deputy took him into custody right quick. So you be careful and let me know if anyone suspicious comes around here asking questions." Mrs. Thorn promised she would, and then her elderly neighbor bid everyone a cheerful good day and went back toward town.

"A spy in Gettysburg!" Betsy exclaimed. "Who would've ever thought such a thing would happen?"

"What will happen next?" Mrs. Thorn asked in a weary tone.

Chapter 8

They opened the windows of the parlor, hoping a little air movement would dispel the muggy heat. "I believe it's going to storm later today," Mother remarked to Mrs. Thorn, looking at the dark clouds beginning to surround the area, contrasting with the dull gray of the overcast sky.

It was nearing eleven and time to prepare dinner when James darted to the window, calling, "Oh, girls, won't you come help us play Blind Man's Bluff? Just for a little while?" Betsy looked questioningly at Mother, who nodded.

The sisters went out and played happily with the little boys, who were very pleased to have more people to try catching when they were blindfolded. "Your turn to be blind-man, Betsy," Frederick called as he grabbed her sleeve and tore off his blindfold to see who he had captured.

Betsy tied the strip of cloth over her eyes and let them spin her around a few times. Her efforts to locate the giggling children were unsuccessful. She groped and stumbled, unsure of where to go and what to do. That was half the fun, though, and she called teasing threats to the little ones until she realized the dark world was silent, and a hush of expectation had fallen on those who could see. "What is it?" she impatiently wondered.

"They're coming again!" James cried jubilantly.

"The Confederates?" Betsy asked in alarm.

"No, silly. Take off your blindfold."

The cloth dropped away from her eyes, and she saw a group of cavalrymen in blue galloping toward the hill. The hooves of their horses made a rumbling crescendo on the green grass as they rode cross-country toward the heights.

"Come on," Frederick shouted, "let's run down to the fence and see them." The boys scurried into the cemetery and flew alongside the fence railing until they neared where the soldiers had halted. Betsy and Rachel followed more slowly.

A man, wearing an old hunting jacket, corduroy pants, western boots, and crushed hat, sat comfortably in his saddle, using a pair of field glasses and peering toward the west. By the others' respectful manners toward him, Betsy guessed he was the commander. That's odd, she thought; don't all commanders wear lots of gold braid on their uniforms? Despite his shabby appearance, the charisma of the man communicated his steadfast and reliable character. His gray horse stood quietly, but, like his rider, seemed to have intense energy reserved for the moment of need.

"Good day," James called, climbing up on the fence so he could see better.

One of the officers smiled at the children and tipped his hat to Betsy and Rachel as they came up. None of the others acknowledged the children. All seemed to have one eye on the distant hills, searching for a hidden foe, and the other on their commander, awaiting a signal for action.

The commander slowly lowered the field glasses from his eyes and tucked them into a holder at his waist. "Well," he said methodically, resting a gloved hand on his hip. "Someone's out there. Who they are or what their intentions, we have yet to find out. How long until Gamble is up?"

"His brigade's about a half-hour behind us, sir," one of the soldiers said.

"Curse it. Of all the…"

Another soldier held up his hand. "Sir, there are children present. Um, you might want to…um…"

The commander stopped whatever he was saying and glanced at the children, the boys on the fence, the girls standing silently near. He had obviously not noticed their approach by the expression of surprise on his face. The worried frown softened, and a half-smile appeared.

"Good day, children," he said, moving his horse closer to the fence. "Do you or your parents know anything about the forces on those distant ridges? Have you seen any Confederates around here lately?"

"Oh, yes, sir!" James exclaimed, eager to share his knowledge. "There were some really mean Rebels here the other day. They took our horses and all our chickens. I was really upset that they stole our horses."

"I see. Miss," he said, looking at Betsy, "could you perhaps clarify what day was 'the other day?' "

"Friday, sir."

"Do you know how many cavalry were here and which unit?"

"No, sir, but my father might. I believe the Confederates left town on Saturday morning."

"Yes, and some Union cavalry came," Frederick put in helpfully. "They came into town as we were leaving church."

"You'll keep the Rebels away, won't you, sir?" Rachel asked hopefully, forgetting her shyness in the excitement.

The commander looked perturbed. "I'll do my best, if we could just figure out where they are. Nobody around here seems to have any idea where that Army of Northern Virginia is!"

"Are you a spy?" piped up George Thorn. "Captain Myers – he's our neighbor – said we had to be careful of spies."

The soldiers exchanged smiles. "No, we're not spies," the commander said. "I am General John Buford. These are my staff officers. We have a division of Union cavalry coming behind us on the road."

James's mouth fell open, and he was speechless for a moment. Betsy felt like she should curtsy or something. A real general?

"Good morning, sir," Father said, coming up quietly behind the astonished children. "I'm Henry Westmore. May I help you with something, General Buford?"

"The first honest, patriotic citizen we've seen for a couple of days," the general muttered. "Yes, I'd be glad of any information that you have about what troops – Union or Confederate – have been in the vicinity of this town. The town is Gettysburg, correct?"

"Yes," Father nodded.

"Nine major roads converge here. And I'd like to know what I've seen on those western ridges. If the Confederate army should come here, it would…well, it wouldn't be good."

Father explained what he knew about the Confederate raiders and the Michigan cavalry. He said Mr. Masser had told him about the campfires on the western ridges and hoped it was part of the Union army.

"It's not Union troops," General Buford said, frowning. "Our force is behind me. Not west of here. We've run into some Confederates to the west earlier today. You know, this whole campaign has been like a blindfolded game! The opposing sides can't seem to find each other. Until now, until here…"

Now? Here? Betsy thought in dismay. Surely there wouldn't be a battle? Battles were fought far away, not here, not close to home.

"And this ground," the general went on, seeming to think aloud as he looked south at Cemetery Ridge, the rocky high ground stretching toward the two rising hills called Round Top and Big Round Top. "This ground is defensive. It's perfect."

Perfect for what? Betsy wondered.

"Thank you, Mr. Westmore, for your information. Be assured that my cavalry division will be coming up, and I'll station them nearby. Do you know of any areas west of your town that could accommodate an encampment?"

Father thought for a moment. "Maybe one of the farmers would lend a field or meadow."

"Or what about the grounds around the Pennsylvania College and the Lutheran Seminary?" Betsy suggested, thinking of the nice grassy lawns surrounding the academic buildings. "I think someone can go up into the cupola of the seminary. Maybe you could see better from up there, sir."

"Thank you, miss."

He was turning to leave when James called, "Excuse me, General Buford, can I please pet your horse?"

The general looked surprised and then chuckled. "Sure. You sound like my little son at home, always wanting to spoil the horses." He guided the gray horse up to the fence.

James considerately let his friends pat the horse first. "What's his name?" he asked General Buford.

"Grey Eagle. He's a good horse."

James sat carefully on the top rail, and Grey Eagle put his muzzle in the boy's lap. The horse's ears were forward in a friendly reaction; he nickered softly while James stroked the face and the drooping forelock. "You take good care of the general, Grey Eagle, you hear?" James murmured. "You keep him safe, so he can keep us safe, alright?" Grey Eagle seemed to nod understandingly.

The general glanced toward the road and then said kindly, "Would you girls like to pet the horse? I wouldn't want two young ladies to be disappointed." Grinning, Betsy and Rachel moved to the fence and patted the horse's soft muzzle.

Betsy looked up at the general. She could see his profile as he gazed toward the western ridges. His face was etched with determination. This man would never give up. "Thank you, God," she whispered, "for sending someone to keep us safe."

General Buford glanced down at them. "We have to go," he said. "There's a war to be won."

"Yes, sir. Thank you," Betsy said politely. He turned Grey Eagle, nodded to Father and the children, and trotted toward town, his officers following behind.

When she glanced at Father, she noticed a concerned expression on his face. "What is it?" she asked. "Isn't it good a whole division of Union cavalry is here?"

"I hope so. But it could also draw the Confederates to this area," he said perceptively.

"They might see how many soldiers General Buford has and go away," Betsy suggested.

"True," Father admitted. Betsy looked at him in dismay when he murmured softly, "Or they'll fight a battle."

Chapter 9

Betsy scrubbed the shirt against the washboard, trying to get all the dirt out of the plaid fabric. Since it had rained on Monday and they had been gone on Tuesday, Mother decided to wash on Wednesday. It had rained the night before, and this morning had been misty, but now the sun was breaking through, and the clothes would dry quickly in the warm weather. If this first day was any indication, it would be a scorching July. Betsy pushed back a strand of brown hair that had escaped her bun and scrubbed harder. Mother and Rachel rinsed the clothes, wrung out the water, and pinned them on the clothesline.

"I wonder if General Buford is still in Gettysburg," Rachel remarked. "Do you suppose the Confederates were really out there?"

"I don't know," Mother said absently, focused on the task at hand.

The previous day, they had watched the long line of cavalrymen enter the town. Last Sunday, they had thought two regiments were a lot of soldiers, but truly it was nothing compared to General Buford's division; he even had an artillery unit. After seeing General Buford's division enter town, the boys had talked constantly about horses and soldiers during dinner at the Thorn's home. The women and girls had felt reassured and confident, though the men had been cautious about being too optimistic.

Betsy picked up the last skirt, thankful they were almost done. By her estimate, it was nearly nine o'clock. They had been working on the laundry since sunrise, about five hours ago, stopping only for a quick breakfast. Betsy agreed with Mother's housework rule: do the harder tasks early. The sun would dry the wet cloth, and they could go into the house and relax with their sewing or knitting during the hot hours of the day.

A dull thud sounded in the summertime scene, breaking the chorus of birds and the buzz of insects. Similar noises followed. "Are Father and James building something in the barn?" Betsy asked.

"No, I don't think so," Mother responded, pausing to listen.

It was like a muffled hammer wielded slowly and with great effort, like a giant edging closer with crushing footsteps, like a cannon shot a long ways off. Cannon shot? Betsy felt cold. There were no mythological hammers or giants in Gettysburg, but there were soldiers. Soldiers with cannons. They didn't shoot cannons near peaceful farms and towns, did they? But General Buford had said there was a Confederate army somewhere nearby.

Mother looked to the west, where Culp's Hill and Cemetery Hill blocked the view toward town, and said cautiously, "Let's finish rinsing and hanging the clothes and go inside, girls."

"Is it a battle, Mother?" Betsy asked uneasily.

"I don't know. I really can't imagine why the Confederates would want to come to Gettysburg, but I'm sure General Buford will keep them away."

They finished hanging the wash on the clothesline, dumped out the dirty water, and put the buckets aside to dry. Mother and the girls went into the sitting room and collected their projects. They worked silently, listening to the noise. Sometimes, they could hardly hear it; other times, it was very distinct. Sometimes, it came in a cadence; other times, it was scattered.

"Do you think we should go away, Mother?" Rachel asked nervously.

"What do you mean?"

"If the soldiers come, will we leave?"

"I don't know. If General Buford thought the Confederates were west of town, I'm sure they won't be near us. Maybe it's just a detachment that he'll drive off easily," Mother replied hopefully.

Betsy's thread knotted constantly this morning as she tried to sew; it twisted and tightened like the fear she felt. She tried to think of something positive. "I'm glad Philip isn't in the cavalry. He's not in this battle."

"Yes," Mother agreed. Rachel nodded as she dropped her thimble for the sixth time that morning.

"There, it stopped," Betsy commented after they had not heard the noise for a while. The steady ticking of the clock was the only sound they heard.

"Praise God, if it was a fight, it must be over now," Mother said.

The silence lasted for over a half-hour; then the disturbance began again. By the time Father and James came in for dinner, the sounds were escalating and seemed closer. Mother and Father spoke quietly in the kitchen while James enlightened his sisters.

"Father thinks it's a battle. Isn't that exciting? I'm going to ask Father if we can walk up and see it. Wouldn't that be wonderful?"

"I don't think a battle is wonderful, and I certainly hope there isn't one near Gettysburg," Betsy replied, trying to ignore the possible danger.

"Are you deaf?" James asked in an unkind tone. "It's definitely a battle."

"How do you know?" Rachel responded doubtfully. "Did you hear or see a battle before?"

"Father said so. You girls don't know anything."

"Children," Father scolded, standing in the doorway of the dining room, "that's enough." He looked calm, but his attitude was tense, and he did not smile.

"Well, can we go and see the battle? Please?" James implored.

"Absolutely not. We don't need to put ourselves in harm's way, and, since we don't know what's happening, it's better to stay here."

"Do you really think it's a battle?" Rachel asked, nervously twisting her braids.

"Yes, but, from the sounds we're hearing, I think the fighting is a distance from where we are. Maybe on the western ridges outside of town."

"What would we do if the battle came near us?" Rachel wondered.

"Obey the officers if they told us to leave, but stay in the cellar otherwise."

"I don't like that we don't know what will happen," Betsy remarked, fearing the unknown danger.

"We'll trust God and act prudently," Father said reassuringly.

Throughout the afternoon, the rumble of fighting came closer, ebbing and rising without pattern or reason. In the sitting room, Mother and Rachel tried to sew. James talked quietly, using his toys to explain his version of the battle, complete with glorious cavalry charges. Father walked to each window, returned to his chair, tried to read, and then paced to the windows again. Betsy gripped her steel knitting needles and knit as though her life depended upon finishing the stocking that day. She thought if she concentrated only on the task at hand maybe she could suppress the growing anxiety in her heart.

About halfway through the afternoon, Mother said they should bring in the dry laundry. Father kept watch while James "helped" Mother and the girls gather the clothing. Glancing toward town, Betsy saw clouds of smoke hanging over the land to the north and west. Deadly thunder rumbled.

"It seems closer," she said to Father as she stood beside him when the work was done.

"Yes," he replied, his hands on his hips as he frowned. "I don't think it's at Hanover Road, directly north of us, but maybe north of town. The smoke and sounds would indicate that."

They went back inside, folded the clothes, and waited. James watched the Baltimore Pike, and, shortly before five o'clock, he announced, "Someone's coming." The family crowded around the window and saw a long column of Union infantry marching past. The flags hung lazily, but still conveyed the might of the United States.

Betsy believed she should have been reassured by the sight of the foot soldiers; Rachel and James obviously were. Yet, with the sounds of fighting drawing closer yet again, she felt as though she was being imprisoned. It felt like being trapped in a box: to see the lid closing slowly, the shadowy darkness creeping around, and knowing there would be no escape until the One controlling fate agreed to lift the lid. The cannon thunder had crept closer throughout the day. The troops moved on the road. Four walls of military forces and a gray sky pressing down. It was a box with no escape. Battle came on July 1, 1863, with the sound of cannons and the sight of marching soldiers. She wondered what would happen next. Could she keep her promise and watch over James and Rachel with war at the doorstep?

Chapter 10

The troops on the Baltimore Pike continued their steady advance toward town. Sometimes, there were breaks when no soldiers could be seen, but then more appeared. Sometimes, military bands played. To Betsy, the rousing songs seemed out of place for men marching toward danger, but maybe it indicated the Union had already won.

Later, the family left the windows and ate supper. The sound of cannons had faded away, but they heard an occasional muffled crash, like someone breaking valuable china dishes. Father thought it was rifle volleys, and James explained to his sisters that it was when a whole unit of soldiers fired their guns at one time.

After the dishes were dried, James went back to his post at the front window. Rachel searched for her thimble again. Thinking of Philip and wishing for his confident reassurance, Betsy gazed out the west window of the dining room into the twilight gloom. Father and Mother talked quietly in the kitchen.

Something appeared from the little hollow at the edge of the field. A minute later, Betsy identified a horseman; Union or Confederate was still a question. As she strained her eyes, he came nearer, cutting cross-country toward the Baltimore Pike and making a destructive trail in the ripe crops. He was close now. His blue coat and his light chestnut horse were plainly seen. Only the rail fence bordering the field and the fence beside the road separated him from the pike. He approached the first fence, intending to jump it. The horse balked at the last second, and the rider pitched forward, catching his leg in the fence and falling heavily on the ground.

"Father!" Betsy called. "A soldier…" He was beside her before she finished speaking and saw the situation in a glance: the trampled trail through the field, the frightened horse, and the figure lying on the ground.

Father said decisively, "James and Rachel, wait by the door unless I call for you. Martha, come with me. Betsy, you come also. We'll see what we can do."

"Is it safe?" Mother asked as they hurried out the door. In the distance, gunfire crackled.

"No one is pursuing him, and the fighting isn't close. Yes, for now, it's safe."

Betsy picked up her skirt's hem to avoid tripping and hurried with her parents to where the soldier lay. Father knelt beside him, and the young man opened his eyes, groaning. Father quickly assessed how the soldier lay and the abnormal position of his left leg, saying, "Sir, I think your leg is broken. Can we help you into the house?"

"These have to get through first," the soldier insisted, holding up a leather messenger satchel. "Take them to the Baltimore Pike. Give them to the first horseman who

comes. I know Hancock will send another courier soon…
before it's dark."

Father took the satchel, nodded, and stood up.
"Martha, stay here with him. Betsy, secure his horse. Take
it to the barn. Tell James to unsaddle the horse. Ask Rachel
to make a pallet bed downstairs. And try to find a board or
something we can use to move him into the house."

Mother sat next to the soldier and talked calmly
while Father rushed toward the road. Betsy chose to do
the unladylike act of climbing the fence so she could get
to the animal more quickly. Although the horse looked
at her with laid-back ears, she saw it was only frightened
and approached slowly. She stroked the horse's soft nose,
gathered the trailing reins, and led it to where she could
remove a fence rail and enter the barnyard.

After tying the horse in the barn, Betsy ran to the house
and gave her siblings Father's orders. James was delighted
to have a cavalry horse to brush and feed, but Rachel was
not happy about having a soldier nearby. "If one comes
inside, then others might come. Why can't they all stay far
away?" Rachel asked, looking alarmed.

"He's hurt," Betsy explained. "Would you leave him
outside? Besides, he's a Union soldier. Now, quickly, obey
Father's directions."

Finding a piece of wood leaning against the chicken
coop and thinking it could be used to transport the
injured man, Betsy returned to Mother and the soldier.
Father joined them.

"He's unconscious," Mother said worriedly. "But his pulse seems strong."

"Let's move him into the house," Father directed and sent Betsy ahead to open the door while he and Mother moved the soldier. Rachel had prepared an improvised bed in the sitting room, but the makeshift stretcher was too wide to fit safely through the sitting room doorway. A few minutes later, he lay on a couple of blankets and a quilt on the dining room floor.

Rachel lit the lamp on the table which had been shoved out of the way toward the back wall. The soft glow of the lamp revealed the appearance of the soldier. It was strange to see a strong, capable young man lying so quietly. He was medium height and had a well-built body. His hair – somewhat unruly from wearing a hat all day – was brown, and a carefully trimmed mustache was surrounded by dark stubble, indicating he had been too busy to shave.

"He's been shot," Mother announced quietly as she unbuttoned his wool jacket. "Rachel, go and get some strips of fabric from our medicine box. Betsy, bring some water." Father helped Mother, and they washed and bandaged the gash on the upper left shoulder between the neck and collar bone.

"I don't think the bullet hit bone. It's a flesh wound," Father remarked.

The soldier twisted under their hands and moaned. Mother spoke gently to him as she smoothed the bandage in place. He opened his eyes and looked at them with confusion. "The orders?"

"I took them and gave them to a messenger on the pike as you told me to," Father said reassuringly. "He saw the papers were addressed to the Fifth Corps and promised to deliver them."

"Thank God," he breathed.

"Your leg is broken, sir, and you have a flesh wound on your left shoulder."

"Yes, I know," he replied, frowning. "Who are you?" Father quickly introduced himself and the family, adding that they were Union supporters.

"Thank you for seeing that the messages got through and for bringing me into your home." He grimaced, took a deep breath, and spoke with effort. "I'm Corporal Thomas Russell. 17th Pennsylvania Cavalry. My company's attached to the Eleventh Corps headquarters. We're couriers."

"Are there any medical staff nearby who could examine and set your leg?"

Corporal Russell frowned. "The medical facilities I've seen today were in town which is now overrun with Confederates. Or they're unorganized back near the hill with the cemetery."

Betsy crossed her arms over her fast-beating heart. Confederates near their friends in town? The Union army at the Thorns' home? The situation grew more dangerous every hour. Would there be fighting in their fields in the morning?

The soldier slid his right arm under his head and thought aloud. "Not sure where the Twelfth Corps ended up or when and where the Fifth will come. No, Mr. Westmore, there are no medical personnel nearby." He looked warily at Father.

"I've taken care of injuries occurring on a farm. I've set broken bones before," Father said. "I believe it'd be best to set the leg before swelling makes more difficulties."

"I agree," the corporal answered resignedly. "If you can do it, go ahead."

When James returned from the barn, Father sent him back to locate wood stakes for splints. Mother instructed Rachel to find an old sheet for wrappings. Betsy retrieved the medicinal alcohol. Corporal Russell watched the preparations uneasily, biting his lip when Father touched the broken leg.

When the supplies were assembled, Father sent the children upstairs. "Do you think he'll be alright?" Rachel asked as they sat nervously on the girls' bed.

"I hope so," Betsy replied sincerely.

"He sure has a nice horse," James informed them. "But it looks like she got grazed with a bullet too. I'll tell Father when…" He stopped as a cry of pain echoed from below. "Will he be alright?" he whispered.

Chapter 11

When the children were allowed back downstairs, they found Corporal Russell lying on his pallet bed, looking pale and exhausted, with his leg splinted and slightly elevated. "Are you alright?" James asked, sitting down cross-legged next to him. Betsy thought that was a tactless question. A man who had cried out in pain and who still had sweat on his forehead was obviously not alright.

The corporal grimaced slightly and replied, "I will be. Could you talk? Keep my mind off the pain. How's Blaze?"

"Is that your horse?" James clarified, and then went on when the soldier nodded. "She's alright, but I think a bullet grazed her. We can check her later. So why'd you name her Blaze?"

"Don't know. The army issues the horses. I thought it'd be silly to call her 'horse' or 'mare' all the time, but I didn't have time to think up a fancy name. She has that long white blaze on her face."

"Are you hungry?" Betsy asked, feeling awkward standing in the doorway watching him.

"An hour ago, I'd have said I was starving. But I'm not hungry anymore. I'd like some water, though, if it's not too much trouble, Miss Westmore."

She brought him a cup of water and sat down near James. "You may call me Betsy, Corporal Russell. I'm not really old enough to be called 'miss' all the time."

"And it's too formal to call me Corporal Russell. Just 'Thomas' is fine with me, unless your parents object." Father and Mother returned to the lamp-lit dining room, sitting down in the chairs at the table. Rachel inched backward until she sat close to Mother.

"How'd you end up here?" James asked.

"Well…I'm a courier. General Hancock gave me orders to take to the Fifth Corps which is supposed to be somewhere called Two Taverns, down the Baltimore Pike a ways. I left the Cemetery Hill area, where the headquarters are, and was heading down the road toward that other hill."

"Culp's Hill," Father put in.

"Thanks. I don't know what landmarks are called 'round here. Anyway, between the two hills, some enemy skirmishers – who'd crept up close to the road – started firing at me. I got hit in the left shoulder which caused some difficulty reining Blaze. I use my left hand for reining, right hand for shooting," he clarified, seeing the girls' confused looks. "Well, Blaze spooked and ran off into the lower woods of Culp's Hill. Lost my hat and had a wild ride. Just when I thought I had Blaze calmed a bit, a low branch I didn't see smacked my left shoulder, causing enough pain that I nearly went off. Blaze ran her own way again until we got to a cleared area. I pulled her up and tried to assess the situation. I could see the pike in the distance and decided to get back there. I did feel bad about riding through the fields, Mr. Westmore, but I couldn't help it."

"It's alright," Father replied, then asked, "How long before the Confederates come here?"

"I don't know. Skirmishers don't necessarily mean the army will follow."

"What happened next?" James questioned eagerly. "You were almost to the fence!"

"Right. The fence," Thomas groaned. "Blaze is a pretty good jumper. I thought she'd clear the fence. But I guess she thought it was too high. She stopped, I didn't. Caught my leg in the fence and hit the ground. Then you found me."

"That was an adventure," James exclaimed in admiration.

"I'd gladly have done without it. Especially considering it cost me a bullet wound, bruised shoulder, broken leg, and a few cracked ribs. All in all, a lot of trouble and pain," Thomas responded ruefully. "No offense to you, kind folks, but I'd much rather be with my company for this battle. I've a feeling they're going to need every messenger they have, if today was any indication."

"What happened?" Father asked anxiously.

"I guess General Buford and his cavalry held off a good part of the Confederate Third Corps for over half the morning. General Reynolds, who commands the First Corps, arrived with his troops in time to keep Buford from losing a place called Seminary Ridge, which is west of town. Reynolds was killed. General Howard – he commands the Eleventh Corps, and I ride for his headquarters – arrived, and there were some Confederates coming from the north toward town. He put his troops out there. We think the troops coming from the north were the Confederate Second Corps. Anyway, those troops attacked most of the afternoon and, around four o'clock, the Eleventh Corps broke lines and retreated, causing the First to do the same."

"Where was General Buford?" Betsy questioned. Everyone else might have fled, but she could not imagine that commander retreating from anything.

"He was the rearguard and made sure our troops got safely up to Cemetery Hill where General Howard had some artillery," Thomas answered, and Betsy felt a little relief; at least part of the army was intact and might keep them safe.

Thomas winced, held his breath for a moment, then continued his report. "General Meade – he's the Union army commander – sent General Hancock to help organize. Hancock's a good leader, and he and Howard got the troops rallied and fortifications started. Sometime after that, the Twelfth Corps came up. You probably saw them marching in. The commanders are sending out messages to all the other corps which will concentrate here at Gettysburg tonight and tomorrow morning."

"That's where you were going?" Rachel asked.

"Yes. It should've been a safer task than the other rides

I had today into the battle lines, but we never know the ways of Providence."

Betsy thought about his last statement. She didn't understand why God let the armies come to Gettysburg. She experienced enough war with Philip in the army; she didn't want to see a battle.

"The Confederates have the town?" Mother said, looking distressed.

"Unfortunately, yes, ma'am," Thomas admitted.

"What will they do to our friends?" Rachel whispered.

"General Lee's troops have a reputation of treating civilians well," Thomas mentioned reassuringly. "Hopefully, your friends will be alright."

Mother asked, "Do you know what happened to the family living at the cemetery gatehouse?"

"Not really. I heard another courier say the lady living there showed an officer where he could see the advancing enemy. So I guess she volunteered for a scouting mission. Is she an acquaintance?"

"Yes, she's a good friend. Her husband is away. I'm worried about her alone with her children and elderly parents and all those troops."

"Though there must be several corps near her home, she'll probably be fine," Thomas predicted. "The men are too tired to cause trouble, and, if officers use her home as headquarters, they'll be respectful." Mother nodded doubtfully.

Trying to understand the situation, Betsy inquired, "What's a corps and how big is it?"

Thomas thought for a moment before explaining. "Alright, there's the Union Army of the Potomac, and it's currently divided into seven corps. Not sequential numbers, though, because some have been destroyed or combined. There's the First, Second, Third, Fifth, Sixth, Eleventh, and Twelfth Corps. Within each corps, there are divisions. Divisions are made of brigades, and brigades are made of regiments."

"And regiments are made of companies, right?" Betsy clarified.

"Correct." Thomas frowned and exhaled hard. "So it's kind of difficult to say exactly how many men are in a corps, but, right now, I think it's between 9,000 and 13,000 depending on the corps. Some have been through more fighting. Others have newer regiments with them. I heard the Eleventh had just over 9,000 before the battle today."

As Thomas detailed the structure of the armies, Betsy twisted her handkerchief nervously. The thought of thousands of troops in the area was no longer comforting.

"Do you think the Union will win?" James asked positively.

"I hope so. I think General Howard and General Hancock will use the hills and ridges to make a defensive position."

Fearfully, Rachel asked, "So you think they'll fight again tomorrow?"

"Probably. We retreated today. But the new position will be much stronger. Though the Confederates may see that and decide to fight somewhere else."

Father tapped his fingers on the table, his gaze shifting between the family, the soldier, and the dark windows. "Do you think my family is safe here, corporal?"

Thomas took another sip of water and spoke solemnly. "I don't know where the Twelfth Corps will end up, but it may be on Culp's Hill or this area. Then it depends where the Confederates put their lines. There could be a battle here, or it may be on another part of the line. It could be somewhere other than Gettysburg altogether."

"I realize you don't know what will happen, but what would you do, if you were in my situation?" Father asked, his expression uncertain.

"I wouldn't leave," Thomas said. "If you leave, more property will be destroyed. I've seen that happen. As for tonight, I doubt there'll be anything more than skirmishing. Both sides need to bring up their troops and reorganize. However, as a precaution, I'd have my family sleep in the cellar."

Father took Corporal Russell's advice and decided Mother and the children would sleep there. He offered to move the soldier to the cellar also, but Thomas refused, and Father chose to stay nearby, in case he needed help during the night.

Mother said it was bedtime, and the children said good-night to Thomas before retreating to the cellar. They spread some old quilts and blankets on the hard-packed floor and lay down. Mother came to say good-night.

"Do you think Philip's here?" Betsy asked as Mother bent over her.

"I don't know," Mother replied. "I'm afraid he might be." Her hand trembled, and she set the lamp down, taking a calming breath. "We'll trust God to keep him safe. Now, rest well."

After Mother returned upstairs, James fell asleep quickly, but Betsy lay awake, staring into the darkness. Rachel tossed beside her.

"You alright?" Betsy murmured.

Rachel whimpered, "No, I'm scared."

"Me too. I didn't know armies were so big."

"And I don't like them so close."

"Well, maybe they'll go away and fight somewhere else," Betsy suggested hopefully.

"What if they don't? They already fought near and in town. What if they don't go away?" Betsy was silent. "Did you hear my question?" Rachel whispered after a while.

"Yes," Betsy replied, turning to lie on her back. "I don't know," she said aloud while her heart added silently, "That's what frightens me. Will I be strong enough to face whatever happens?"

Chapter 12

"It was only a dream," Betsy thought, trying to calm her fast-beating heart after she had jerked awake. The dream had been terrifying. Philip had been shot in battle; Philip died in front of their house. She sat up, rubbing her eyes. The darkness of the cellar made it difficult to know the time, but she could not sleep after that nightmare.

Silently, she pushed aside the blanket, found her skirt and bodice, and slipped them over the underclothes and petticoats she had slept in. The trapdoor was open, and she climbed out of the underground chamber. Hardly any light came through the kitchen windows; she guessed it was four in the morning since sunrise was about half-past four. Betsy looked into the shadowy dining room. Father slept on a blanket on the floor, and Corporal Russell rested on his pallet.

She sat down quietly near them, her back against the wall, her arms wrapped around her knees, and her long skirts trailing around. July 2nd – what would happen today? She tried to pray, but did not know what to ask. Her thoughts whirled in confusion: fear for Philip's safety, concern for friends in town, apprehension about more fighting, and dread of the unknown outcome awaiting them.

In the strengthening light, Betsy observed Thomas as he lay on his pallet. She saw the splinted leg. His shirt flopped open, revealing thick wrappings around his ribs and the bandage on his left shoulder. He frowned in his sleep, and his rest had not been peaceful, indicated by the twisted blankets and quilt.

Something in his manner reminds me of Philip, she thought, recalling Thomas's conversation last night. His words had been more terse and to the point than her brother's, but there was the same honest practicality in his speech. Although his other features were different, Thomas's blue eyes had the same ability to betray thoughts. She had seen the pain, the determination, the hope of ultimate victory. Where was Philip? Was he with the Union army in the Gettysburg area? Would he fight a battle in their or the neighbors' fields? Oh, if only he was safely home. Sending him to war had been hard enough, but now fearing his injury or death in their own community was dreadful.

A loud blast shattered the morning stillness and was rapidly followed by more, causing the windows to rattle. Betsy recognized cannon fire; this time, it was close. Terrified, she sprang up to flee to the cellar when a calm voice said, "No need to run, Miss Betsy."

She turned and saw Thomas had awoken. "But it's cannon fire," she protested.

"Yes, I know what it is," he replied with a small smirk, amused, but not unkind. "And yes, it's closer than yesterday, but we don't hear the shells shrieking, so they aren't firing toward the house or this area."

Father sat up and rubbed his neck. "You're sure?"

"Positive."

"How do you know?" Betsy responded, not wholly convinced.

"I've been on a few battlefields and heard artillery a few times," Thomas replied. "We'll know in a minute or two if the battle is on or if some unit is just testing their range." A few moments later, the firing ceased.

"Well…good morning," Thomas said, trying to smile.

"Did you sleep well?" Betsy asked.

"I managed to doze off a couple of times," he replied, attempting to shift more comfortably on the pillow, but stopping with a grimace.

"Let me help," Father said. He adjusted the support under the young soldier's head and shoulders so it propped him up more comfortably.

After asking if it was safe, Mother, Rachel, and James emerged from the cellar. Father went out to the barn to complete the few chores, and the others prepared a simple breakfast and brought it into the dining room. James suggested they eat picnic style so Thomas would not feel lonely on the floor. Mother agreed it would be alright for the morning meal. During breakfast, the sound of occasional rifle shots could be heard, and Thomas informed them it was light skirmishing. Neither army had retreated during the night.

"Today is Thursday," Father remarked. "I guess we won't be harvesting the west field."

"No," Mother replied sharply, "our ordinary routine has certainly been disrupted this last week. I just hope the armies will go away and fight their battle somewhere else." She rested her hand on her head wearily. "I'm sorry. I shouldn't have spoken harshly. I'm worried and didn't sleep well."

Father reached out and held her hand. "They still might go away," he said. Betsy saw Thomas shake his head in disagreement. She wondered if crying would release her suppressed fears.

In a moment, Mother regained her composure and gave directions. While Father and Mother redressed Thomas's wound, the children were sent into the kitchen to wash the dishes and complete the other morning tasks. The blankets and old quilts in the cellar were neatly folded, the floors were swept, and a fresh bucket of water was drawn. When the chores were finished, they gathered in the dining room; the girls brought their knitting, and James was anxious to talk.

"You're not tired, are you?" James asked, plopping down near Thomas's head.

"Can't sleep anyway. Why?"

"Could I ask some questions, Mr. Russell?" he said hopefully.

"Sure, ask some questions." He looked weary, but seemed to welcome conversation.

"Well, I'm wondering what it's like to be a cavalryman."

Thomas smiled weakly. "Exhilarating and scary, to be

honest. But, you see, my current assignment isn't what you think of when you think of cavalry. My company got selected for courier duty at headquarters, supposedly because we were brave or something like that. But we'd rather be with the rest of the regiment doing the traditional scouting, raiding, and skirmishing."

"Oh." James picked at a loose button on his shirt. "So what do you do?"

"Take pieces of paper with scrawled writing on them from one officer to another and get shot at in the meantime. Actually, the task is important. If those messages don't get through, a battle could be lost or more men killed. So it's important, and I really don't mind. It's been interesting working at headquarters and with the infantry, and, I suppose, at this time, there's more riding involved with being a messenger than a regular cavalryman."

"Where did you learn to ride?" Betsy asked, genuinely interested in the conversation and thankful for the distraction from the war outside.

"I rode a lot at home. My father's a Pennsylvania farmer. I grew up helping with the farm horses. My uncle owns a blacksmith shop and is also a horse trader, an honest and respected one. When I finished going to school, Uncle Adam hired me to help with the horses – grooming them, feeding them, cleaning stalls – in the afternoons after I worked around our farm. Uncle Adam let me start riding just for fun, but I eventually got pretty good. He'd have me test new horses for saddle skills or wagon driving."

By his expression, Betsy thought James was calculating his own path to joining the cavalry. "So you decided to be a cavalryman because you liked horses and could ride?" James questioned.

"Mainly. It was my duty to enlist to help defend the unity of the nation, and, since I could ride, cavalry was a natural choice."

"Do you have any brothers or sisters?" Rachel asked, shyly glancing up from her sewing.

"Two older sisters. I'm the youngest in the Russell family."

"What are their names?"

"Mary Jane is the oldest, and she's married and has two little children. Eliza got married last year," Thomas answered, smiling briefly.

"That's nice," Rachel commented. "He's not scary," she whispered in Betsy's ear. "I'm sorry I thought we shouldn't help him last evening."

Betsy nodded and replied in an undertone. "Yes. His confidence reminds me of Philip."

"How old are you, Thomas?" James demanded.

"James," Mother scolded, "you don't ask that."

"It's alright, Mrs. Westmore. I don't mind. I'm twenty-two. I can read, write, and do arithmetic. I'm a bachelor and intend to stay that way through the war. Anything else you'd like to know, James?"

"Nope. You and me will get along real well."

Thomas started to laugh, then groaned, "Ugh…broken ribs. Don't make me laugh." James nodded solemnly.

They were silent for a few minutes, listening to the sounds of the skirmishing and the occasional blast of a cannon finding range. Then Father asked, "You mentioned you are with the Eleventh Corps and General Howard. What do you think of them?"

"Well, the Eleventh is a good fighting unit, despite this reputation they've gained after the Chancellorsville battle in May. A lot of people blame them, but really I think they're quite patriotic and determined fighters when they have good commanders. General Howard's a good man. He's a Christian and is always encouraging the troops to attend prayer meetings, avoid drinking, and such. He gives tracts away and sets a good example. I've never heard him use a swear word, but he's courageous and forceful. You should've seen him yesterday when he rallied the troops at Cemetery Hill. Grabbed a battle flag and shouted encouragement to his men. He lost an arm earlier in the war. I think he's determined to prove that a Christian man can be a good military commander."

"There are troops on the road," Mother remarked uneasily as she returned carrying a spool of thread. "Union troops."

"Any flags?" Thomas questioned, restlessly gripping the quilt.

"United States flag and an odd flag with a Maltese cross were being carried behind some mounted officers."

"The Fifth Corps is here," he announced.

"How do you know?" Betsy asked.

"Each Union corps has a different insignia that they

use on brigade or division flags. The Maltese cross is the Fifth Corps. It makes it easier in a line of march or battle lines to know who is where."

When Thomas asked if they had anyone with the army, Betsy told him about Philip. "I don't know where the 138th is…" he said. "I'd heard they were guarding supplies earlier in the campaign, but I don't know now."

Guarding supplies…safe…and far away from the battle. Philip would claim it was boring, but he would be unharmed. Betsy clung to that shred of hope and prayed Thomas was right.

The day wore on, warm and sunny. The staccato echoes of skirmishing continued, but nothing else. Sometimes, they could hear a faint chopping sound; Thomas and Father surmised that someone was building fortifications on Culp's Hill. More troops marched on the road.

Except when Father went to check Blaze or get more water, the family stayed indoors. The ladies worked on their handiwork. James played quietly with his wooden toys while Father kept watch at the windows. Thomas dozed, watched the others, or stared at the ceiling; his jaw clenched against the pain. He didn't talk much after the morning conversation, but politely thanked anyone who brought him water or food or adjusted his pillow.

A little before four, as Mother and the girls were folding up their work and planning supper, a single cannon blast resounded, followed by a crescendo of artillery barrage. "That's close and to the north of us," Father estimated.

Betsy heard the insecurity in his voice and saw the nervous touch of his hand as he closed the window curtains. She could not remember Father seeming afraid of anything in the past. Now, though he tried to conceal it, she saw he was doubtful and concerned about the developing situation. He hardly touched the food they prepared and moved restlessly around the interior perimeter of the house, watching and anticipating.

In some ways, it seemed surreal…such a thing – a battle – could never happen in Gettysburg. In other ways, it was a grim reality, and Betsy feared the unknown aftermath of the fighting. Later, more cannon, farther away, joined in the tumult. Then rifle volleys. It was horrifying to hear. Rachel shrank fearfully in the corner, covering her ears. Betsy sat close to her, resolutely continuing to knit, though carefully watching Thomas to see how he reacted to the unfolding battle. Innocently imagining a general would ask his opinion for a winning maneuver, James prepared a new strategy with his toys. While Father paced from window to window, Mother tried to read the Bible, but eventually closed it and stared at the photograph of Philip she had taken from the desk.

The closer cannons' fire ended after about two hours, but the fighting elsewhere still raged. James reported more troops on the Baltimore Pike and identified the symbol on the brigade flag as a cross.

"The Sixth Corps," Thomas said quietly. "I expect the whole Army of the Potomac is here now."

Twilight settled, and the terrific confusion of battle noise diminished. Relief was short-lived. The uproar began again, this time, sounding like it was in the backyard. "Culp's Hill? Cemetery Hill?" Father wondered.

"Probably," Thomas answered. "The Confederates must have tried the other flank first. Whether it held or not, we don't know. Now, they'll try here."

The darkness deepened, and the fighting intensified. The drawn curtains did not block the sounds, but gave an illusion that the battle was in the outside world and could not touch the quiet interior. Father and Mother spoke in low, urgent tones in the shadowy kitchen. James had put away his toys and joined the girls; they inched closer to the corporal. For some reason, Betsy only felt safe near Father or Thomas. Father was the most trustworthy person she knew, and she supposed Thomas's knowledge and brotherly attitude made him reassuring.

Thomas frowned, but Betsy was uncertain if he experienced intense pain or was thinking. "Mr. Westmore," he said when Father entered the dining room, "I believe you may want to make some preparations…"

"To leave?" Father questioned with dread. "I thought you advised against that."

"No, sir. With the nearby fighting, there's a very real possibility your property and home may be used as a field hospital."

Chapter 13

A cannon shot exploding into the kitchen would not have been as shocking to Betsy as Thomas's words. A field hospital? Here? And what exactly is a field hospital?

Thomas explained. "Surgeons and medical staff will take any solid structure and use it as shelter for a field hospital. I've seen it happen many times. If prepared, you may reduce some of the damage to the house and your possessions. Roll up your good carpets. You could lay straw on the floors. Prepare bandages and draw extra water."

Betsy stabbed her knitting needles into the ball of wool. If more danger loomed, she did not want to sit knitting and be caught unprepared. Father and Mother looked at each other for a long moment, and then Father spoke resolutely. "James, come with me. We're going to bring a couple wheelbarrows of straw to the house. Martha, why don't you roll the rugs in the sitting room and parlor?"

Betsy went upstairs to collect some of the older quilts and blankets. She peered out the window in the hall toward the sound of the battle. Sometimes a flash appeared, but mostly there were only frightful echoes of dreadful shooting. Men were being injured. Was Philip somewhere nearby in this dark fight? He'd never desert, but she wished he would, so they'd know he was safe. She remembered the dream, closed her eyes to erase the memory, and turned away from the window. Hurriedly, she gathered the blankets and returned downstairs. The clock struck nine as they spread the straw in the rooms.

When the preparations were finished, Betsy hoped it would be adequate for whatever happened. A layer of straw had been spread on the floors of the sitting room, parlor, and dining room. A stack of old blankets and a few quilts were waiting to be used. Buckets of water stood ready.

Surely we won't need it, Betsy thought. We'll be able to clean up in a day or two. Maybe a dozen injured men will come, but nothing too serious. Fearing the unknown, she tried to deny reality, but, deep inside, she knew something terrible approached; the truth reflected in Thomas's straightforward words and worried gaze.

They gathered in the dining room again, listening to the explosions and rapid firing in the darkness outside. "We'll pray together, and then, children, I want you to rest in the cellar," Father said calmly. The family sat or knelt close together and held hands while Father prayed God's will would be done, the Union would win the battle, Philip and their friends would be kept safe, and they would have courage for tomorrow.

As the lamp cast weird shadows on the hard-packed earth walls, the children crept into the cellar. Soon their preparations were finished, and they lay down in the darkness. James's even breathing told that he was asleep almost instantly, but Rachel cried. "I'm so scared. I've tried to be brave all day, but I'm afraid. Something bad is going to happen to me…"

Betsy held her sister, letting her cry on her shoulder. "Shh…" she whispered. "God will take care of us." Betsy continued to talk comfortingly, trying to hide her own fears to help her sister. Eventually, Rachel quieted.

Betsy did not remember falling asleep, but she was jolted awake by the crash of artillery hours later. Stumbling, she straightened her clothing and climbed out of the cellar. At first, it seemed like repeating the previous morning: dawn breaking, cannons firing, Thomas lying silent. However, it was July 3rd: a new day with more dangers and difficulties. Father stood at the kitchen window, watching and expecting something.

The door burst open, and a tall man in a uniform stood silhouetted in the shadowy light. "Can I help you?" Father asked.

"I'm Dr. Barnes, surgeon with the Union Twelfth Corps. We're requisitioning your barn and home to be used as a field hospital, sir," the man said brusquely. Betsy shivered at his announcement.

"I'm Henry Westmore," Father responded soberly, motioning the man inside. "We've made some preparations."

Dr. Barnes brushed by Betsy and looked into the dining room. "That's a start. Wait a minute," he spoke critically, seeing Thomas. "A deserter?"

"No, sir," Thomas answered quietly. "Corporal Thomas Russell, 17th Pennsylvania Cavalry. I was wounded and broke my leg on July 1st while on messenger duty. The Westmores moved me inside to safety."

"Light the lamp," the surgeon ordered, his tone hasty and harsh.

Father obeyed, and the surgeon made a hurried, but careful, examination of Thomas's wound and leg. "Set the leg yourself?" he asked Father.

"Yes."

"It's a good job. You'll be alright, corporal. A little feverish, but I expect you'll pull through." He stood up, replacing the lamp on the table. "Dr. Elder – another surgeon – will set up in the barn. I'll be here at the house. We expect the wounded who can walk to arrive as soon as it is light enough for them to see. Others will come by ambulance when the vehicles can evacuate them." The cold expression in his brown eyes told that he would accept no arguments to his orders, and the firm line of his mouth, partially hidden by a short, trimmed beard, showed his decisive control of the situation.

Dr. Barnes walked through the house and then went outside to speak with some other uniformed men. Two entered the house. "Um, Mr. Westmore," said one of them, a tall, lanky man with blond hair and sideburns, "we need your dining room table. We're going to take it outside, alright?" Father only nodded.

Confused by the entire situation and the need for the table, Betsy leaned against the wall. When the men had gone outside, she asked, "Why?"

Father put his arm around her. "If we don't cooperate, wounded men will suffer even more. And, ultimately, we have no choice."

No choice. Those sounded like final words. "But why would they want the table?" she questioned again.

"Operating table," Thomas said impassively.

"Not on our table!" Betsy exclaimed in horror. "Father made it. We've eaten every meal at it for as long as I can remember. What else will they want to use?"

Father looked distressed, as if he did not know what to say. Thomas spoke softly; Betsy knelt beside him to hear better. "Betsy, this is war. To you, the table is an heirloom. To them, it is a piece of functional furniture they can use in their efforts to help the wounded. If your brother was injured, wouldn't you want the surgeons to do everything they could to help him?"

"Yes."

"Then remember that," Thomas advised. Betsy stared at him, and he gazed back at her, his blue eyes never wavering. "Be brave and make your brother proud," he whispered, not knowing his words were exactly what she needed to hear, reminding her of her promise.

The tromping of the surgeon's and orderlies' boots woke the others, and they came from the cellar. James bounded into the dining room, convinced the generals had arrived to hear his strategy, but quickly realized the surgeon did not look friendly. As if fearing any significant movement would send a cannon shot crashing toward her,

Rachel tiptoed into the kitchen. Mother tied on her apron and began preparing breakfast; she seemed determined to act normally no matter what occurred outside.

Through the windows, they saw Dr. Barnes and his orderlies bringing crates of supplies from a nearby wagon. An assistant had set up a makeshift table of barrels and boards near the requisitioned dining table and covered it with a stained cloth. Dr. Barnes worked methodically, and Betsy watched as he removed instruments from a wooden case: knives, saws, probes, spools of thread, prepared needles. A couple boxes of bandages stood ready for use. It appeared that similar preparations were being made just inside the barn door.

By the time their hasty breakfast of cold cornbread with honey concluded, wounded men were staggering from the road toward the house while the sound of the guns was incessant. The walking wounded were awful and mesmerizing: how they limped, struggled, stumbled, or fell in their quest for aid. The orderlies quickly met them and helped them to the shade of the barn where Dr. Elder and his assistants waited.

"We can't just stand here watching," Mother exclaimed.

"No, we cannot," Father replied. "Children, stay in the house and look after Corporal Russell. Your mother and I will see what we can do."

With her parents away from the house, Betsy felt that yet another piece of her formerly safe world was torn away. Would the war take all the security she had known? First

Philip, then peaceful surroundings, next home safety, now her parents' calm stability. She thought about her promise to her brother; in the last year, it had seemed rather simple to be brave, responsible, and look after Rachel and James. Could she still fulfill those duties as her protected world was invaded? She felt Rachel and James watching her, hoping to see reassuring confidence. Who could she look to? God? For the first time, He seemed far away. She had prayed none of this would happen, but it did. Did He care? Why did He let this frightful battle happen? Still, she silently reached out, praying for it all to end and for God to help her be brave.

Betsy suggested they wash the plates from breakfast, but after that there was not much to do. It made no sense to sweep the straw-covered floor, and she would not go out to the barn or garden. They gathered by the window, watching their parents help the hurting men toward the barn. The cannon and gunfire continued, rattling the windows. Smoke drifted in the fields and yard. Betsy finally turned away; she was afraid and could not watch.

She brought a cup of water to Thomas and sat down next to him. He was awake, and, despite the warm morning, he shivered. Betsy laid her hand gently on his flushed forehead. Feverish, she thought, and dipped a handkerchief in the water remaining in the cup. Rachel came, and Betsy motioned her to draw up the quilt while she placed the cool cloth on Thomas's forehead. "Thank you," he whispered.

James hovered near them, unsure what to do. "Do you think he wants to play with my toys?" he whispered in Betsy's ear. "I like to do that when I'm sick and can't get up." Betsy tried not to laugh as she shook her head, but she acknowledged it was a thoughtful idea.

A shrieking artillery shell sounded nearby, followed by a loud explosion. "Go to the cellar," Thomas ordered. Rachel fled, but James jumped toward the window. "Get away from there, James Westmore. Go below." Another artillery shell screamed as it tore a deadly trail in the air before exploding in the field. "Those are close. Get to safety now," he shouted. James obeyed, looking frightened.

"I'm not going," Betsy said. "I won't leave you, Thomas."

He started to protest as two more explosions rocked the ground, but, before he said anything, the kitchen door burst open, and the tall orderly rushed in, shouting, "D'you have some red cloth?"

"What for?" Betsy asked, raising her voice to be heard.

"We need to identify these buildings as hospitals so the Confederates will stop targeting this location. Red cloth has been the accepted identifying sign."

"We don't have any." She stopped, thinking quickly. "Wait! I forgot." She ran through the sitting room and hall into the parlor, snatched the brown paper parcel from the cutting table, and tore it open. The beautiful brick red fabric for her new dress tumbled to the floor, but she grabbed it and raced back. "Here."

Eight yards was too much fabric, but the orderly tore off several long strips and dashed outside, leaving the rest of the fabric crumpled on the floor. Sadly, Betsy picked it up and refolded it, thinking there might still be enough for her dress. She laid it at the foot of Thomas's pallet.

"Go below," he ordered her again.

She shook her head and, picking up the damp handkerchief, continued using it to try lowering his fever. The minutes stretched endlessly as the shells continued their blasts; then they stopped. "Your fabric must have got the signal through," Thomas said.

"I'm glad. I just wish something that simple could stop the whole battle."

Dr. Barnes came in and stood in the doorway, his tall frame making the room seem small. "Miss Westmore, I presume?" he said, his tone gruff and unfriendly.

"Yes, sir," she answered coldly.

"It has been brought to my attention that some of the wounded have not eaten a full meal in the last two days and are literally starving. Your mother is busy assisting Dr. Elder and his staff. You need to prepare some food."

Cook a meal in the middle of a battle for who knows how many men? she thought numbly. "Is it safe?" she wondered aloud

"You should be safe. The artillery fire has been directed elsewhere. The food doesn't need to be fancy. Just bake bread for a start. You can do that, right?"

"Yes," Betsy answered, and he turned abruptly and

marched out. I don't like the way he orders people around, she thought. It doesn't matter, she decided quickly. Men are starving. Mother would want me to be responsible, and I can help by cooking. At least that's not scary...

In the kitchen, Betsy worked the ingredients into a stiff dough the way Mother had taught her. When the dough was ready, she set it to rise and waited, wandering to the windows, checking on Thomas, and going down to see Rachel and James in the cellar. Her sister and brother were fine, but decided they wanted to stay there for a while; Betsy wished she could too. The cellar was somewhat quieter, and there were no surgeons venturing in with orders.

After sufficient time had gone by, she punched the dough and began kneading it. She set the dough to rise one more time, prepared the pans, and brought the oven to the proper temperature, adding more wood and monitoring it carefully. When she slid the pans into the oven and went into the sitting room to check the time on the clock, she was astonished to see it was already mid-morning. Time had moved quickly with the startling explosions and the task of preparing the food. Betsy decided to prepare more bread dough since she was not certain how many men had arrived.

The dining table was unused thus far. Dr. Barnes and his orderlies had gone to the barn and could be seen assisting the others there. Betsy frowned. She did not like that doctor. He seemed rough, and she hoped if Philip was ever hurt he would not have a doctor like him.

Mercifully, the sound of the fighting died away, and,

when the clock struck half-past ten, the chime was clearly heard. Betsy breathed a sigh of relief. At least for now, it's over, she thought, leaning idly by the west window in the sitting room. She saw a wagon jolting down the dirt road, its square canvas cover flapping. A long strip of her red calico fluttered on the fence, and the vehicle turned into the front yard and went hurriedly by the window. She saw men lying in the back of the wagon. With suspicious curiosity, she hastened to the back dining room window. The wagon had stopped near the barn and orderlies moved around it, lifting out men on stretchers and laying them side by side in the shade. She could not see Dr. Elder's makeshift table because of where the ambulance had stopped.

A little while later, another ambulance came, then another, and another. The last one stopped in front of the house and the requisitioned dining table. Dr. Barnes and his assistants waited at their posts.

Betsy suppressed a horrified scream as they moved the first wounded man from the ambulance. His shirt and some bandages around his upper torso were soaked with blood. He was so pale that he appeared dead. They laid him on the table. Dr. Barnes felt for a pulse, waited a moment, and callously shook his head, even as the soldier's chest moved with shallow breaths. They moved the man to the shade at the side of the house and laid another on the table. Betsy turned away, unable to watch and hating that doctor for not even trying to save the man's life. What if this happened to Philip?

Chapter 14

An orderly came and took the loaves of bread from where they cooled on the kitchen table. Betsy was kneading the dough for another batch when the tall blond assistant pushed open the door, and two others entered carrying a wounded man on a stretcher. This soldier had obviously been cared for by the doctor since a clean bandage was wrapped around his head, concealing his face. "Put him in the front room," the assistant ordered. "And with the others, come through the front door to stay out of the young lady's way."

At a quarter to one, Thomas woke from a light sleep and asked for a drink and "some of that good-smelling bread." Betsy brought him a thick slice from a warm loaf, and James, who, with Rachel, had ventured upstairs, handed him another cup of water.

Glancing into the sitting room, Betsy saw the wounded men on the straw-covered floor and the tall orderly moving along the row. "Can I do anything to help?" she asked.

He looked at her, perhaps trying to appraise her skill. "No," he said decidedly. "Baking bread is a good task for you. There will be more wounded arriving later."

"What?"

"You really didn't think these were all the wounded on that wretched hill after all the fighting, did you? The front-line aid stations can't even get many soldiers to safety because those...um...Confederates are firing at medical personnel. The ambulances are having difficulties too. No, you innocent, naïve little girl, there will be more wounded coming here."

Betsy blushed angrily at his last sarcastic comment. "I may be innocent and naïve, but at least I care!" she retorted.

"And what's that supposed to mean?" he responded, raising his eyebrows.

She took a deep breath and asked sternly, "What is your name?"

"Lamar. Sergeant Lamar, field hospital orderly. Why?"

"Nothing."

"What did you want to say?"

Although she knew it was rude, she walked away, afraid she would say something she would later regret. "Oh, bring me a clean bucket of water, please," Orderly Lamar called, but not unkindly.

She marched outside toward the well, resolutely looking away from the operating table. If she did not see it, could she ignore that it was there? Returning, Betsy handed the full bucket to the orderly, who accepted it with a half-smile. "Thanks. I'm sorry for what I said, miss. I truly am." She nodded, accepting his apology. "I know there's a lot of things happening right now that you don't understand. But you're brave, and – "

A single cannon blast interrupted anything else he was going to say. Betsy glanced at the clock; it was seven minutes after one. The echo had barely died away when many cannons discharged a fiery sound. The ground shook. Completely terrified by this new development, Betsy fled, colliding in the dining room with Rachel and James, who were looking for her.

Somehow, they ended up sitting against the wall near Thomas. He had tried to motion them to go below, but Betsy knew she could not move. Her terror kept her magnetized to someone she trusted. With Father and Mother still helping in the barn, Thomas was the next reliable person.

James covered his ears and curled up with his head on his older sister's lap. Rachel leaned against Betsy's shoulder. Thomas lay quiet, his eyes worried, and his expression betraying the pain he suffered.

The walls of the house – walls Betsy had always thought were strong – shook. The ground trembled. The air turned smoky outside, and, even in the house, it was hazy. Never in her life had Betsy felt so terrified.

This is the end of the world, she thought. Please, God, help us! Then the words she had put to memory came to her mind. She knew no one could hear her because of the tremendous crashing outside, but she spoke the words aloud anyway. One voice against the furies of war:

"God is our refuge and strength,
A very present help in trouble.

Therefore we will not fear,
Even though the earth be removed,
And though the mountains be carried into the midst of the sea;
Though its waters roar and be troubled,
Though the mountains shake with its swelling."

The mountains were shaking. She sensed that the world as she knew it would never be the same again. God was their stronghold; the outcome did not matter. He was her refuge. Her help in trouble. "Therefore we will not fear," she said over and over. Though nothing could drown out the monstrous noise, she felt an indescribable peace conquer the fear in her soul. God was in charge, and nothing could happen without His knowledge. She was safe and secure in the palm of His mighty, invisible hand. There was truly nothing to fear. Her world of sunlight, security, and smiles was falling apart, but God was her refuge. She would hope in Him.

Time ceased. Only the shaking ground, crashing weaponry, and the awful smell of battle smoke existed. She held her siblings close, feeling James's trembling and Rachel's sobs, but to try to speak would be in vain. It seemed as if all the fury of a judgment day was being unleashed. How many men were marching into eternity? The horror of the aftermath of this immense battle would be beyond words, but Betsy pushed that thought away for the time and continued to recite her scripture verse.

Then there was silence. Thought-provoking, deadly, and chilling. They looked at each other, afraid to speak, ears aching, heads pounding, eyes watering, and hearts burning. The tense silence stretched forever. Only the steady ticking of the old clock could be heard; how many hours had slipped by? They waited, hardly daring to breathe. It was an ominous silence, as though every living thing in the outside world had perished.

It came, faintly at first, then growing into a mighty crescendo. A cheer of triumph – low, resounding, manly – echoed from the woods of Culp's Hill and ran to the south where the Round Top hills stood. "Thank God," Thomas whispered reverently. "We've won."

"How do you know?" Betsy breathed.

"That's not a Rebel yell. That's a Union cheer, and they would not cheer if they were retreating or defeated. Oh, thank God, thank God!"

Chapter 15

As Thomas finished speaking, Father and Mother came in quickly, and the children ran to them. Held tight in her mother's arms, Betsy breathed a silent prayer of thanks for their safety. "Why didn't you come back to the house?" she asked, seeing Mother's worried expression and the blood stains on her sleeves and apron.

"Some of the wounded were agitated by the cannonade, and Dr. Elder insisted that he needed our help. I'm sorry you were alone here with Rachel and James." Mother sighed wearily.

Betsy nodded. "I just kept thinking about the psalm I memorized, and it helped me to have courage."

Father scrubbed his hands in a basin of water. He looked determined and sad as he prepared to return to the barn hospital. "You children stay inside," he ordered. "You don't need to see what's happening."

James started to ask what he couldn't see, but Betsy motioned him to be quiet. "I won't even look out a window," Rachel promised, resolutely studying the ground. Betsy thought that was a little extreme, but was thankful she didn't have to see the badly wounded men.

Betsy noticed the bowl of bread dough she had set to

rise several hours ago. The dough had overflowed the bowl and now lay limp. "Oh dear," she sighed, and then smiled at the funny sight.

"Never mind," Mother said encouragingly as she hurried into the sitting room, carrying a pitcher of water. "It may end up a little flat, but it will still be food."

Though she wanted to sleep and awake to a clean, beautiful world, forgetting the terrible battle and the injured men nearby, Betsy knew she could not ignore the responsibility she had been assigned. She baked more bread and, anticipating Orderly Lamar's requests, drew more water from the well. The sun dropped lower as silence dominated the world, and dark rain-clouds rolled in.

As the sun set, the aftermath invasion began again. Quick glances out the windows revealed ambulances traveling along the pike, some coming to the Westmores' house, others moving farther down the road. The surgeons were busy, the tromp of the assistants' boots reported the continuous procession of wounded carried into the house through the front door and hallways.

In the overcast twilight, Orderly Lamar appeared in the kitchen, his sleeves rolled up and blood splattered on his hands and arms. Betsy thought he looked like the butchers at Mr. Pierce's shop in town. "Miss Westmore," he said, "our supply of bandages will not last long. Does your mother have cloth we could use?"

"I'll go ask her," Betsy responded as she slid more bread into the oven.

She had not realized how many wounded had been moved into the house in the last couple of hours until she stood at the sitting room threshold. They lay in neat rows, but the room was still crowded. The hallway was filled, and a glance into the parlor revealed the same conditions there. Betsy climbed the wooden steps. Mother was at the far end of the upstairs hall, kneeling by the chest under the window, and Betsy approached quietly.

A young man lay on the chest. His brown eyes were open, and his kepi had been removed as Mother smoothed his dark hair. The blue uniform had been unbuttoned, and the bloody bandage on his chest shifted with each ragged breath.

"It's right kind of you, ma'am, to stay with me," he murmured. "You remind me of my mother."

"Rest now," Mother whispered.

"No, there'll be time to do that later," he answered, reaching out a trembling hand to hold her sleeve. "Won't you button my jacket properly? Always hated a sloppy uniform."

"How old are you?" Mother asked, beginning the desired task.

"Seventeen, ma'am. Been a bugler for the regiment."

"There," Mother said, fastening the last button. "I had a son, who, if he had lived, would have been your age."

"Then you understand, ma'am. Can you kiss me the way my mother would if she was here?"

Mother nodded and tried to wipe away the tears on her face. She kissed him gently on the forehead and smoothed his unruly hair again. "My son's name was Charles," she whispered. "What is your name?"

He looked beyond her and seemed to see something beautiful and glorious. His drawn face broke into a smile, but he glanced at Mother one last time. "Charlie…" he whispered, answering her question. Then his eyes fixed beyond her and seemed to freeze as his last breath gently exhaled.

He was dead. Betsy covered her face and trembled. She could not cry even though she wanted to; she could not move or make a sound. A seventeen year old had died, and for what purpose?

She felt Mother's arms around her. They stood there for a long time. "What can I say to help you?" Mother finally asked.

"I don't know," Betsy answered hollowly.

An assistant came from one of the bedrooms and paused near where the boy lay. "What was his name?" he asked Mother.

"Charlie."

"No last name known?"

"Only Charlie…"

Betsy looked once more at the young soldier. His blue uniform was neatly buttoned, and, in the semi-darkness, he appeared to sleep. A single bullet had caused the torn hole in his coat and this eternal slumber.

"He could've been my son," Mother murmured as an orderly carried him downstairs. "Same age, same name. His mother will never see him again. I know that pain. Oh, Charlie…"

Later, they went downstairs, and Mother silently took the sheets from the linen cupboard. She hesitated before adding her good linen tablecloths to the stack, but emptied the entire shelf. They picked up the large pile to carry it to the kitchen, but as they passed through the sitting room, Orderly Lamar asked Mother to come and help calm a young man who was panicking and calling a woman's name.

Betsy fled to the safety of the kitchen, grateful her baking task was comparatively easy. She did not want to see any more of this dreadful war conquering her home. The young soldier's death haunted her, and she desperately thought of Philip. Where was he? And where were Rachel and James? They should be in the kitchen or the cellar, not exposed to the war scenes; she would go and look for them in a moment. Betsy laid the linens on the table by the window and was turning to check the bread when Dr. Barnes opened the door and ordered, "Miss Westmore, come outside. I need your help."

Remembering Father's instructions to stay inside, Betsy tried to think of a way to refuse. "Sir, I'm sorry...but..."

"Miss Westmore, I don't have time to reason," he replied sternly. "I'm in charge of this field hospital and the efforts to care for these wounded. I need your help. Come outside."

Conflicted, but seeing no choice, Betsy obeyed his command. It was raining, but someone had rigged a canvas cover over the operating table. In the darkness, she saw the shadowy outlines of injured men waiting for medical assistance.

"I can't see," Dr. Barnes explained brusquely. "They're

looking for my lanterns, but, until they find them, I need someone to hold this lamp." He pointed to a flickering lamp on the instrument table. "Can you do this?"

No! Betsy's mind screamed. I've seen enough awful things. I've seen a young man die, and there are wounded all over my house. She recalled Thomas's words. If her brother was injured and waiting for care, wouldn't she want someone to hold a light for the doctor? These men lying in the darkness were somebody's brothers. "Yes," she whispered, reaching for the oil lamp and twisting the wick to give more light.

The surgeon did not reply. Two assistants lifted a young soldier onto the table. His uniform was gray. There was a makeshift tourniquet on his right leg and a bandage on his right shoulder. In the flickering light, Dr. Barnes cut the coat and lower pant leg and examined the wounds. "Chloroform," he said tersely. As the assistants administered the anesthetic, the doctor ordered Betsy to stand to the side of the table where the light would not be blocked by their movements.

I can't do this, Betsy thought. I'm going to be sick. He's going to amputate this soldier's leg. She swallowed hard, willing herself not to drop the lamp and flee. In horror, she saw the doctor preparing the shattered limb, but, when he picked up a sharp knife, she closed her eyes. How long she stood there, she did not know. She focused on not thinking about what was happening until an awful rasping sound and a cry from the patient made her open her eyes.

One glance at what the surgeon was doing sickened her, and she looked away, trying to calm the nauseous feeling. The patient lay still, but his brown eyes were open, focused on her and seeming to never blink. His sandy blond hair was plastered to his forehead. His body trembled. She wondered why he was awake and if he could feel the pain.

The surgeon finished the amputation and bandaging and moved to examine the wounded shoulder. The soldier did not move and continued to stare at Betsy. She never let her eyes leave his face, fearing she would faint or be sick if she saw what the doctor was doing.

"Finished," Dr. Barnes announced. "Move him inside, and let him rest. Monitor him as the chloroform wears off." He wiped his instruments on his bloody apron and used an already saturated rag to wipe a pool of blood off the table.

"He wasn't unconscious…" Betsy said, partly as an observation, partly as a question.

"No. But he didn't feel pain," the surgeon remarked absently. "We don't want to give enough chloroform to make them unconscious because we don't understand when unconsciousness becomes death. My assistant's careful, and we've not lost a patient to chloroform overdose yet. That last patient was brave. Some of them struggle and fight us because they don't want the operation or they've gone temporarily mad in battle shock." By this time, the next wounded man had been moved to the table, and the surgeon silently began the examination.

Betsy willed herself not to watch and again focused on the soldier's face. This man, a Union soldier, suffered intensely. The pain reflected in his light brown eyes, and the set expression of his squared jaw and almost bloodless lips revealed his efforts to not cry out or complain. His kepi remained on his head, but some sweat-soaked reddish-brown hair escaped.

An assistant placed bloody fingers on the soldier's neck to check for a pulse. "It's steady, sir, but not strong."

"I think we can remove the bullet. Miss Westmore, stand closer," Dr. Barnes ordered.

Betsy heard him, but she seemed rooted to the ground. Someone pushed her until she stood against the table. It was unavoidable to see the wound, tearing into the soldier's abdomen. The smell of blood and the strange odor of chloroform affected her as much as the sight of the injury. She tried to look away and breathe calmly, but the lamp wavered. "I…I'm…"

Someone took the lamp from her hands and held her by the waist. "Go inside and sit down, Daughter," Father's voice said. "Can you walk?"

She nodded and ran, slamming the kitchen door behind her and leaning against the wall, shaking and trembling, her empty stomach turning. She wanted to cry, but no tears would come. It was a revolting nightmare: the cannonade in the afternoon, Charlie's death, and the two wounded men she had seen.

Small arms wrapped around her, and, glancing down, she saw James crying. Betsy knelt down and held him, her own eyes still tearless and staring. "Where have you been?" she asked, anxiously. "I was going to look for you."

"I obeyed Father and didn't go outside, but I wandered around to see what was happening." James sniffled. "I didn't know that war was like this. I thought it was glorious and exciting." He took a shaky breath and, looking her in the eyes, asked, "What will happen to Philip?"

"I don't know," Betsy answered hopelessly. Knowing that the wounded men lying in the house were somebody's brothers did not give her confidence about Philip's safety. Was he lying in someone's house, hurting or dying? "Where's Rachel?" she asked after a long moment.

"In the cellar. She's afraid and hiding."

I don't blame her, Betsy thought. I'm ready to run away and hide too. "It's late," she said aloud. "Why don't you go down and sleep? God will take care of Philip."

"Alright," James responded and moved slowly to the entrance of the cellar.

There was not time to ponder deep questions or thoughts. Betsy forced herself to stand and moved to the doorway of the dining room. Thomas slept, and near him lay the Confederate soldier whose leg had been amputated. Between them there was room for one other man while maintaining a clear walkway into the kitchen. The red calico for her new dress still lay at Thomas's feet. She picked it up and returned to the kitchen, surveying the stack of linens waiting on the table.

She walked to the window and looked out at the surgical scene. Someone had found lanterns, and Father was hanging them at the corners and ridgepole of the canvas structure. The surgeon was wiping his hands as an assistant secured a bandage around the Union soldier's torso. Other assistants carried the next patient toward the operating table. The wounded men lay as far as she could see, and there must be more in the darkness because the upright figures of orderlies moved through the drizzling rain.

Betsy looked back at the pile of linens. She glanced down at the fabric in her hands. She tried to reason that there would never be enough bandages anyway, so why should she sacrifice more of her dress material? As she stood there thinking, orderlies carried in a stretcher with the Union soldier; they gently laid him in the open area in the dining room. He's been wounded, she thought. Others are dying, and I'm reluctant to give my dress fabric.

The thought was despicable to her patriotic heart, and, after retrieving a small pair of scissors, she made cuts at the edge of the fabric. Then she tore the beautiful cloth into long strips: bandages. When her fabric was shredded, she began on the sheets and heirloom tablecloths. She felt regret, but self had no place in this new world of misery. Relentlessly, she cut and tore the cloth as though it was the only thing that mattered. Her fingers worked, but her mind seemed dead.

Betsy was tearing the last sheet and leaning against the table when someone lifted the fabric from her hands and said gently, "Go to bed, Daughter. You've done all you can."

"Oh, Father," she whispered, turning as he embraced her. "I don't even know what to think or say."

She saw how tired and sorrowful he was, but he tried to speak hopefully. " 'Cast all your cares on Him because God cares for you...' Take comfort in His promises. I cannot control the situation or turn it into something good, but He can. Trust the Lord." He smoothed the escaping strands of her hair and kissed her on the forehead. "Now, go and sleep."

She nodded and answered softly, "Yes, Father…" From habit rather than determined faith, she repeated the first line of her psalm to herself as she went into the darkness of the cellar, found a blanket, and lay down, too tired to undress or even take off her shoes. Sleep came quickly, and, mercifully, it was dreamless.

Chapter 16

Betsy sat up in alarm. Someone was screaming. Then she remembered: home was a field hospital. There were injured men upstairs. She covered her face with her hands and prayed for it all to end. Somehow, her siblings still slept, but Betsy decided to get up. She straightened her clothing, and finger-combed her hair, twisting it into a neat bun.

The kitchen looked the same as the night before, except the two loaves of bread and the bandages had disappeared. As though in a dream, she wandered through the house, dazed and unsure what to do. In the dining room, Thomas was awake, but he looked at her with staring, unseeing eyes as he shivered under his blanket. The other Union soldier lay tensely, his arm shielding his eyes from the light. The Confederate still slept, frowning and clutching his wounded shoulder. How did enemy soldiers end up in their house? Why had the war invaded this formerly happy place? What was the reason for all this?

Shrugging away the questions, Betsy continued, reality settling as she walked into the next room. The sitting room was filled with injured men, most lying on the straw-covered floor or leaning against the walls. There was hardly room to walk between them. The wounded had been placed in the hallway and the parlor, where they used the embroidered chair cushions as pillows or limb supports. Soldiers in blue and gray crowded together; some lay perfectly still and had died in the night.

She moved upstairs, following a trail of splattered crimson on the wooden steps. A few wounded lay in the hall, but quick glances into the bedrooms revealed that these had been requisitioned for officers or critically injured. The beautiful quilt she had made was blood soaked, and Dr. Barnes and an assistant bent over a man, trying to stop a fast-flowing stream of blood. Oddly, Betsy was not upset at the condition of her quilt; she felt a pang of sadness, but her mind could not process the disappointment.

She wandered back downstairs and out the front door where she stopped in shock. Men had been laid on the porch to avoid the rain, but one step off the porch lay a motionless row. Dead. The dead, in blue and gray, had been laid there, waiting for burial.

Betsy glanced at the strip of cloth hanging limply from the porch pillar and touched it regretfully. It was the red calico from her dress; that red flag indicated the location of a field hospital. What was supposed to be beautiful and charming had become a symbol for misery.

She felt like she was falling. There was nothing to grasp. The safe world had vanished and been replaced with a world of suffering. Her bright and happy home had become a house of blood, pain, and death. Betsy caught the one lifeline she knew: her faith. "God is my refuge and strength," she said aloud, causing one or two wounded to look at her strangely. "I won't fear, even though the world as I knew it has been destroyed." She added under her breath, "But please help me, God. I don't know what to do. I'm so scared."

Turning, Betsy slowly re-entered the house and retreated to the kitchen; at least there were no wounded or dead there. Orderly Lamar was waiting. "We need you to continue baking, and you can prepare some soup. Your mother said you should work on this. She and your father are helping us with the wounded in the barn. And Mr. Westmore told me to bring these pails of fresh milk in. Maybe you could strain it and pour it into pitchers for distribution."

"Alright. How much bread should I make?"

"Cook all you can. It won't be too much."

After he left, Betsy rubbed her eyes and tried to form a plan. She brought more flour and collected the last root vegetables from the bins in the cellar. James woke up and asked if he could help; Betsy motioned for him to come upstairs. "I could get some more vegetables from the garden," he suggested.

Betsy hesitated. She didn't want to send him outside, but knew she would not have time to go. Finally, she agreed, after making him promise to stay away from the wounded, the operating tables, and the barn.

"I don't want to see the hurt men or the doctor," James admitted solemnly, marching outside.

She started the bread dough and washed a few used dishes left on the table. When James returned with the basket of produce, he was promptly instructed by an orderly to start hauling buckets of water to the barn. "Can I, Betsy?" James asked. "Father said…"

"I know," Betsy replied. "I don't really want to send you there, but the doctors and orderlies need help. I think Father and Mother would want us to assist so the wounded men will feel better." James nodded and started on his new task.

Betsy was chopping the vegetables when Rachel climbed timidly up the cellar stairs and sat on the top step, looking around as if expecting a beast to seize her and force her to work. "Do you want to help me with the food?" Betsy said, worried about the traces of tears on her sister's face and the dark circles under her eyes.

"No. I just came to get some water and something to eat. May I have that heel of bread?"

"Sure."

Rachel snatched the bread and disappeared into the cellar like a frightened mouse. Betsy sighed, envious of and annoyed by Rachel's fear which kept her sister from responsible work. How could she help Rachel understand hiding in the cellar did not change the situation? Hiding did not cook meals for starving soldiers, haul water for the wounded, or help more directly like Father and Mother. How could she make Rachel understand her fear was paralyzing her usefulness?

Too busy to reason with Rachel at the moment, Betsy found the largest kettle, filled it with the vegetables, water, and a few herbs, and prepared it to simmer slowly all day, ready for use at any time. By mid-morning, a glance from the window showed that tiny tents and canvas shelters had been erected in the yard and along the house, and the wounded had been moved there to avoid the drizzly rain. In the house, the medical staff tramped in and out through the kitchen, carrying basins of water, bandages, or surgical supplies. Occasionally, the mutter of skirmishing could be heard in the distance or a single cannon shot was fired, but no large-scale fighting seemed to be occurring today.

As she turned and punched more bread dough, Betsy thought about Philip and felt like crying. Where was he? Was he hurt? Was he like some of the poor men here, with a painful injury or missing limb? She would not allow herself to think he would not return. Worry tightened in her chest, and she tried to think of something else. Betsy remembered the diminishing level of the flour in the barrel and wondered how long it would last while baking so much bread. What would happen to the wounded and her family if the entire food supply was used up? The dull ache in her arms from kneading added to her gloomy feelings.

Noon approached. The tired orderlies came and ladled small portions of the soup into cups and went to feed the wounded a meager dinner. A few of the assistants expressed their gratitude for Betsy's management of the cooking. "Oh, Miss Westmore, can you take some soup to the three men in this first room?" one asked as he rushed out toward the barn with a small pot of soup in his hands and two loaves of bread under his arm.

She ladled the soup, feeling a little nervous; she knew Thomas, but the other two were strangers. One was a Confederate. What would he be like?

James staggered in. "I've never hauled so much water in my life," he moaned. "Look, the bucket ropes blistered my hands." Betsy wrapped a scrap of cloth around each sore hand and reminded him not to complain: what were blisters compared to wounds?

"I know," he said sadly, looking many years older and wiser. "I'll never think war is fun ever again." He wandered into the dining room, and, when Betsy entered a moment later, balancing three cups of soup, James was saying, "Thomas, I made sure Blaze got a bucket of water this morning. She's doing alright, but Father put her out in the rain with the cows 'cause there's wounded men in the barn."

Thomas blinked and said slowly, "Thank you. That's good."

"Are you alright?" James demanded, alarmed at the shallow response.

"No. Sorry. I can't think."

"I'll go away and let you rest," James murmured. "That doctor wanted me to go pick some of the cherries and plums anyway."

Betsy set down the bowls and knelt by Thomas. He sighed as she touched his forehead. "Your hand's cool."

"You're burning up," she exclaimed.

"I know. When you see him, ask the doctor if he'll examine me."

"I will," Betsy replied. "Do you want some soup? It's mostly broth."

"Sure. I should eat something."

She handed him the tin cup and smiled encouragingly before turning to the other Union soldier. "Would you like some too?"

"No, thank you. Not now," he replied with a forced smile. "It does smell good. I hope you won't be offended. I can't eat right now."

"Not at all," Betsy answered reassuringly. He seems kindhearted, she thought, but he looks very uncomfortable. Aloud, she said, "Do you want some water instead?"

He nodded, and she brought some. "Thank you, Miss…?"

"Westmore. But you can call me Betsy, if you prefer. And you are?"

"Sergeant Edward Morten, 27th Indiana," he replied formally.

Chapter 17

"Well, I'll have some of that soup," the Confederate announced in his Southern accent. The lonely expression on his face was chased away by a friendly grin. "I'm right starved. General Lee can fight, but he sure does have trouble keeping us fed." He blushed a little and said, "I did think you were real plucky, miss, standing there through the surgery last night."

"Well, I thought you were brave also," she answered sincerely.

"Never thought I'd hear a Yankee girl say that. I'm a Confederate you know."

"I know." Betsy handed him the soup. She sat down, feeling surprised an enemy soldier was so friendly and eager for conversation.

"I'm Harold Cooper, a private in the 10th Virginia Infantry," he added with pride. "And we almost whipped the Yankees."

"Did you now?" Thomas muttered.

"Yeah, we captured their position on the night of July 2nd."

"Only because we were called away," Sergeant Morten murmured. He shifted uncomfortably, stopping suddenly with a startled gasp.

Alerted by his quick inhale, Betsy watched him. He swallowed hard, and his jaw clenched before he exhaled slowly; his controlled expression returned, and whatever he felt was concealed by an immovable mask. She waited, then continued the conversation, asking, "Called away?"

"Yes," the sergeant responded, his voice low, but steady. "To my understanding, the three brigades of the Twelfth Corps were on Culp's Hill, but two of the brigades were ordered to go elsewhere as reinforcements." He paused for an instant as if distracted, then refocused and continued. "The 27th is in the Third Brigade of the First Division, and we marched double-quick toward the south, over a little ridge, and saw the fighting, but were too late to help our comrades. In the failing light, we could see that the fighting had been savage out in a wheat field and peach orchard and near a big pile of rocks in front of a little mountain."

"Devil's Den and Round Top," Betsy said, recognizing the landmarks from his description.

"When we got back to the Culp's Hill area, night fighting had begun, and we couldn't find our position or determine who held it," the sergeant finished.

"Then you all attacked in the morning and spoiled our plans," the Confederate complained. "That fighting on Culp's Hill was some of the worst I've seen yet, and the 10th has been through a lot. In the end, we couldn't drive the Yankees out, but we sure tried our...um...hardest. Where was the 27th anyway?"

"Near the creek to the southeast of the hill. Some of the Confederates sniped at us when we were in the woods. Someone with shoulder bar insignia thought it was a good idea to charge across an open meadow with the enemy waiting on the other side of a stone wall. The 27th and one of our sister regiments, the 2nd Massachusetts, made the charge." Sergeant Morten's eyes shown with pride as he told the next event. "Our regiment got farther into the field. The fire was dreadful. I saw our flag, torn with bullets, fall from the bearers' hands as they were shot, but I thought that flag was worth fighting for."

Private Cooper snorted in disgust. "Lincoln's fool," he said derogatorily. "Well, when'd you get wounded? Out in the field?"

"No." Sergeant Morten frowned, as though he did not want to recall this part of his story. "We retreated, and I was wounded only a little ways from the cover of the trees, but they couldn't get to me during the whole day because the Confederates started sniping at the medical personnel."

"Well...I don't do that," the private commented self-righteously, and the sergeant did not respond.

Betsy listened to the discussion, curious to learn more about the battle and what had happened to these men. They, like Thomas, only knew what they saw or heard, not an overall strategy or outcome. Still, from Sergeant Morten's words, she guessed the Union had successfully held the Culp's Hill area. Philip wasn't in the Twelfth Corps, so she reasoned he could not have been there.

Sergeant Morten restlessly turned his head on the pillow. Betsy noted the rigid position of his body and his clenched fists at his sides. "Can I do anything for you?" she asked, touching his shoulder.

His expression betrayed momentary confusion at her question. "No, there's nothing to be done…except endure." He looked away.

Sensing he did not want her to remain, Betsy returned to the kitchen. She thought Sergeant Morten detected her inexperience and did not trust her. She pushed aside those thoughts and determined to focus on her assigned task.

Betsy spent the afternoon continuing to bake bread and adding more vegetables and water to the soup kettle. Mother and Father came and went, helping mostly in the barn where the need seemed greater because of the primitive facilities and fewer orderlies for the large number of wounded men. James kept busy hauling buckets of water and running simple errands.

When Betsy realized the day was July 4th, she did not believe it at first. Of course, the calendar was correct, but she had never imagined spending the holiday this way. There were no picnics, games, visits, or fun; it was simply another day in this post-battle world. However, if the Union had won the battle and if home was not permanently doomed as a hospital, then maybe next year they could celebrate in a peaceful America.

In the late afternoon, kitchen work lulled, and Betsy decided to talk with Rachel. It would feel good to sit down for a couple of minutes, and maybe she could encourage her sister. However, when she carried a lamp into the cellar, Rachel was not there. Slightly alarmed, Betsy returned to the kitchen; Mother was there, slicing another loaf of bread. "Have you seen Rachel, Mother?"

"No, I thought she was in the cellar," Mother replied, concerned.

"I thought so too," Betsy admitted. "Yet she could have slipped out several hours ago when I asked the doctor to check Corporal Russell. I'll find her and make sure she's alright."

"Thank you," Mother sighed wearily and rubbed her forehead. "How's the food supply holding out?"

"I cut the last of the vegetables. I'm going to prepare the basket of fruit James picked and boil it for a sort of jam sauce. Tomorrow, I'll cook the beans for soup, but I don't know how long the flour will last for bread."

"One day, one hour at a time, Daughter," Mother said, trying to speak encouragingly.

"Yes," Betsy murmured. "Now, I'm going to find Rachel."

She walked through the dining room and sitting room, glanced into the parlor and onto the porch. "Have you seen my sister?" Betsy asked a soldier with a bandaged arm, who seemed to be guarding the stairs. He shook his head, but she went up anyway.

In the boys' room, Betsy found her. Timid Rachel sat on the bed next to a wounded officer, and she placed a folded cloth over the blood soaked bandages covering a bad wound. Then, she took a scrap of material from the washbasin and wiped away the sweat on his forehead. Wondering at the change in her sister, Betsy leaned against the doorframe and observed, unwilling to intrude.

"You are kind to sit with me these last few hours. You look like my daughter," the officer said quietly. "I wanted to see her and her mother again."

"You will, sir," Rachel spoke with soft confidence.

"That's correct," he sighed. "But in heaven. Not here." His face contorted with sudden pain, and his hand reached gropingly.

Rachel gently held his hand and bent over him. "I don't know what to say to comfort you, sir. But my father says that the words of scripture comfort and heal." In a reverent voice, she began:

"The Lord is my shepherd; I shall not want.
He makes me to lie down in green pastures;
He leads me beside the still waters.
He restores my soul.
He leads me in the paths of righteousness
for His name's sake..."

The officer listened intently and began reciting the words with Rachel.

"Yea, though I walk through
the valley of the shadow of death,

I will fear no evil; for You are with me;
Your rod and Your staff, they comfort me.
You prepare a table before me
in the presence of my enemies;
You anoint my head with oil; My cup runs over.
Surely goodness and mercy shall follow me
all the days of my life;
and I will dwell in the house of the Lord forever…"

Only Rachel's voice spoke the final line. The officer had gone to dwell with the Lord. Rachel sat motionless for a moment, then she laid his hand at his side. Moving slowly and almost with an angel-like benediction, she picked up his sword from the floor and placed it beside him before covering his pale face with a clean handkerchief left on the bedside table. Not until she finished these ritual-like duties did she notice Betsy and, going to her older sister, hid her face and sobbed the grief of a torn heart.

Betsy could not think of anything to say. Her throat was too tight. A few tears ran down her cheeks. It was the second death she had witnessed in less than twenty-four hours.

"I don't even know his name. I forgot to ask," Rachel cried. "We can't even write to his family. When the doctor asked me to sit with him, I didn't realize he was going to die."

"How long were you with him?" Betsy whispered.

"Several hours, I think. He slept a while, and then we

talked a little." She sobbed, "He has a little girl who's my age, and now her father isn't coming home."

Betsy held her. She felt useless because she could not think of anything comforting to say. She thought she had failed her siblings; they had seen war, and she had not protected them. Philip would be disappointed because she had not kept her promise.

Finally, Rachel calmed and dried her eyes, saying, "I'm sorry for hiding. My shyness was selfish, and being selfish doesn't help anyone, does it?" Betsy shook her head. "I'll help you in the kitchen, if you want."

Sadly, they returned to the work waiting for them downstairs. Night came, and the girls still toiled. Mother and Father remained in the barn, returning to get what they needed and check on the children, but with no time to stay and talk. As twilight came, James was reassigned from hauling water to sit beside Thomas and wipe his forehead with a cool cloth, with strict orders to avoid talking.

The clock had struck nine a long time before. Betsy leaned on the kitchen table, idly watching Rachel pit the last of the cherries. Betsy could hardly keep her eyes open or stand upright, but she managed to pull the latest batch of bread from the oven.

Orderly Lamar entered leading James. "Children, you've done all you could today. Go to bed," he said wearily, but with sympathy in his tone. Betsy nodded. James nearly fell into her arms and started crying. Rachel came, and they huddled together.

As the flickering lamps cast gloomy light over the spectacle and the moans and cries of the wounded echoed through the once-cheerful home, Betsy felt helpless. There was so much to be done, so many men needing help. The wretchedness of sin displayed in war had its consequences, and she shed tears for the helpless men who lay within the walls of the house. The rain came down more heavily, pattering on the roof. With tears in his eyes, James looked up at his sisters and whispered, "I think God is crying too."

Chapter 18

The next day – July 5, 1863 – was Sunday, but it was unlike any Sunday Betsy had ever known. There were no church services. It was not a day of rest. She rose at sunrise, preparing more food and seeing with consternation the flour supply would only last the day and maybe one baking of bread tomorrow. What were they going to feed the men? As Mother had said: one day, one hour at a time. Yet, every hour brought new challenges.

By late morning, rain-clouds hid the sun, and the heavens wept as Dr. Barnes had a soldier carried to the operation table and performed another surgery. Betsy resolutely stayed away from the window, turning and punching the bread dough, while trying to block out the poor soldier's screams. They carried him back inside, and the assistants returned to their tasks.

She glanced out the window a few minutes later and was shocked to see Dr. Barnes on his knees, his face covered by his bloody hands, and his shoulders shaking with sobs. What had happened? Where was the fierce, callous doctor who had amputated countless limbs, set aside mortally wounded men without a thought, and ordered people around harshly?

"Take him some food, Miss Westmore, and a cup of that coffee you've made for us," Orderly Lamar directed, glancing at the situation as he rinsed some sponges in a basin of already bloody water.

Nervously, she stepped out into the rain and hastened under the frail shelter of the canvas. The doctor did not hear her approach. He continued a mumbled monologue. "Oh God! What can I do? Three days I've worked with little food and no sleep, trying to save these men. What more can I do? There aren't enough supplies. I have to do this work knowing not all can survive. It eats at my soul, but if I leave my post, more men will die. I…"

Betsy felt ashamed. She had thought this man was a brute who did not care about the soldiers. How wrong she had been! He cared, and perhaps it was because he cared so much that he steeled himself to be strong and unbending which she, in harsh judgment, had labeled cruel.

She put the plate and cup on the stained table and said hastily, "Here's some food and coffee, sir. Mr. Lamar asked me to bring it to you."

A moment later, he glanced up at her and said in his gruff voice, "My thanks."

"You're welcome. Please forgive me for misjudging you." She fled back to the house, glad she had apologized, but unwilling to stay, supposing he might prefer to be alone. As she cut some herbs for the soup, she reconsidered Dr. Barnes's previous actions when he set up the field hospital and took care of the wounded. Now, she realized he was very focused and dedicated. How much worse the situation could have been if he had truly been uncaring and unskilled. She started praying for strength for the tired doctor and the assistants.

At noon, she offered food to the three in the dining room. Thomas and Sergeant Morten refused, but Private Cooper accepted. Betsy returned with a bowl and spoon; all the cups were in use and it might be a while before Rachel washed them.

"Could you help me?" he asked, embarrassed. "I'm not good with my left hand, and my right's useless."

"Yes, Mr. Cooper."

"I'd like it better if you called me Harold."

Betsy found it was awkward for both of them. He was mortified at not being able to do the simple task by himself. She felt disconcerted by his bashfulness, the fear of spilling the soup, and the oddity of feeding a grown man like a toddler. Harold started a conversation as a way out of their predicament. "Have you always lived in Pennsylvania?"

"Yes," she replied. "This farm has been in my father's family for several generations."

"I'm a farmer back home too. I'm from Virginia…the Shenandoah Valley. There's lots of farms there. My ma's the best cook in the world, but your soup is pretty good too."

"Do you have siblings?" Betsy asked.

"Yeah. A younger sister, who's fifteen, and two little brothers, who are twelve and nine. I'm nineteen."

"And is your father at home or fighting in the war?"

"He died." Harold's brown eyes clouded with sorrow. "At the Battle of Malvern Hill last year. I buried him."

"I'm so sorry," Betsy said, regretting her question.

"I have to get better. Ma needs my help. Though I don't know how much help I'll be with only one leg," he added bitterly. "It might be kind of hard to hop on one leg while plowing the fields," he mentioned sarcastically after some consideration. In spite of herself, Betsy laughed at the idea, and then Harold smiled. "No, I know what I'll do. I'll get a wooden leg, and my brothers will call me a pirate. What do you think?" he asked with a teasing grin.

Before she thought of a suitable reply, Betsy was distracted by Dr. Barnes bending over Thomas, who lay wrapped in the quilt. Making a quick excuse and taking the empty bowl, she left Harold and approached the doctor, who looked up and saw her worried expression.

"It's a bad fever," Dr. Barnes declared. He checked the splinted leg. "Normal swelling, no infection there." He examined the bullet graze on the shoulder. "Not good. Slight inflammation, but I think he's sick with something else." The doctor rubbed his head as if trying to think what to do. Thomas, weary and ill, looked at them and waited.

"Sir," Betsy said quietly, "my mother uses dried herbs to brew teas that can lower fever. Would you like me to make some for Corporal Russell, and it would be available for other soldiers too?"

"It can't harm," Dr. Barnes admitted, turning toward Sergeant Morten. He lifted the soldier's wrist and checked his pulse, asking something in a barely audible tone. The sergeant glanced at Betsy as though he wanted her to leave, and, confused by his wordless command, she went to prepare the herbs and boil the water.

A tall, dark-haired soldier, in a dusty blue uniform with no bloodstains, stood awkwardly in the kitchen when Betsy entered. "Excuse me, ma'am?" he said quietly. "I heard Corporal Thomas Russell was here. May I see him?"

"May I ask who you are?" Betsy responded politely.

"Sergeant William Saylor, at your service. I'm Russell's cousin and a courier for the Second Corps headquarters." He nervously turned his hat in his hand. "Do you know Russell? Is he alright?"

"Yes, he's here. I don't know if he's alright," Betsy admitted.

He looked at his dirty boots and mumbled, "Is he dying?"

Betsy quickly reassured him. "I don't think so, but he has a high fever. I'm sure he'd be glad to see you." She motioned him into the dining room, then filled the tea kettle and put it on the stove to boil.

"Yes, we won," Sergeant Saylor said as she entered the dining room a few minutes later. "The second day was a draw, but the third day was clearly a Union victory."

Harold scowled fiercely from his corner, but the other two listened with interest.

"Union lines held on Culp's Hill from what I heard. Then there was two hours of cannon fire, but the Confederates overshot most of the time and didn't do much damage to the fighting lines. After that cannonade, the smoke cleared a little, and we saw long lines of Confederates marching across those open fields – fifteen thousand of them, if I had to guess. It was an awe-inspiring sight for a few minutes, but ultimately they were defeated, though a few did make it over the stone wall. General Hancock was wounded and quite a few of the couriers, but I was lucky this time."

"Then the fight was not in vain," Sergeant Morten said with triumph in his quiet voice.

"No," Sergeant Saylor responded. "We won, but the cost to America – North and South – is terrible. The dead lie in heaps all over the fields of fighting, the wounded are countless, and the hospitals are horribly undersupplied. The destruction has been complete. Worse, I believe, than any battlefield we've seen before. You're fortunate here. Second Corps hospital is flooded by the creek after all the rain. I understand only the Twelfth Corps medical staff disobeyed orders and got their supply wagons in. None of the medical wagons were supposed to come up to keep the roads clear for the ammunition wagons."

Betsy shuddered at the account. It really was over – this world of sunshine and smiles she had known. Darkness, gloom, and death haunted the endless path. And where was Philip? In a field hospital cared for by another soldier's sister? Or in the "heaps of dead" still on the field? When would they know? The suspense was almost worse than knowing.

The cousins talked quietly for a little while, reviewing what had happened to Thomas, the news from their homes, and Sergeant Saylor's plans to marry his sweetheart next winter. Thomas took interest in the conversation, but his replies were slow and forced.

"Well, I've got to go," he finally said. "I'll ride by the Eleventh headquarters and let your comrades know you're still here and doing as well as can be expected. Smith took the message from the farmer and noted where you were, so he told me when he rode over to the Second Corps today. Do you think you'll be able to rejoin?"

Thomas sighed. "I hope so. But right now, I'm so dizzy with fever and pain that I feel sick even thinking about riding."

"Get well. I need you to teach me some more riding tricks, alright?" He grinned teasingly.

"I'll at least be able to teach you not to try to jump high fences," Thomas groaned. "Write home for me when you have time. I'll write as soon as I can."

"Will do. Get well, old man." Sergeant Saylor shook Thomas's good hand and smiled encouragingly before leaving.

"Excuse me," Betsy said, following him into the kitchen. "I was wondering if you knew...was the 138th Pennsylvania at this battle?"

The sergeant thought for a moment. "Haven't seen or heard of them, but they're not in our corps. I really don't know. Do you have someone in that unit?"

"My brother."

He nodded awkwardly. "I hope he'll be alright. Thanks for letting me see Russell. Take care of him," he said, moving toward the door.

"We will. He'll ride again, if we can help him." Betsy felt a little surge of hope as she said it, but it faded when she returned to Thomas's bedside and noticed that the eagerness in his countenance when his cousin was there had only been a façade. She saw he was in restless pain and seemed slightly disoriented by the fever. Patiently, she coaxed him to drink the tea and prayed God would heal his broken body.

The day wore on, and, despite Betsy's efforts to conserve, the food supply continued to diminish. Wearily, she wondered how much longer the food would last and what would happen when it ran out. She wanted to tell Mother and ask for reassurance, but knew there was nothing to make the situation better at this time; she decided her parents and the medical staff knew of the shortage, and it would not be helpful to bother them about it.

Rachel and James were hauling water in the late afternoon when Orderly Lamar stepped into the kitchen and said, "Miss Westmore, I'm sorry, but we need help."

She looked at him, puzzled. Wasn't she baking bread and cooking food? What more did they need her to do?

"I've spoken to your mother. Miss Rachel will come to the kitchen to continue the food preparation. We need you to help dress wounds."

Shivering, Betsy remembered her experiences at the operating table. "I can't," she stated.

The orderly did not waste time arguing with her. He looked her in the eye, saying, "Then many of them will die from lack of care. There aren't enough doctors, assistants, or orderlies to take care of all these wounded."

Betsy looked at the ground. Every emotion in her heart and every fiber of her body wanted to run, wanted to refuse, wanted to ignore this need in an effort to preserve her safety and her ignorance about wounds. But how could she let men die simply from lack of care? How could she face God on Judgment Day and offer feeble excuses for these soldiers' deaths? Could she live with the knowledge that she could have saved someone's brother and didn't because she was afraid and selfish?

"I don't know what to do," she admitted. "But, if you will show me, I'll try."

After Rachel came to the kitchen, Betsy slowly made her way through the house, being careful not to step on the injured men lying in the pathway and eventually finding Orderly Lamar in the parlor. He showed her how to unfasten the bandages, clean the wounds, and properly apply the wrappings, giving careful instructions about not pulling ligatures or breaking open healing wounds. She was too busy trying to remember everything he said to feel sick or nervous.

"There. Do you understand, Miss Westmore?"

"I think so."

"Good. Start in the dining room and work through the sitting room. The soldiers in those rooms mostly have had amputations or more basic wounds. No head or abdominal wounds, except that sergeant in the dining room. If something seems wrong, call me or Doctor Barnes, alright?"

"How will I know if something is wrong?" Betsy worried.

"You'll know. Basins, cloths, and bandages are on the table in the hallway. Get clean water from the buckets in the kitchen."

Chapter 19

Betsy entered the dining room and set down the basin of water before her trembling hands spilled it. She suddenly realized what she had to do, and fears of incompetence overwhelmed her. But she had promised to help, and she would try.

The doctor had examined and re-bandaged Thomas's injuries earlier in the day so she approached Harold first. He watched her warily. She tried to smile, but failed, finally saying, "They've asked me to help clean and redress wounds."

Maybe it was her nervousness or her attempt to be brave that made Harold reply, "Alright. You can do this, Miss Betsy. I promise not to move or trouble you."

She rolled up the thin gray blanket covering his leg and, steeling herself, untied the wrappings around the stump of his right leg. The cloth removed, Betsy snapped her eyes shut and took a deep breath as her stomach turned at the sight. She started crying and refused to open her eyes.

"Come on," Harold spoke softly. "You can do it."

Betsy finally looked up and into Harold's brown eyes. He's trying to be brave to help me, she thought. He's trying to encourage me, and he's the one who's hurt.

She soaked a sponge in the water and carefully dabbed the wound clean. Harold did not move. She did not look at him, afraid that if she saw she was causing him pain, she would not be able to continue. Putting a cloth pad and wrapping on the wound was not hard, and she finished quickly. She felt sweat running down her body and knew it was from nervousness rather than the heat of the day. Without speaking, she cleaned and re-bandaged the injured shoulder and finally rinsed out the sponge a last time. "There, finished," she whispered.

"Thank you. It'll feel better," Harold replied.

"I didn't hurt you much, I hope?"

"Not more than anyone else would've. You're gentle which is better than some rough orderly. You did fine."

Too dazed to realize the compliment, she turned to the sergeant, folded back his coat and, with shaking hands, untied the long strips around his torso. "You shouldn't do this," he said firmly.

"I don't want to. But the wound must be cleaned and re-bandaged, and there's no one else to do it."

Sergeant Morten frowned, but he did not try to stop her, and Betsy forced herself to continue. She used water to ease the pad away from the wound, but the oozing hole, so deep into the body, was too much for her. With a gasped "excuse me," she fled, barely making it outside before losing the meal she had eaten a few hours before.

Silently, Rachel brought her water, and, a few minutes later, she braced herself and returned. Sergeant Morten had picked up the used linen and pressed it against the wound. "Alright?" he asked, concerned.

Betsy nodded weakly. "I'm sorry. I think I can finish."

"I'm the one who's sorry. You shouldn't be exposed to all this." He glanced at the wound and at the basin of scarlet water.

"You're from Indiana, right?" Betsy asked, hoping an ordinary conversation might distract her from the awful task.

"Yes," he gasped as she gently cleaned around the injury. She glanced up; he had turned his face into the pillow and fought to lie motionless. Frightened by his pain, she swallowed hard and finished as quickly as she could.

"I'm sorry," she whispered as she wiped the sweat off his face with a clean cloth.

"Not your fault," he murmured through clenched teeth. "It'll subside. Go on. Take care of the others."

Betsy moved into the sitting room where a blue and gray army waited with crimson wounds. She worked carefully, and her mind began to numb to any reality other than the precise steps for cleansing and re-bandaging injuries. This world was made of gray uniforms, ashen faces, blue bedrolls, stained bandages, and red blood. Before her tired eyes, the men and objects seemed to twist and blend into a sea of color: revolting colors because of what they represented. Twilight came, and she was two-thirds through the room. Someone lit the lanterns hung from the ceiling. She continued. The only definitive thing her dazed mind could recall about those hours was the gratitude shining through the soldiers' pained expressions.

"Finished, Miss Westmore?" Orderly Lamar's voice said close to her.

Betsy tucked the strip of bandage in place and stood up. "I…I don't know. I think I've taken care of all the men in this room." She felt physically and emotionally exhausted.

"Yes, you have. Go rest."

"Aren't there more wounded?" Betsy asked, confused.

"Yes, but we've nearly finished with the injured inside. It's late. I've sent your siblings to bed, and your parents are still in the barn. You're asleep as you stand, Miss Westmore. Go rest."

Betsy moved slowly through the rows of wounded on the floor. She glanced at the three in the dining room. Harold slept, snoring lightly. Thomas seemed worse and moved feverishly on his pallet. Sergeant Morten was silent, though his tortured expression betrayed his suffering. I can't leave them alone, Betsy thought. Thomas should have more of the tea, and I could at least sit with the sergeant.

Outside, lanterns sputtered as the orderlies' shadowy forms moved toward the barn or among the low canvas shelters which protected the wounded in the yard. There were so many injured. Betsy felt like crying; she had worked for several hours tending to the wounded and spent the rest of the day cooking. It was so inadequate. Yet she could not give up. She remembered promising Sergeant Saylor that

Thomas Russell would get better; if that meant she had to sit with him half the night, then she resolved to do it.

Betsy sat down against the wall between Russell and Morten. The sergeant had turned his face away and seemed to be resting or ignoring her. She coaxed Thomas to drink the cold tea and bathed his forehead and arms, trying to break the fever. She succeeded in quieting him, but was uncertain whether he was getting better or simply responding to her presence. Thomas eventually relaxed in sleep, and she watched his calm, even breathing.

When a low, agonized moan escaped the sergeant, Betsy turned to him quickly. "Shh..." she soothed, touching his shoulder and noting his uneven breathing. "Can I do anything for you?"

His eyes focused on her. "No," he whispered, his stoic expression wavering. "They must be running low on the painkilling medicine, and someone else will need it more than me."

"Do you want me to ask the surgeon?" Betsy responded, amazed by his unselfishness.

"No. Just stay with me, please," he entreated. "I'm sorry, but I need help, and you remind me of..." He turned away without finishing, gritting his teeth.

If Philip was hurting like this, what would I do for him? she wondered. She moved closer until she sat beside him, leaning protectively over him.

"I'm sorry," he whispered, glancing up at her. "I tried to shield you from all this, but..."

"Shh…" Betsy motioned. "Sometimes there's no choice." She saw he was listening, though preoccupied with the painful struggle. "Maybe you're thinking of your mother? Or perhaps you have a dear sister?" He gave a brief nod. "I have an older brother. He's a soldier too. I'll take care of you as though you were my brother."

He hesitated with uncertainty and finally nodded. "Then you can call me Edward," he breathed, surrendering his formal, indifferent manner.

Betsy reached out and wiped away the sweat on his face, then smoothed his dark chestnut hair, persisting with a gentle touch until every rebellious lock surrendered. He turned his face toward her and looked somewhat relaxed. Edward extended his hand. She grasped it reassuringly, and he responded with controlled pressure. They did not speak. She could not tell if his pain lessened or if it only helped to know he was not alone.

After a long while, she thought he slept, but when she tried to release her hand, he opened his eyes and looked at her so imploringly she could not leave him. Silence reigned, except for the steady footsteps of the surgeon and an occasional groan or cry from elsewhere in the house; the clock ticked endlessly. She stared at the lantern burning above them, mesmerized by its unfailing light in a world of darkness. A lone, frail beacon in a world threatening to overwhelm it.

"God," she whispered, "I don't even know what to pray anymore. But I'll still trust You to be my refuge. Please show me something to give me hope."

When Betsy opened her eyes, the candle had burned out, but the faint light of coming morning drifted through the now curtain-less windows. Edward was really asleep, and she let go of his hand, stretched her cramped legs, and stood slowly. Strands of hair had loosened as she had rested against the wall. She brushed them back and tiptoed into the kitchen to find a drink of water.

All the water buckets were empty. She seized one and stepped into the cool morning. A shadowy figure, sitting wearily near the well, announced, "It's dry. There's no water."

"No water?" Betsy repeated, confused.

"Used so much the last few days, the well has gone dry."

"Oh," she said. We have to have water, she thought. Water for cooking, drinking, cleaning and re-bandaging wounds. We have to find more water. I know, Rock Creek. With all the rain there will be more than enough water there.

Too tired to run, Betsy trekked determinedly toward the southeast, taking a path near the somehow un-ruined field beyond the barn and garden. The light of morning grew stronger, and the sky turned gray. Hurriedly, she entered the woods; the creek was not far ahead.

She recoiled, horrified. Even in the dim light, she could see the creek water had a slightly reddish hue. Rock Creek was contaminated. They could not get water here. Afraid of what else she might see, she ran the opposite direction.

Betsy felt like panicking, giving up, sitting down, and crying. Then she remembered a tiny spring at the northern edge of the west field. Years ago, she and Philip had found it and had thought it was more convenient than the well when bringing water to Father in the field. She took a deep, steadying breath. Maybe the water there would still be clean. She went back along the path, skirted the barn, and climbed the fence into the ruined west field.

Until this time, she had not noticed that the surgeons had turned their horses into the fenced field when they arrived. It appeared the animals had spooked during the battle and the field was mostly trampled, though patches of grain still stood in some places. Betsy sighed; more change…more damage. The horses looked at her curiously as she went through the field toward the little spring.

The water was clear. Betsy breathed a prayer of thanksgiving for a single blessing in this scourged world. Cupping her hands, she took a drink of the sweet water and then filled the pail. Taking the bucket, she turned and began trudging up the slight incline through the ruined field and toward the house. She kept her eyes on the ground and bucket, trying to avoid spilling any water. As she reached the top of the incline, she glanced up to see how far away the house was. Betsy pushed back the strands of hair in her face and gasped.

The sunrise lit the eastern sky and spread like a glorious canopy. Illuminated storm clouds shone with jewel colors. Fiery red, victorious blue, and fleeting gray mixed and swirled on the canvas of the sky as if daubed by a master painter. The beauty of the scene took Betsy's breath away.

"Blue, gray, and crimson," she murmured, gazing upward. "I never thought those colors could be beautiful again…" The magnificence of the sunrise brought tears to her eyes – such splendor above such earthly misery.

Words from her psalm echoed in her mind. She said them aloud.

"There is a river whose streams shall make glad the city of God,
  The holy place of the tabernacle of the Most High.
God is in the midst of her, she shall not be moved;
  God shall help her just at the break of dawn."

Betsy started crying as she finished the words. Though she knew that the psalm literally referred to God's presence in the tabernacle, at that moment, the verse was for her. God was helping her, just at the break of dawn. He gave her a gift of beauty in a world of gloominess. He gave an answer to her prayer the previous evening: hope. Tears of sorrow mingled with tears of thankfulness at the overwhelming power of God's protection and strength.

The brilliant colors faded as the sun rose a little higher, and she continued on her journey back to the field hospital, carrying with her the gift of hope. God had shown her that blue, gray, and crimson could be beautiful.

Chapter 20

The rest of the day passed, and Betsy was occupied with tending to the wounded, cooking food, and trying to avoid gagging with each breath as the horrid stench of blood in the house and decomposing bodies on the battlefield filled the air. Harold slept most of the time, claiming exhaustion after the long march from Virginia. Edward continued to endure the pain and discomfort of his wound stoically, again collapsing in sleep after hours of fatiguing distress. Betsy watched over him and Thomas, re-bandaged wounds, and helped Rachel cook a rationed meal.

"What will happen, now, Betsy?" Rachel asked, looking at the empty food storage bins.

Betsy did not know what to say. They might starve, but telling Rachel would not help matters. She had overheard Father and Dr. Barnes talking earlier in the day. Messages had been sent to other field hospitals, but all were in the same situation: no food, no extra supplies.

The following day – Tuesday, July 7th – Betsy ladled the last bowl of soup from the kettle; it wasn't much, some half-ripe garden vegetables cooked in water. Her stomach rumbled.

"Can I eat it?" James asked. Rachel watched, looking hungry.

Betsy shook her head and whispered, "We must make sure the recovering soldiers have food."

"But what about us?" James questioned. Betsy closed the door, preventing the soldiers from hearing.

Father came inside, and Rachel said, "Father, there's one bowl of soup left. No more flour. No more fruit in the orchard. No more vegetables in the garden."

"I know." He leaned against the wall, looking disheartened and fatigued. "We need to trust the Lord. He will provide for us. Don't give up faith because it's hard to understand His reasons."

"Too bad Moses isn't here. Then we could get some manna, like in the Bible story," James commented.

"Or water from a rock," Rachel added. "Then we wouldn't have to haul the water across a big field."

"Who's the soup for, Betsy?" Father asked, eyeing the mug in her hands.

"Thomas," Betsy answered almost regretfully as the tempting aroma tickled her nose. "His fever broke this morning, and Dr. Barnes said he should eat."

"Then take it to him," Father instructed kindly. The worried expression slipped from his blue eyes for a second as he said, "Or else we just might have to find four spoons and eat it now."

It took an effort to hand over the mug of soup, but, in the end, Betsy rejoiced. Though weak and exhausted, Thomas was much better, and she smiled at his cheery ideas. According to his own estimation, he'd be walking in three days and riding in a week because of all the good care he'd had. Dr. Barnes overheard as he passed through the room, and, though he shook his head, the grim doctor chuckled.

Later, Betsy was hauling buckets of water from the precious spring; Rachel, James, and a couple of medical assistants passed her, returning to the spring with empty pails. The day was warm, and her buckets seemed to get heavier with each step. As she stopped to rest in the yard, it surprised her to see a couple of families, dressed in their Sunday clothes, wandering down the Baltimore Pike. They were not people who lived in or near Gettysburg, and she watched them, wondering who they might be.

They meandered into the front yard where they stared at the wounded on the porch and at the dead being buried in the orchard before strolling toward where Betsy stood. One of the ladies fluttered a fan and loudly proclaimed to her husband she was going to faint at the sight of all the blood. The other two ladies saw Betsy carrying the water and stared at her, exclaiming over "that poor girl's dress, all stained with blood. And her hair! Has it been brushed in a week?"

Betsy wanted to say insulting things to them, but she held her tongue, picked up the buckets, and turned to walk away, bumping into Orderly Lamar and splashing water on both of them. "Sorry," he said.

"Who are they?" she asked, nodding toward the richly attired spectators.

"That's what Dr. Barnes has sent me to find out." He advanced toward them, causing the "fainting lady" to shriek at the sight of his bloodstained clothes. "Excuse me, who are you and what do you want?"

"We have come from the city to see the sights of the battlefield," one of the portly gentlemen said haughtily. "Quite fascinating, quite fascinating. We found bullets and even some shrapnel in the woods back there. But this," and he waved his hand toward the field hospital, "is truly extraordinary. I've never seen anything so gruesome in my life." He spoke as though he was commenting on the latest play in a New York theater.

"I don't care about your 'sight-seeing' party. I've been instructed by Dr. Barnes, who is in charge of this field hospital, to tell you that you may either leave these premises immediately or roll up your fine sleeves and assist with the care of our wounded," Orderly Lamar responded, controlled anger in his voice.

Hearing their fine clothing might be soiled, the party retreated hastily, leaving Betsy and Orderly Lamar looking at them in disgust. "I'll never understand some people," the assistant fumed. Betsy only sighed in frustration and wondered if they had any food in those picnic hampers; her stomach rumbled, and she felt a little faint with hunger at times.

In the late afternoon, Betsy stood in the hallway, counting the few remaining bandages, when a knock sounded on the front door. Wondering who would bother knocking, she went and opened it. A man in a dark civilian suit stood there.

"I'm sorry this isn't a museum," Betsy said, before he had a chance to speak. "If you're here to sight-see, the doctor's orders are to leave or come in and help us."

The man chuckled. His blue eyes sparkled for a moment, and the corners of his mouth, half-hidden by a full white beard, turned into a smile. "Very good, miss. But I assure you I'm here to assist. I am Reverend Elisha Tennant, an agent with the United States Christian Commission."

Betsy blushed. "I'm so sorry for my rude greeting, sir. There were some people here earlier today…"

He held up his hand and interrupted. "I know. I've seen people like them all over this area, and I understand your frustration. May I speak with your parents or the surgeon?"

"Yes, won't you come in?" Betsy opened the door wider and motioned him inside.

Dr. Barnes and Father were coming down the stairs; they introduced themselves and greeted Reverend Tennant, inviting him to step into the kitchen where they could talk without disturbing the soldiers. Betsy followed to refill her water pitcher.

Reverend Tennant informed them of the situation. "The Christian Commission is establishing a supply warehouse in town. They've assigned their delegates to oversee certain parts of this disaster area. At this time, I'm ascertaining how many patients are here, what supplies are needed, and will make arrangements for you to receive the needed items. The railroad will be completely repaired soon, but, even now, there are many supplies available for distribution. Also, our brothers in this work, the United States Sanitary Commission, are arriving and will be able to assist if the Christian Commission should fall short in any supplies. Now, what is most needed?"

"Food," Dr. Barnes and Father said almost at the same time.

"Medical supplies are the next priority," the surgeon went on. "Later, clothing for the soldiers if it is available."

"The first two we have in abundance," Reverend Tennant replied. "The commission stockpiles donated items for such times, and the ladies of the north have been very generous in their contributions."

Dr. Barnes leaned against the empty kitchen table and gave a relieved sigh. Betsy glanced at Father; his tense expression relaxed, and, for the first time in several days, she saw him smile. She remembered his confidence in God's provision and felt stronger. God had not abandoned them; the beautiful sunrise and the arrival of Reverend Tennant when they needed supplies amazed her. God answered their prayers!

Reverend Tennant continued in his practical, efficient way. "Do you have a wagon, Mr. Westmore?"

"Yes, but no horses. They were taken in a Confederate raid. Oh, we do have one horse in the stable, though it belongs to an injured courier."

"And you could use my horse," Dr. Barnes added. "Now, you have two horses on loan."

"Good," Reverend Tennant replied. "Do you think you could drive the wagon into town and bring supplies from our station?" Father nodded. "Very well. In a moment, Dr. Barnes and I will calculate how many wounded are here, and I'll make a list of supplies you'll receive. You must request more, if you need it." He turned to Father and added kindly, "Mr. Westmore, since your home is being used as a field hospital, the Christian Commission will provide basic food for your family."

"Thank you," Father said sincerely, clearly surprised by the generosity. "Where should I go to get the supplies?"

Reverend Tennant gave directions and added that the commission hoped to obtain the use of one of the stores in town for their warehouse, but was still making arrangements. The gentlemen discussed other transportation details, and Betsy returned to her work with a full pitcher of water and a singing heart. She took half the bandages in the remaining pile and started tending to the wounded; more supplies were coming. Soon, the doctors would have medicines for the soldiers, and, best of all, there would be food.

It was nearly sundown when Father returned, the wagon filled with wooden barrels and crates labeled with their contents: food, bandages, medicine. The orderlies unloaded the wagon. James scurried around, helping Orderly Lamar unpack and organize the medical supplies. Mother came to work in the kitchen, and cooking began at once. To Betsy, it was wonderful to work alongside her mother again. It was a feeling of normality in a chaotic world. Mother was there; everything would be alright.

"I'm proud of you, Betsy. And you also, Rachel," Mother said quietly as she prepared bread dough. The girls looked up from the dried beans they were checking, surprised at her comment. "Orderly Lamar has told me how helpful and reliable you've been. I know it's difficult, but I'm pleased you've handled the situations responsibly."

"It's been so hard," Rachel replied with tears in her eyes. "It's all scary."

Mother covered the bread bowl and hugged her youngest daughter. "I know. But it's going to be alright. We have to keep working hard and being strong. Dr. Barnes and Dr. Elder are good managers, and, now that we have food and supplies, some things will get better." Betsy put her arms around both of them and leaned her head on Mother's shoulder.

Finally, Mother said cheerfully, "Alright. We're safe and together. And now we need to keep working. There are some hungry boys who need to eat."

Betsy smiled at Mother's words. Hungry boys…that was the way she talked about Philip and James. The smile froze and faded: Philip! "Where do you think Philip is?" she blurted.

"I don't know." Mother gripped her knife tighter and continued chopping the salted meat.

"He can't be wounded or…dead," Rachel insisted.

Betsy wanted to believe her sister's words, but again she wondered how many families had loved ones here in the Westmore home.

"We can't do anything for Philip except pray for his safety," Mother said, her voice shaky. "But we can take care of the men here. As I've worked among the wounded, I keep thinking: I hope, if Philip is hurt, somebody's sister, daughter, mother, or wife would care for him."

In a low tone, Betsy told about Edward and Harold, the little she knew about the Confederate's family, and the sisterly attitude she had adopted with the Union sergeant. Mother approved of her actions and encouraged her to be friendly or supportive in a sisterly way to help the lonely soldiers.

By late evening, the soldiers were fed and settled for the night. The family and some of the medical staff gathered in the kitchen to eat a hearty meal. The exhausted assistants and orderlies were appreciative of the Westmores' help; they were a bloodstained crew, but, from their honest conversation and previously observed actions, Betsy knew they were kindhearted men with nerves of steel to accomplish their mission of healing. Orderly Lamar asked for news, and Father shared what he had heard in town.

Virginia Wade, a young lady who worked as a seamstress to help her struggling family, had been killed by a stray bullet while she was kneading bread to bake for the soldiers. A few other civilians had been wounded, homes had been struck with shells, and supplies were taken, but overall the town had escaped destruction. Old John Burns, a cobbler at Kendlehart's, had decided to go out and fight on July 1st. He'd been wounded, but managed to get home.

Gettysburg and the surrounding area were under martial law with Union troops left behind to maintain order and collect the government property scattered across the fields. Notices were posted around the town, calling for able-bodied men to assist burying the dead. The Union troops had interred most of their dead, but many of the Confederates still lay where they fell; there was also the difficulty of the heavy rains reopening the shallow graves.

"How is the Pierce Family?" Betsy asked, hoping her friend was alright.

"I saw Mr. Pierce briefly, but didn't have much time to talk," Father said. "They're fine, but have a few wounded officers in their home."

"Did you see Mrs. Thorn?" Mother questioned in a concerned tone.

"Oh, yes, are Frederick and George alright?" James inquired.

"I didn't see the Thorns. The gatehouse is still standing, but isn't fit to live in. There are…" He stopped suddenly, then said, "At least the building is still standing. They'll have shelter in the winter." Betsy wondered what he did not tell them, but did not want to ask.

The days passed. Sometimes, the hours dragged; other times, the day disappeared in a blink. A sort of routine was established. In the early morning, Father and Mother assisted in the barn while Betsy and Rachel prepared food and James hauled water or brought in firewood. In the late morning,

Betsy tended to the wounded in the dining room and sitting room who seemed to be assigned to her particular care.

Some of the soldiers seemed to be recovering; others were feverish, lonely, or depressed. Sometimes, a soldier would be missing from his resting place. He had perished and been carried out to be buried near the orchard. If they knew his name, the orderlies marked the grave, and Father tried to make notes in a little book about each buried soldier.

Everyone helped distribute the noon meal, but, in the afternoon, the children got a little rest from the work. James usually curled up in the cool cellar and slept. Rachel did odd little tasks for the soldiers, bringing them paper to write letters, tiny bouquets of summer flowers to brighten a dreary room, or a juicy piece of fruit to enjoy. Betsy sat by lonely soldiers, talked or read to them, or wrote letters to their families.

In those quiet afternoons, Father would take a shovel and depart for a few hours to help other men bury the dead that lay in the woods around Culp's Hill. He always returned to help serve the final meal and assist the medical staff in checking the soldiers for the last time that day. Father never said what he saw in those afternoons. Once James asked him, and Father shook his head and looked away. Father was always very quiet in the evenings; sometimes, in the summer's late twilight, he split wood with angry energy or paced alone in the ruined west field.

The routine was odd, tiring, and often unpleasant. However, with better organization and consistent supplies, the medical staff and the Westmore family assisted each other. The farm chores, the extra water hauling, and wood chopping were completed by whoever was available to do the tasks, and the orderlies helped. Together, the family and the medical staff – former strangers – became a focused unit. They worked unselfishly, trying not to complain and attempting to raise the spirits of the lonely, hurting soldiers in their care.

Chapter 21

By Friday, July 10th – one week after the battle had ended – the awful smell of decaying flesh mixed with the stench of the burning horse carcasses. They kept the windows closed, and the air inside the house was stiflingly warm. The odor of blood, infection, and human bodies lying close together polluted the indoor air. The smells made Betsy gag, and other times she feared the food she ate would not stay in her stomach.

The afternoon, the least busy time of the day, had come. Betsy took some of the paper and pencils from a box sent by the Christian Commission to a few of the officers upstairs who had expressed a desire to write to their loved ones. Returning from this errand, she passed through the dining room where Thomas dozed, Harold scowled at the ceiling, and Edward waited expectantly. "Miss Westmore," he said quietly, "could you write a letter for me if I dictated the words to you?"

"Of course," she replied, retrieving some paper, a pencil, and a small breadboard for a desk. She sat down on the floor and glanced at the sergeant who lay propped on a pillow. During the last couple of days, Edward had seemed physically stronger and more relaxed. Perhaps his wound was healing, or maybe the regular doses of medicine reduced the pain so he could rest comfortably.

"I have a younger sister named Allison." He kept his voice low to avoid disturbing the other men. "Could you write her a letter for me? There are some things I need to tell her."

"Should this be to Allison or to Allison and your parents?" Betsy asked, wondering how to begin the note.

"My parents are dead," Edward replied sadly, glancing down.

"I'm so sorry. I know you're from Indiana. What did you do before the war?"

"I was a storekeeper. Family business that I inherited at my father's death. We had a nice town home, and Allison kept house. We managed."

"Is Miss Morten running the store now?" Betsy inquired, straightening the crooked folds in his blanket.

"No, my grandfather and an elderly friend oversee it while I'm away. Allison's twenty-three, and she's engaged to a young man who would have partnered in the store with me." Edward looked uneasy and focused on buttoning the cuffs of his worn shirt. "We had plans to expand the business, using his skills and investment resources."

"What do you mean 'had plans?'" Betsy wondered.

"I'm seriously wounded, and he's a prisoner. Only God knows how all this will turn out."

"I see. Your sister will be worried when she hears you're injured."

"Yes. And she may have already heard, depending on how quickly the papers reported the regiment casualties."

"What shall I write?" Betsy asked, pushing back a wisp of her hair.

"*Dear Allison,*" Edward began. He spoke slowly, giving Betsy time to write down the words in even lines. "*Forgive me for not sending word earlier. It is difficult for me to write, and, until this time, everyone has been too busy to write for me. You may have already received word that I've been wounded in this fight near Gettysburg. I have received good medical care and am at Mr. Henry Westmore's home. The family is very kind to me.*

"*How are Grandfather and Mr. Klutzman doing with the store? I hope Mr. Klutzman's harmless grumblings do not drive away customers. How is the extended family? There was no mail delivered during the campaign, so I haven't heard anything since the beginning of June. Most importantly, how are you?*

"*Do you hear anything about Lieutenant Carver? I know you are concerned about him, but remember to keep your trust in God. I believe he will return safely to you. I think you should marry as soon as he returns, if that is what you both desire. I'll try to be there to give you to him, but, if I should not, don't let any sadness keep you from marrying. When the war is over, he'll do a fine job running the business, and I have no doubt he will keep you comfortable and dressed in fashionable clothes to your heart's content. I am teasing you, dearest sister. I know you understand there is more to life than new clothes.*

"There are many things I wish I could tell you, but I don't want to weary my cheerful scribe, Miss Westmore. You have always been a good sister. You're younger than me, but you taught me so many things about family and life. You are a beautiful girl, especially in your faith. No matter what happens, Jesus is always there for you. I learned that when Papa died. I have experienced it many times during this war. Let Him carry you when the road seems too hard.

"I wish you could come here. Ask uncle to bring you. Maybe I will be able to go home. But, dearest sister, always remember, heaven is our real home. Jesus is waiting there and our loved ones who have gone before.

"I trust you are well and that these words will be encouraging to you in the unknown future. Keep your faith, your hope, and your love. Your affectionate brother..."

"Do you want to sign it?" Betsy asked as he paused.

He nodded, taking the offered pencil. "I hope she'll be able to come in time to see me," he said wistfully, handing back the page and pencil.

"I'm sure she will. I don't think the surgeons will want to move you anywhere for a while." Betsy folded the papers neatly, slipped them inside the envelope, and wrote the address he dictated. "You're a Christian?" she asked.

"Yes," he replied with a warm smile. "I love Christ and am His soldier first." He picked up some small items lying by his side. "The Bible and my packet of letters are always with me," he said. "They symbolize what's important to me: my faith and my family."

Betsy nodded understandingly. For a few minutes, they talked about their love for the Savior and how He was their hope in life's hard times. The bond of friendship between them strengthened as they talked encouragingly.

The next day, Father took the notes the soldiers had written to the post office on his regular trip to town. When he returned, he brought two letters; the first he handed to Mother and the second went to Thomas.

Mother's hands trembled as she held the letter. "It's Philip's handwriting," she murmured. Betsy tried to think positively. It was her brother's penmanship; he couldn't be hurt badly. Rachel twisted her braids' ends, and James's eyes were tightly shut, as if a quick prayer could change any bad news the letter might contain.

Hastily, Mother slit the envelope with a knife and drew out two sheets of paper. She scanned it quickly. Father stood behind her, reading over her shoulder. "He's safe, and he wasn't here," she announced, before hiding her face and crying with relief. Father held her comfortingly.

James's eyes popped open, and he smiled. "I don't want Philip to tell me about battles. I'd be happy to hear about guarding supplies if that's what he's been doing."

Rachel hugged Betsy, whispering over and over, "He's safe."

Betsy wanted to run into the yard and do fifty cartwheels, even though it would have been very unladylike. The burden of worry was gone, and her heart rejoiced. "May I read it?" Betsy asked, wanting to know everything her brother had written. Father nodded, and she read the letter aloud.

July 1863
Dear Family,

I read in the papers about the three-day battle near Gettysburg and am most anxious to hear that you are safe. From the paper reports, it seems there was fighting near Culp's Hill, but I do not hear that any civilians were killed or injured.

I wasn't at the battle. The 138th is guarding supplies, which is boring, but safe. I was ill for a few days at the end of June, but seem to have recovered pretty well. Corporal Thorn is well, but very concerned about his family.

The troops are wild with joy at the victory. Our army has lost so many times that to have a real victory brings up the morale. Rumors say President Lincoln wants General Meade to hurry up and fight again before Lee can retreat into Virginia.

I'm sure you've been writing, but I haven't received any letters for a long time. I think the campaign marching slows the mail. Write soon, and tell me you are alright. I am praying you will have courage for the many challenges you must be facing. My love to all.

Your son and brother,
Philip Westmore

Chapter 22

"So, who's your letter from, Yankee?" Harold asked with jealousy in his voice. "A sweetheart anxious to marry her soldier who's been hurt in Lincoln's cause?"

"From my mother," Thomas answered shortly, refolding the letter.

"Oh, mama's boy, then," Harold shot back. Edward rolled his eyes at the squabble.

"Gentlemen," Betsy scolded from the kitchen doorway, "you sound like two year olds."

"Got nothing else to do ma'am," Harold said, sounding guiltless. "Just want to know why these Yanks are so bent on fighting us."

"Well, if you really wanted to know, why don't you ask nicely?"

"It's more fun to start a quarrel, and I'm bored just lying here," Harold admitted contentiously. "You know, I've been so good the last week my mama wouldn't recognize me. So don't start fussing if I misbehave."

"If you're unruly, Private Cooper, the surgeon can move you to a different location," Betsy said firmly.

"Well, then I'll have to be good enough not to get moved away from my pretty nurse, but bad enough to bother the enemy." Harold winked at her.

Harold Cooper was pesky for the rest of the afternoon. He kept Betsy running to fetch him different items: a book, another blanket, more water, and paper for letters. She went sweetly, but, after several hours, she was ready to quit.

"That's enough, Private Cooper," Edward ordered after the Confederate had requested Betsy to bring him a sachet of herbs because the room had the stench of Yankees. "I don't know what your goal is, but Betsy Westmore has catered to your whims this afternoon and hasn't had a moment's peace."

Harold looked innocently at her with pleading brown eyes and drawled in his Southern accent, "Oh, dear, I'm so sorry, madam. I'd no idea I was causing trouble."

"Thank you, Edward," Betsy said and, ignoring Harold, walked out of the room.

When she returned with supper in the late evening, a pile of small paper balls lay between Thomas and Edward. Harold had tucked himself into his blankets and appeared to be angelically sleeping. The other two looked grim and annoyed. "What's all this?" she asked, pointing to the paper balls.

Edward sighed, but Thomas spoke up. "Spitballs. After Morten defended you, Cooper though it'd be fun to bother us. He's lucky neither of us could move, or we'd have tossed him out of here."

"That...that's awful!" Betsy exclaimed. She glanced at Harold who smiled in his sleep. "What should we do?"

"Lower your voice," Thomas whispered. "Cooper's not really asleep. We think you should kill him," he paused, and Betsy stared at him, "with kindness," he finished.

With a conspirator's smile, Edward handed her a Bible and pointed out a verse in Proverbs Twenty-five. "We devised a strategy for you already."

" 'Heap coals of fire on his head,' " Betsy read and smirked.

"We'll run interference if he starts bugging you too much," Thomas assured. "But scolding him, ignoring him, or moving him won't change the problem."

"And it won't change his heart," Edward added seriously.

Since Harold was pretending to sleep, Betsy ignored him and gave the others their mugs of soup, chatting with them in a low tone. "We heard from my brother. He's safe and wasn't in this battle," Betsy announced. The men expressed their gladness, and then she asked, "Did you have a good letter from home, Thomas?"

"Yeah. They obviously received the letter from my cousin, but not the one I wrote recently. They want to travel here, but don't think they'll be able to," Thomas replied forlornly. "Our crops weren't good last year. Father's been ill. So Mother can't come, even if the money was available. In the letter I sent, I told them I was doing alright. So, hopefully, they won't feel bad." Though disappointed, he attempted to smile.

"You'll get better and be able to see them," Edward said, trying to speak positively while his hand settled near his wound. To Betsy's surprise, Thomas looked at Edward regretfully, and, from their expressions, she felt they knew something she did not.

Later that evening when the last dish had been washed and Betsy was ready to stumble into the cellar and collapse in much-needed sleep, Harold called, "Oh, Miss Betsy, I'm hungry."

Thomas smirked, and Edward rolled his eyes when she stepped to the door with a smile, saying, "I thought you weren't hungry since you were sleeping, but I'll get you some food, if you like."

The first victory was won when she saw his sheepish look as he took the slice of bread. "I hope you rest well tonight. If you need anything more, you'll have to ask one of the orderlies. Good-night."

Harold stared at her, but Thomas gave her a salute with his uninjured hand, and Edward said quietly, "Good-night. The fire's kindled." The war of kindness to the enemy had begun.

The next day was a busy Sunday and one of those days when everything took longer than it should. When the tasks were finally finished and Betsy was contemplating a nap in the cool cellar, Harold needed attention. "Betsy, they're ignoring me," he stated, glancing at Thomas and Edward and wrinkling his nose.

Thomas cleared his throat. "Edward and I were reading the Bible together. We offered to read louder if Cooper wanted to hear, but he refused."

"Well, it sounds like you chose to keep your own company, Harold," Betsy said reasonably. Inwardly, she was irritated by Harold's needy attitude.

He shrugged. "Not fond of that old book anyways. Nothing exciting in it at all. Just a bunch of righteous rules."

"I'm sorry you think that," Edward said sincerely. "There is great comfort and hope in God's Word. Knowing God as Savior, Lord, and Friend is what makes life worth living."

"It obviously doesn't make you better soldiers," Harold jabbed.

"Actually," Thomas spoke up, "fearless men make the best soldiers. I won't do foolish things. But I don't fear dying. I know Christ has forgiven my sins. I'll go to heaven."

"Yeah, I bet you think you've really earned your way, fighting to end slavery and all."

"I didn't enlist to end slavery," Thomas replied. "I enlisted because I thought the United States should be one nation. Not two separate countries. If the slaves are freed through the war, that's fine. But it's not why I enlisted to fight." Edward expressed agreement, but allowed Thomas to continue the defense.

"But there's states' rights! You legally can't invade a seceding state," the Confederate exclaimed.

"Yes, I know your arguments, but each man must make a decision based on what he believes. It's the same with God. We make a choice. But with God, if we make the wrong choice, we'll spend eternity remembering in torment."

"You sound like a preacher," Harold scoffed and turned his face toward the wall, evidently not anxious to continue the conversation.

"Join us for prayer?" Edward invited Betsy. She sat on the floor and joined them in praying for God's strength for themselves and His mercy on those who needed it most. The prayers were simple, straightforward and not self-righteous.

"How did you discover you were both Christians?" Betsy asked.

"We both read our pocket testaments, and, lying next to each other, a simple action soon became topic of conversation. It was interesting to find how God has taught us similar lessons, but in different ways during this time in the army," Edward commented.

"What was the most important thing you learned?" Betsy wondered.

"Two things, actually," Thomas answered. "God is merciful…"

"And all things will happen in His time," Edward finished.

Betsy felt surprised. "You learned that in war? How?"

The soldiers glanced at each other. Finally, Thomas said, "I'm not going to tell you about the fighting we've seen, but I'll tell you this. When there's no safety, when time seems to end, then you see the power of God and learn to rely on His strength."

"I think I understand that from my experiences during the battle, but I still don't see God's mercy or any good in the situation," Betsy admitted.

Edward started to say something, but Orderly Lamar called urgently from the sitting room, "Miss Westmore, bring me two roller bandages and my kit; look on the table in the hall."

"Sorry, I have to go," Betsy apologized and rushed to bring the items to the orderly. She spent the rest of the day helping the wounded or cooking in the kitchen and wondering how anything good could be accomplished through the horrors of war.

Tuesday morning – July 13th – brought a change to the established routine. Ambulances creaked into the yard, and any wounded the surgeons thought could make the journey were moved to town, where they would be placed in train cars and taken to base hospitals in large cities. By late morning, many of the wounded departed, and those remaining were transported into the house or under a few canvas tents in the yard. Dr. Elder and his assistants packed and went to a different location. Betsy felt relieved to see some of the wounded and one medical unit leaving; now Mother and Father would not have to work in the barn, and, with fewer wounded nearby, the quantity of work would decrease.

Dr. Barnes refused to move Corporal Russell, saying the broken limb might not heal properly if jostled in travel. Sergeant Morten stayed too, but the surgeon did not state why. Private Cooper had started a fever the previous day, and the doctor did not want to send him to prison when he still needed medical attention.

Blankets had arrived from the Christian Commission, and Mother collected the quilts and bedding, replacing them with the wool blankets. The linens were filthy and spotted with dried blood. "The first thing to do is to wash them," Mother announced, her voice overly determined as if to disguise her sadness. "Tomorrow, unless the surgeon tells us otherwise, we're going to scrub these linens so they can be used again. I know some of the men prefer the quilts because it's more homelike, but they can't use them when they are this dirty."

In the dusky twilight, Betsy and Rachel sat by the backdoor. There was still a nasty stench in the air, but the coolness of the outdoors persuaded them to rest there for a few minutes. James came, carrying a basket, and plopped down beside them.

"So, I had to help Father rake out all the stinky straw into the barnyard. He's going to burn it tomorrow. Then Father sent me up to the loft to toss down a little clean straw and guess what I found!"

"Mice?" Rachel guessed, sounding disgusted.

"Nope. Let's go inside so you can see them."

Curious, the girls followed, and James took the cover off the basket in the lamp-lit kitchen. "Oh, baby chicks!" Betsy exclaimed.

"They're so cute," Rachel said, picking up one of the little birds. "Where'd you find them?"

"In the loft. I guess those Rebels didn't catch one hen. She'd been up there all this time, setting a nest, and now we have ten chicks."

"It's a new flock," Mother said, coming in behind them and seeing the baby birds.

"It's a new start," Betsy murmured, stroking the down of the tiny chick that Rachel held in her hand. The lamplight did not brighten, the wounded tossed on their hard beds, and the smell of death still permeated the land, but, somehow, the fuzzy chick with shiny bead eyes promised that brighter days would come.

Chapter 23

The hot sun made Betsy wish they had started the washing earlier, but the wounded had needed care and their food had to be cooked, which had taken up the whole morning, forcing the Westmore ladies to do the washing in the afternoon. A couple of the orderlies had hauled the water for them which was a blessing. Now they scrubbed, rinsed, and scrubbed again trying to reduce the stains in their quilts and remaining clothes.

When the linens hung on the line, Mother commented, "Well, the quilts will never look the same again, but at least they'll be useable until we can begin replacing them." Grandmother's heirloom quilt and Betsy's quilt had the worst stains, a constant reminder of the soldiers' sufferings. Betsy felt melancholy as she looked at the quilts, but ruined linens seemed insignificant compared to the misery around them and the sorrow in mourning households.

As they rinsed the clothing, four blue-clad cavalrymen rode into the barnyard. Father came from the woodpile and met them. "We're here to make sure you aren't hiding any government property," the officer announced, dismounting from his black horse.

"What do you mean?" Father asked, confused.

"Horses, blankets, cartridge boxes, weapons, tents, wagons, and such that you may have collected on the battlefield are the property of the United States government, and you aren't supposed to have them," the lieutenant explained impatiently.

"I haven't gone to the battle areas except to help bury the dead," Father stated. "My family and I haven't taken anything."

"Alright. Then you won't object to a brief search, will you?" He sounded doubtful.

"No, of course not," Father said. "As you see, our home is a field hospital. Dr. Barnes of the Twelfth Corps is in charge, if you wish to speak with him. The blankets used by the soldiers were provided by the Christian Commission. There are some soldiers' knapsacks stored neatly in the barn, but their owners are still here and will reclaim them when they are moved."

"That's not a problem," the lieutenant said, tying his horse near the well. "The trouble's the civilians who deliberately disobey the provost marshal's orders and collect and hoard government property for their own use or to sell."

The soldiers walked through the house, and, when they returned to the yard, Betsy knew by their conversation they had found nothing questionable. Three of them went to the barn while the officer talked with Father. As she clipped the last shirt to the clothesline, the others came from the barn, leading Thomas's chestnut mare. "Lieutenant, he ain't as honest as he says," one called. "Here's a horse with the U.S. brand."

"How do you explain this, sir?" the lieutenant asked angrily, turning to Father. "I almost believed you were an honest man."

Father crossed his arms and said truthfully, "The mare belongs to an injured courier in the house. His horse and Surgeon Barnes's horse have been used with their permission to haul supplies from the commission headquarters. The horse will either leave with the courier when he returns to duty, or I'll return her to the army if Corporal Russell is unfit for active service."

"Smooth talking! Almost sounds like the truth," the lieutenant sneered.

Betsy watched the nearby interaction and felt angry that the officer would accuse Father of stealing. Father's stance became defensive, but he asked calmly, "Would you like to speak with the courier?"

A few minutes later, a shamefaced lieutenant walked out of the house and briefly apologized. "We've dealt with a lot of liars and thieves the last few days. Apologies for my unkindness. Here's a paper detailing that you have permission to use the courier's horse until he recovers or is sent home." The officer and his men mounted their horses. "You should have no more trouble," he called as they rode away.

Father sighed and walked to where Mother and the girls were watching. Mother was very upset. "Why do they accuse without knowing the facts?" she stormed.

"There now, no reason to get angry," Father reassured her. "I'd seen the notices in town about not taking army property, but I didn't realize people were actually stealing it and trying to sell it for a profit." He glanced at the house, the empty water buckets, the supply wagon needing to be completely unloaded, the stacked shovels from digging graves, and said softly, "How does anyone have time to plunder the battlefield?"

The quilts dried quickly during the warm day. By evening, they were taken from the clothesline, folded neatly, carried inside, and distributed to the soldiers who seemed most chilled or homesick. The one Thomas had used was lent to someone else since he said he would be more comfortable with a thinner blanket. The stains in Betsy's quilt would always remain, but it was still useable; carefully, they folded it and laid part of it under Edward, letting the rest be a comfortable cover for him.

Betsy offered an extra quilt to Harold who occasionally shivered with fever chills. He declined, making it clear only his gray blanket was good enough for him, then apologizing for any offense. Harold's fever diminished his pesky actions, but he still had sarcastic comments which he tried to smooth over with exaggerated apologies.

Between finishing chores and bedtime, Mother and the girls collected a few uniforms and mended the bullet holes or campaign tears. They talked with the soldiers as they worked, and James carried around a couple of the fuzzy chicks so the men could see them. It was interesting to see how amused they were by the awkward baby birds, how something so small brought a smile to a face usually drawn with pain. The orderlies told the Westmores these simple activities were effective in keeping the men's spirits up, and Dr. Barnes said, with one of his rare smiles, it was the best medicine for loneliness.

The following day – Thursday, July 16th – marked nearly two weeks of bloody aftermath. "I don't think I can do this another day," Betsy groaned, tossing a stained sponge into the empty basin, relieved to have finished her morning work, but hating the thought of doing it again the next day… next day…and next day. "I'm tired of being brave and responsible. I wish someone would come and help us," she told the hallway walls.

"Why don't you come with me, Daughter?" Father suggested, stepping out of the parlor with a covered basin. "I have to go into town to get the supplies. Perhaps seeing how people are helping and the change of scenery would be good for you."

"But I'm filthy. I can't go anywhere," Betsy grumbled, glancing at her stained dress and apron.

"Go change into your clean dress. We'll leave for town as soon as Dr. Barnes and I are finished in here."

"I want to go with you," Rachel said, coming in the front door with a basket of fresh fruit and hearing Father's last sentence.

"Me too! Me too!" James shouted, hopping down the hallway.

"Shh…not so loud," Father instructed. "I'll take you another time. This time, Betsy needs to go. Besides, James, didn't you promise to play checkers with Thomas this afternoon?"

An hour later, the wagon jolted along the Baltimore Pike, Father driving the borrowed horses and Betsy sitting beside him on the seat. As they left the farm behind and headed northwest, it seemed to Betsy that she had never seen these places before. A little over two weeks ago, it was beautiful. Now, grass and fields were trampled and still muddy from the rain. Rows and rows of headboards stood in regiment clusters, marking gravesites. Outside crowded houses, where red flags flew from porches or windows, wounded lay on the grass. Trees on Culp's Hill were stripped of leaves. Rocks were bullet marked. Some trees had fallen, shot by cannon or numerous bullets.

The gatehouse of the cemetery had all the glass windows blown out, but the structure seemed undamaged. Over a dozen dead horses lay bloated in the yard, and the stench was so awful that Betsy gagged and covered her nose. Two figures appeared to be digging graves, but Betsy could not tell who they were.

Looking to the south along Cemetery Ridge and its surrounding fields, she noticed most of the fences had been destroyed. A smoking pile in the distance showed where dead horses were being burned. Groups of men still buried the dead soldiers, and others reclaimed the government property, stacking rifles in long rows like corn shocks. The crops were destroyed, and in their place was a harvest of death.

Betsy shivered. The chilling words of the psalm crept to her mind:

"Come, behold the works of the Lord,
who has made desolations in the earth.
He makes wars cease to the end of the earth;
He breaks the bow and cuts the spear in two;
He burns the chariot in the fire."

With the scattered weapons, scarred landscape, and unfinished graves, Gettysburg's post-battle desolation seemed like a monument to man's sinfulness, but could it have been God's work? If so, why? What good could come from this stark and fatal landscape? She thought about Thomas and Edward's conclusion about God and war, but doubted there could be mercy and a divine purpose in the Gettysburg battle.

They reached the outskirts of town where blue-clad sentries stood guard. The streets were crowded with ambulances, wagons, and many strangers. Father halted the horses near Mr. Schick's store. Crates, boxes, and barrels of supplies overflowed on the streets. "This is the headquarters of the Christian Commission," he explained. "It'll take a little while to get the supplies since they're so busy. Do you want to wait here or come with me?"

"I'll come," she said, climbing down carefully and smoothing her faded burgundy dress, hoping no one would notice its shabbiness.

Betsy stood quietly, observing the busy scene. Agents inventoried supplies, loaded waiting wagons, or located specifically requested items. No one was idle. They worked together to accomplish the task of supplying the hospitals.

"Miss Westmore!"

Betsy turned. "Miss Pierce. I'm so glad to see you're safe."

"Yes. Oh, good day, Mr. Westmore. Are you waiting for your supplies?" Father nodded, and Tillie asked quickly, "May Betsy walk with Mother and me up to the Sanitary Commission's camp near the train station? We won't be very long, but we must take these things, and I'd so like to talk with your daughter."

Father gave his permission. The two girls followed Mrs. Pierce, wading through the crowds and keeping close to the buildings to avoid being crushed by wagons.

"What did you and your family do during the battle?" Betsy asked when they turned into a quiet alley.

"I wasn't home," Tillie answered. "You see, Mrs. Shriver, our neighbor, asked me to go with her to her parents' home down south of the Round Tops, and my parents, thinking the battle would be fought in town, said it would be best for me to go with her. As it turned out, the battle shifted, and some of it was fought close to the farm. It was frightful. Then the wounded came. For days, I could not get home. I was so worried my family had been hurt. What happened to you? Is your brother alright?"

Betsy briefly told what had happened and shared the good news that Philip was safe.

"We have wounded soldiers at our home too," Tillie mentioned. "One of them is the commander of the 1st Minnesota Regiment, Colonel Colvill. Oh, and I nearly forgot to tell you, I met General Meade, the Union army commander! Well, I guess I didn't really meet him, but I gave him a cup of water when he stopped at the farm."

"I heard about poor Miss Wade," Betsy remarked sadly. "How did other civilians fare here in town?"

"We're too busy to visit, but I've heard some news. Laura, the Methodist minister's daughter, was standing in an upstairs room of the house when a cannonball flew in. Miraculously, it didn't explode. Many families hid Union soldiers while the Confederates occupied the town. I hear that one soldier hid in a cabbage bin and successfully avoided capture. Miss Anna Garlach, our neighbor, says a Union general hid in their woodshed for three days. Mrs. Garlach took him some food. He avoided capture and rejoined his men who were so happy that he would continue to lead them. Many homes have wounded in them. The churches are filled and so are the college buildings, I hear. Mrs. Sarah Broadhead went to the Lutheran Seminary and found the basement flooded by the rain. There were dozens of men nearly drowning in that water. She helped to move them to safety on a higher floor." Tillie paused and then smiled. "I did hear one amusing story. A few young ladies had been obliged to cook for a Confederate soldier. After the meal, they played and sang some Union songs. He obviously didn't like it and offered to teach them a Rebel song, but then the girls played to be dense and couldn't learn the words or constantly changed them to support the Union. He left very disappointed, I understand." Betsy giggled and then shared her trials with troublesome Harold.

There was still confusion in the town and smoke from the burning horses. Wounded were still in the homes, and caskets were drawn through the streets, followed by mourning family members. But there was a glimmer of hope. They could smile after all they had been through. It felt good to laugh again, to feel the sunshine, and to be with a friend. Betsy smiled.

Chapter 24

They neared the train station. Betsy stared in amazement at the scene before them. Railroad cars had been unloaded, and boxes, barrels, crates, and chests stood in neat piles, waiting to be hauled to the distribution locations. Wounded men hobbled or were carried into the empty cars to go to base hospitals farther east in Philadelphia, New York, Baltimore, or Washington City. The train whistle shrieked, the car doors slammed shut, and the train began its lumbering journey away from Gettysburg.

Before crossing the street, Mrs. Pierce and the girls stopped to let a couple of wagons pass. "Aw, shucks!" said a frustrated voice close to them. Two soldiers, one on crutches and the other looking exhausted and cradling a bandaged arm, leaned against the side of the brick building. "We missed the train. Now what?"

"You could go to the Sanitary Commission tents," Mrs. Pierce suggested. "We're heading there now, if you want us to show you the way."

"Good enough," the soldier on crutches groaned. They moved on with Mrs. Pierce and Tillie as guides. Large hospital tents stood near the tracks, not far from the station. Wounded men lay in the shelters or sat on the grass.

"You'll be fine here," Tillie said as the two soldiers sank wearily onto the ground in the shade. "The ladies who work here are nice and motherly. They'll look after you and make sure you have a good meal. Hopefully, you'll be able to get on a train tomorrow." The soldiers thanked them.

Mrs. Pierce and the girls approached the tables and cook stoves where some ladies and a couple of freedmen bustled around, preparing food. "Miss Woolsey," Mrs. Pierce called, approaching a pretty lady, "here are the bandages and herbs we promised to send."

"Many thanks, Mrs. Pierce."

"We met a couple of soldiers on our way," Tillie said. "They were so disappointed at missing the train, but we brought them here."

"That's good of you. It's sad how these poor wounded hobble here, using all their strength, and then find they are too late or the trains are full. Poor fellows! But that's why we're here. So they don't have to spend the night without food or medical attention," Miss Woolsey explained, a satisfied smile on her tired face. "I'm glad Mr. Olmstead insisted Mother and I start a food station when we first arrived." Betsy was impressed with the lady's kindness, her willingness to serve others, and her dependable character while overseeing such important work.

"Who is Mr. Olmstead?" Betsy asked. "His name sounds familiar, but I really can't remember…"

Miss Woolsey replied, "Mr. Olmstead is in charge of the United States Sanitary Commission which brings supplies to the troops, provides medical care when necessary, and, in camps, tries to oversee the cleanliness of the facilities."

"Yes, I know about the Sanitary Commission," Betsy commented. "My mother has sometimes sent a box of food supplies to them for the soldiers."

"That's good of her," Miss Woolsey responded. "We women cannot fight, but we can do our best to support our soldiers. I was a hospital nurse last year, and, oh, how desperately our brave soldiers need good care and supplies." She looked sadly at the open tents where the suffering men lay, then glanced back to the work at hand. "You must excuse me. I've work to finish. There's no time to stand talking. My thanks for the supplies, Mrs. and Miss Pierce, and good day to you, Miss…?" she looked questioningly at Betsy.

"Westmore." Impulsively, she added, "Miss Woolsey, I wish I was brave and unselfish, like you."

"You are," the lady replied. "I can see by your countenance that you have sacrificed much. We all serve and give in our own ways."

Reflectively, the girls followed Mrs. Pierce through the streets and arrived as Father and another man loaded the last crates into the wagon. As Father and Betsy drove slowly back toward home, Father said, "Was it helpful to see we aren't alone in this unfinished work?"

"Yes," Betsy answered solemnly. "A lady told me 'we all serve and give in our own ways.' There must be supplies in Gettysburg from nearly all of the states in the Union and people – distributors, nurses, doctors – from many places too."

"Indeed. The Christian Commission and Sanitary Commission do a fine job in transporting supplies and getting personnel to a battle area. Until now, I never fully understood how effectively they worked. And you are right. Those supplies they distribute have been sent by families throughout all the northern states. People, who days before never knew Gettysburg existed, now send supplies and pray for their loved ones' return from this place. Others," Father commented, looking sadly at a woman dressed in mourning and leading two little children, "have come to find their earthly hopes shattered because of what happened."

"I never thought something like this would happen here," Betsy said, looking back at the scarred landscape south of Cemetery Hill. "Gettysburg will never be the same again."

"No. But our hope isn't in a place or community. Our hope is in God. He never changes."

"I know that now," Betsy answered softly. "I understand why you and Mother wanted us to memorize Bible verses. My psalm reminded me that God is my strength and refuge no matter what happens." Father spoke reassuringly, and, by the time they reached home, Betsy was ready to help once again.

Orderly Lamar met her at the door. "Miss Westmore, I need you to reason with Cooper, that Confederate. He won't listen to me, Dr. Barnes, or your mother. He refuses to let us examine his leg wound, and we're concerned an infection is causing his fever. Maybe you can convince him. Sergeant Morten's observant and told us Cooper listens to you sometimes."

Betsy nodded, took a deep breath, and marched into the dining room to face this new challenge. Harold was worse than in the morning; she could see the fever flush now, and his eyes had a sick stare. "Harold," she said gently, kneeling beside him.

"You went away," he said accusingly.

"Only for a couple of hours. I went with my father to get supplies in town. Now I'm back. The surgeon wants –"

"I'm not letting anyone touch my leg," he interrupted defensively. "It's burning and painful, and they'll just make it hurt worse." He stopped her as she started to speak. "Nothing you say is going to change that, Miss Betsy."

"Very well," Betsy said resignedly. "I'll tell Dr. Barnes." She went and found the surgeon; he was in the downstairs hallway filling out some paperwork at a desk. He glanced up with a pleased expression when he saw Betsy, and she told him about Harold.

The surgeon frowned. "Listen, Miss Westmore, if the wound is burning and painful, I believe infection has started. You tell him that if the wound isn't examined, he may lose his life to gangrene."

Betsy returned, and Harold scowled at her. "Well?"

"You once told me you wanted to go home, see your family, and be able to help your mother on the farm." His expression softened. "Dr. Barnes is concerned that you may have an infection which could lead to death, if not examined properly." Harold started to protest, but she held up her hand. "I know you don't want more pain, and you don't want anyone to touch the wound, but your family needs you to come home. Would you risk not returning?"

He huffed. "Alright. You're persuasive. I'll let you redress the wound."

"And you'll let the doctor examine you?" Betsy bargained. Harold glowered at her, but gave a quick nod.

A few minutes later, with Dr. Barnes close by, Betsy un-wrapped the leg stump and looked away. Dr. Barnes ordered, "Lie still. This needs closer examination."

"No!" Harold protested, struggling to sit up.

"Harold, don't," Betsy commanded, pushing him to lie down again. "The surgeon knows what he's doing. He won't cause you unnecessary pain."

"I have to use a medicine to clean the wound," Dr. Barnes said. "You've got an infection in the stump. We need to try to prevent it from spreading. We'll try medicine first."

"What's second?" Harold muttered. "Maybe I'd like that better."

"Surgery," he answered bluntly.

Betsy stayed while the surgeon cleaned and re-bandaged the wound. When it was finished and the surgeon had left, Harold looked at her and gasped, "I really hate you."

"Well, I'm not fond of your annoyances these last few days, and I certainly don't like what the Confederate raiders did…but…I don't hate you or your comrades." It took an effort to say the words, but they were true. Confederates weren't monsters. Betsy believed they didn't have the right principles to be fighting for, but who could say they were not brave and determined?

"I don't care. I still hate you," Harold muttered, turning his face toward the wall.

Betsy got up and stumbled away. How could he say that? Why would he hate her personally? She could understand his mistrust or dislike of Union supporters, but why would he hate her, especially when she was taking care of him?

"I don't think he really means it," Edward whispered to her later. She only shrugged. Though he could be friendly at times, there was something different about Harold, something beyond the color of his uniform and Southern accent. Something hidden bothered him; she sensed it during the conversation about religion a few days ago, and she felt it in his hate-filled words. Could she help him?

Chapter 25

By the next day, Dr. Barnes had heard about Harold's words to Betsy, and Orderly Lamar not-so-gently persuaded Harold to lie still while the surgeon did the examination. Betsy still took Harold his food and brought water, but he refused to eat, moaned that he felt sick, and then rudely refused to drink the tea which might reduce his fever.

"I give up," Dr. Barnes announced quietly, coming into the kitchen where Betsy, Rachel, and Mother were washing dishes. He closed the door, helped himself to a bowl of soup for a late dinner, and sat down wearily. "Harold Cooper refuses to drink the herbal tea and seems unresponsive to any efforts we make to help him."

"Do you want me to try?" Mother asked.

"No offense, ma'am, but the only one who seems to have any influence with him is Miss Westmore. No," the surgeon said decidedly. "Leave him alone until evening, then, if you're willing to try, Miss Westmore, you may see what you can do. The wound is worse. The fever is higher. If he doesn't drink the tea and a dose of medicine, I fear he'll be delirious by midnight."

The door burst open, and James and a couple of boys from town ran in. "Oh, Mother," James exclaimed, "the

boys asked me to go collecting with them on Culp's Hill.
We're going to find bullets, artillery shells, and all kinds
of interesting things. Maybe we can explode some of the
shells. Please can I go? Please, Mother, please…"

"I'm sorry, James, but you may not go. I need you to
help me this afternoon." She turned to the other boys, "Do
your parents know what you're planning to do?" The boys
shrugged in an I-don't-care fashion. "Well, it was considerate
of you to ask James to go with you. Be careful out there."

The others slipped out, disappointed. Dr. Barnes
rolled his eyes and sighed. James leaned on the table and
complained about Mother's decision. "That's enough,
James," Mother said. "I don't think playing with artillery
shells is a good thing for little boys to be doing. They're
dangerous, and I don't want you to get hurt." James tried
to explain collecting bullets was not dangerous. "That
may be," Mother admitted, "but you aren't going to do it
without an adult's supervision. I know you don't like my
decision, but I want to keep you safe."

James went into the dining room, told Thomas and
Edward his tale of woe, and then said, "When we're not
so busy and all you soldiers are feeling better, Father'll
take me up to Culp's Hill, and we'll find tons and tons of
bullets. And maybe I'll find some shrapnel. I'm going to
have a really interesting collection."

Betsy looked into the room as she put the dishes away,
wondering how the soldiers would respond to James's new
idea. Both seemed amused, and Edward said to Thomas,

"I wish I'd had a little brother. We would've had plenty of mischievous adventures." Thomas grinned and nodded.

Later in the day, Betsy helped haul water. Some of the water could be drawn from the well, but they brought extra water from the spring to avoid draining the well again. The sun was dropping behind the hills as she returned from the last trip and encountered Mr. Lightner storming into the yard. "Where's your father?" he barked.

Father came from the house, and the neighbor divulged his tale of woe. "You just won't believe this, Westmore. I was arrested, just released today! Look, my entire house and barn were taken over as a field hospital. My family and I have been forced to live in a tiny shed while the medical butchers literally destroyed the house. My crops are completely trampled. So I thought I could collect a few blankets and other little things to replace what we'd lost and maybe sell to make a little money to get us through the winter. I'd not been to town and didn't know that'd be a problem. Anyway, this awful man, Colonel Blood, comes down and says I'm hoarding government property. I had absolutely no idea I'd done anything wrong. But what does he do? Arrests me! Hauls me off to town and throws me in jail. Only today a couple of my neighbors came and got me bailed out by explaining the whole situation and that I'm a man of good character."

Father made a sympathizing comment, but Mr. Lightner was too irate to listen. "I wasn't angry about the house or the barn or the fields or all the stuff that got destroyed. I figured why should I complain about little things when soldiers are dying? So I give everything I've got, and then they haul me off for trying to provide for my family when I've got nothing left. Oh, I'm so angry I could…" he glanced at Betsy and stopped. "And then you should see what the papers are printing about us!"

"I know. I saw a paper in town the other day," Father replied, motioning Betsy inside.

After Mr. Lightner calmed down and started home, Betsy asked Father about the newspapers as the family and a couple orderlies sat at the kitchen table, eating a quick supper. "Well," he replied slowly, "the large national papers say that the people of Gettysburg – farmers, in particular – are being stingy and charging the wounded for food, shelter, and bandages."

Mother held up her hands in disbelief. "Truly? I guess the reporters didn't come here."

"No, they didn't," Father said. "Our local papers in town are trying to counter these stories, but the large presses still delight in reporting infamies and putting down the people living in this area." He paused and added, "I think perhaps there were a few farmers or households who were self-seeking, perhaps others were trying to find a way to make up for losses, but many, probably even the majority, of the farmers and families have done what we have: given free of charge to make the situation better and to help the wounded soldiers."

"It is like that with everything," one of the orderlies admitted angrily. "Medical staffs are accused of stealing supplies, neglecting the wounded, and showing incompetence because there are a few out there who do that."

"Isn't it sad how the press twists stories or takes a handful of incidents and applies it as a generality to a whole area, population, or group?" Mother remarked unhappily.

"Well, I hope someday people will learn the truth," Rachel said.

"Yes," Betsy sighed. "Like how we're so tired and want to sit here all evening, but we get up and go help the wounded settle comfortably for the night?" Wearily, she started her evening duties.

What a long day this has been, she thought, as she finally sat down near Harold, preparing for a battle of wills. Edward dozed uncomfortably beside them, and Thomas had given her his now customary salute for encouragement. "Harold," she whispered, shaking his uninjured shoulder. "Wake up."

He opened his eyes and looked at her in confusion. "Patty?"

"No, Betsy Westmore."

"Oh, sorry," he murmured. "The light's dim. I thought you were my sister."

"I want you to drink this," she said and put the cup to his lips without waiting for him to protest.

He took a sip and made a face, saying childishly, "I don't like the taste."

"I'm sorry, but you need to drink it." She put the cup to his mouth again.

This pattern repeated: he protested, she answered and made him drink more. Finally, the cup was empty. "Tyrant," he said bitterly. "I just want to die."

"Don't say that, Harold," she replied, hoping he was only confused by the fever. His words hurt her.

"You don't understand, and you never will," he hissed. "For a year, I've lived without my Pa. He died in my arms. I buried him and wrote the news to Ma, knowing that her heartbreak would be worse than mine. Now, here I am: wounded. Amputated leg makes me no good to anyone. I've been in unending pain for two weeks. I wouldn't call myself a coward, but I can't take it any longer. I just want the fever to kill me. It'd be better for my family if I'm gone. Then I wouldn't be a burden." He tried to stifle the pain, but started crying.

Stunned by his vehemence and hopeless words, Betsy watched him try to hide his tears by keeping his face toward the wall while his chest heaved with sobs. Finally, unable to just sit there and unwilling to leave him, she touched his shoulder and then turned his face toward her, using her clean handkerchief to wipe away his tears. "No, Harold. You aren't a burden to us, and you won't be a burden to your family. I know your body and soul are hurting. I don't know why God let all this happen to you. But I know your family loves you. Your ma needs you to come home. Your siblings need their older brother. And there's Someone who loves you more than you'll ever know."

"Who?" he asked, frowning.

"God."

"I don't know if I believe that," he admitted.

She ignored his statement. "Then live for your family. No matter what happens, I want you to remember that you have to go home to them. I want you to fight to live. Can you promise me you'll try?"

Harold looked at her doubtfully as if torn between painful reality and hopeful future. An expression of trust flickered in his eyes. "I promise," he whispered.

Chapter 26

"I don't want him to give up," Betsy explained earnestly, after she had told Mother about Harold's reaction. They were sitting in a corner of the dimly lit cellar, talking quietly while James and Rachel slept. "He's so bitter…he needs God. But he doesn't want to talk about that."

"I think you did the right thing in reminding him about his family, Betsy," Mother said.

"I know he's a Confederate, but he's not bad," Betsy admitted. "He's been annoying, but he's like a silly older brother, not an enemy."

"We should pray for him. And you should continue to serve him kindly."

"But how can I help him?" Betsy said uncertainly. "How can I help someone else be brave, responsible, and caring?"

"By continuing to show those qualities in your actions. You've been very brave helping to care for physical wounds. Don't lose your courage now when one of your soldiers struggles with emotional or spiritual pain. Maybe God can use this situation for His glory." Mother brushed back the loose strands of Betsy's hair.

The next morning, Harold still seemed to suffer intense pain in his leg. Betsy forced him to drink another cup of cold tea which seemed to help to reduce the fever. He refused to talk and stared at her hollowly, as if he regretted revealing his hurting soul.

Confidentially, Betsy and her parents informed Dr. Barnes of the situation. He shook his head when he heard, but then commended Betsy for reminding Harold what was left to live for. The surgeon said to Father, "Your daughter has some influence over Cooper. Why this is I don't know, but probably because she's been kind to him. Maybe she reminds him of someone at home. Miss Westmore could be the one who can save him," he finished.

"No, sir. Only God can save him," Betsy said quietly.

"That's true," Dr. Barnes replied sincerely. "But you may be the one to save his earthly life, simply by reminding him he has a reason to live. Remember that, especially later."

In the afternoon, when Betsy had finished her routine tasks, she sat in her parents' room, reading to two wounded brothers who lay on the bed. The next thing she knew, someone tapped her arm, saying, "Betsy, wake up. Dr. Barnes needs you."

She woke with a start. "Oh, goodness, I'm sorry. I didn't mean to fall asleep in the middle of the story," she said to the soldiers. They chuckled and assured her it was alright, hoping her short nap was refreshing. Orderly Lamar repeated his message, and she followed him downstairs. Mother and Dr. Barnes met them.

"Miss Westmore," the surgeon said gravely, "the infection in Private Cooper's leg reached a point where we had to either amputate again or he would die."

Betsy covered her mouth in horror. "What did I do wrong? Did I not take care of the wound properly?"

"No, no," the doctor answered quickly. "This isn't your fault. Sometimes the infection is too deep or beyond medical control. There's something – we don't really understand what – that causes these bad infections. His fever isn't as high today, but he isn't strong in mind or body. The surgery is over. We think it'd be best if you were near him as he recovers and the chloroform wears off."

Betsy felt tears in her eyes as she thought of Harold's plight. Mother said gently, "We don't know why Harold listens to you and trusts you the way he does, but maybe God made this opportunity. The surgeon, Father, and I agree that you are the best person to be near him."

"Does he know the surgery was going to be done?" Betsy asked, trying to prepare for what Harold's attitude might be.

"Yes," Dr. Barnes replied. "As before, he was given chloroform so there was no pain, but he was conscious. I didn't give him any choices, and, surprisingly, he did not resist."

"I'll try," Betsy said. "I don't know what good I'll be able to do, but I'll sit with him." She walked toward the dining room. "Dear God," she breathed. "Help me to know how to act. Harold needs You. Help me to know how to comfort him and how to show him that You love and care for him."

Thomas gave her a quick, encouraging smile. Edward looked at her with compassionate concern as she sat down beside Harold's pallet bed. The Confederate had half-buried himself in his gray blanket; his face was turned toward the wall, and his body shook.

"I don't want to talk," he said through gritted teeth.

"Alright. I just want you to know I'm here, and I've been asked to sit near you for the rest of the day."

They were silent for a long while. Choking back frustrated tears, Betsy watched him. She didn't know what to do. Absently, she wondered what Philip would say if he saw her now. Would he be shocked that she cared for an enemy soldier? In some ways, I'm now responsible for Harold, she thought. I'm trying to be brave, but I don't know how to care for him right now. Would you be proud of me, Philip?

Edward handed Betsy his Bible and said quietly, "Cooper, could Betsy read to us for a little while?"

"Fine," he growled.

When Betsy asked what she should read, Edward responded, "I think the third chapter of John would be a good place to start."

Surprised that Edward had observed the difficulties his wounded companion faced, Betsy half-smiled and started reading in a clear, low voice. Four chapters later, Harold turned toward them and seemed contemplative. "It hurts," he moaned as Betsy put down the Bible to take a sip of water.

"Shh…" Betsy motioned, "it'll be alright."

Uncertainly, he held out his hand. For an instant, Betsy hesitated. He was a Confederate, and he had come north intending to fight and kill Union boys like Philip, Thomas, or Edward. It doesn't matter, she thought quickly. He's in pain, and it doesn't matter what color his coat is. She took his hand and responded to his firm grip. He looked at her with surprise.

They stayed that way for a couple of hours. At times, his pressure on her hand made her wince, but he relaxed his grip when he realized he hurt her. Suppertime came. Betsy fed him broth and made him drink another cup of tea. Orderly Lamar came and redressed the wound; Harold stoically survived the process, falling asleep shortly afterward.

"Did he say anything?" Dr. Barnes wanted to know as Betsy washed her sweaty hands.

"No. He seems depressed." She felt discouraged again.

"We'll have to wait and see what tomorrow brings," Dr. Barnes said, touching her shoulder. "He knows he's not alone. And he knows you care. That's important."

By mid-morning the next day, Betsy had finished tending to the other wounded men and she went to the dining room to sit near Harold, who was sleeping. Thomas leaned against the wall, quietly reading an outdated newspaper. Restless and withdrawn, Edward lay propped on pillows. When Betsy asked if he was alright, he admitted the medicine did not completely mask the intensifying pain. She read a couple of chapters from the Bible to him, and they talked quietly.

"I'm hoping my sister will come soon," he said anxiously.

Betsy wiped away his sweat with a cool cloth. "That'd be nice. Who would travel with her or would she travel alone?"

"No, she wouldn't travel alone. Probably with our uncle. He's a lawyer, though, so I hope he's not busy with an important case."

"What does Miss Morten look like?" she asked, sensing he wanted distracting conversation.

Edward smiled faintly. "Allison is beautiful. She's twenty-three, two years younger than me. She has blue eyes and curly hair that's a little more red than mine. 'Dark auburn' is her way of describing it. She's tall. I used to tease her that her clothes made her look like a fashion plate. But she's practical, too, and much smarter than me. You'd like her. At our church, she helps with the ladies' aid society for the soldiers. She likes children and sometimes goes to an orphanage to read with the little ones or teach the girls how to sew. I miss her, and I fear that she will come too late to…" he paused, and then shook his head. "I may get better yet."

"You will, Edward," Betsy said confidently.

Beside them, Harold moaned and opened his eyes. "Good morning," Betsy said. "I hope you feel better after sleeping."

Harold shrugged his good shoulder and replied, "I'm hungry. I'm sorry."

"I'll get you some broth and maybe some bread. Why would you be sorry?"

"For troubling you."

"I'm glad you feel like eating." She brushed away the light colored hair and felt his forehead. "I think your fever is nearly gone too. Well, I'll be back." Betsy skipped into the kitchen with the good news.

Chapter 27

Harold was frowning when she came back; he looked confused, but not hostile. "Why?" he asked. "Why do you treat me the same as the Union men?" She was puzzled by his question, but he went on. "I'm a Confederate. You're a Union girl. I thought you would've treated these other men," he glanced at Thomas and Edward, "with great care and only taken care of me because you had to. But you cared for me the same as them. You didn't leave me alone when I was suffering. Why?"

Betsy thought about her momentary conflict when she had almost refused to hold his hand and answered, "God doesn't think of you differently because you're a Confederate, so why should I? Jesus said Christians should live like He did. He helped all who came. He said we are supposed to love our enemies. I never really thought of you as my enemy, though some other Confederates weren't nice to my family."

"But many other people would have," Harold acknowledged.

"I suppose," Betsy said slowly. "But even though I don't agree with what you and your friends are fighting for, and I certainly don't like some of the things the Rebels – I mean,

Confederates – have done, I can't hate you. God says we are supposed to forgive and love like Christ did for us."

Harold appeared thoughtful. "My ma always tried to teach me to love God, but I never really cared or had time for all that religious stuff. I've seen something different in your life, Betsy. Your actions show me something I don't have and something I need. You've been through an awful experience for anyone, but especially for a young girl. I've seen you cry, and I've seen you close to despair, but you never gave up. You never got angry about the battle and all of us wounded in your home. I just don't understand."

"God is my refuge and strength," Betsy answered simply. "It's been hard and the experiences have been terrible, but I trust Him." She began to understand more clearly as she put her thoughts into words. "It's not fate that brought the war here. It's not fate that brought you to our home. It was God."

"And you're not mad at Him for all this?"

"No. I don't understand why, but I'm not angry with God. The Bible says His plans are greater than ours and also He can work all things for good." She started to comprehend what Edward and Thomas meant when they talked about what they had learned in war.

"So you think my pa's death and this wound I've got could be used for good," Harold asked incredulously after a moment's thought.

"Yes," Betsy replied confidently. "It's part of a plan God has for your life."

"You have faith," Harold stated flatly. "And that makes the difference in your life. My life's a mess. I'm angry with God because my pa died, and now my future's hopeless because of this wound."

"But God still loves you," Betsy said, earnestly repeating what she knew well. "He loves you so much that He sent His Son to die for the sins of those who will believe. Sin – those wrong thoughts, words, and actions – would separate us eternally from God, but He made a way we can be saved."

"Isn't being good enough?" Harold reasoned.

Betsy easily recalled the scripture verses she had learned through the years. "No. The Bible says our goodness is like filthy rags and sin has no place in God's presence."

"Then it's hopeless," Harold said, frustration in his voice, while he aimlessly twisted the corner of his blanket.

"No, it's not. Jesus died to pay for the sins of all who would believe. If you ask Him to save you from sin and accept Him as Lord of your life, then you are saved and made righteous before God. Accepting Christ as Lord means you desire to live a pure and righteous life, following His will."

"It's that simple?" Harold asked doubtfully.

"Yes," Betsy answered, "but it takes faith to believe Jesus is the only way to God."

"And does God punish you if you sin after you're a Christian?"

"If you're not obeying His Word, sometimes He has to bring trials of correction. It's not easy to live a life of obedience to God, but we do it because we love Him. As it says in First John, chapter four, 'we love Him because He first loved us.' "

Harold frowned at her. "You sure know a lot for being…how old are you?"

"Fourteen. My parents believe it's important for us children to explain and defend our faith." Betsy fully realized why her parents wanted her to memorize scripture.

Harold looked away for a moment and then reached for the slice of bread. He ate in silence, only requesting Betsy to help him with the soup. When he finished eating, he said quietly, "I'd like to be left alone for a while. I just want to think."

As Betsy left the room, she noticed Thomas and Edward were praying silently, and she thought she knew who they prayed for. She found Mother and Rachel and told them about the conversation. A few minutes later, Father and James joined them, and they prayed for Harold.

In the late afternoon, as she was coming from the garden with a basket of vegetables, Betsy met Reverend Tennant. After pleasant greetings, he asked, "Do you know of any soldiers who might wish to talk or pray with a minister?"

Betsy smiled eagerly and told him about Harold. Reverend Tennant said he would speak with him. Father joined them and asked, "Reverend Tennant, can we pray for you and that you will have the right words to encourage the soldiers?" The minister was surprised and pleased by Father's suggestion, and they prayed together before he went to the house.

Though she could not go with Reverend Tennant and talk to Harold, Betsy prayed for them as she worked to accomplish her assignment. It was relaxing to pick the ripe fruit and fill the baskets, but Betsy didn't enjoy the task. The graves near the trees in the orchard made her uneasy. It was disconcerting to know that dead men were buried under those numerous mounds of dirt.

When she returned to the house, Harold was asleep, but Reverend Tennant said they had talked. Betsy was finishing her evening work when Orderly Lamar told her Harold was awake, needed his wound redressed, and was asking to see her. Anxiously, she entered the room and was surprised by the joyous smile on Harold's face. "You're better, Harold?" she asked, setting down the basin and bandages.

He held out his hand, and she took it. "The wounds still hurt, but I'm better. I've repented of my sins. God has forgiven me and healed my soul! The bitterness in my heart is gone. I'm not angry at God anymore." The look of peace, the firm grasp of his hand, and the sincerity of his voice brought tears of happiness to Betsy's eyes. "You're crying," he said, confused.

"Yes," Betsy replied, quickly wiping away the tears. "I never thought I'd cry because I was happy. May I tell my family your good news?" He agreed, and she went and told them.

They came, crowded into the room, thanked God for His mercies, and prayed that Harold would be a strong soldier for Christ. Thomas and Edward joined in the joy and thanksgiving of the evening. It was a time of happiness.

The crimson sacrifice of Christ had brought another soul to God, another brother to God's family.

Harold was tired and still weak, and, after a time of prayer and rejoicing, Father suggested Betsy should proceed with re-dressing the wound so Harold could rest. The task was gruesome as always, but Betsy did not seem to notice. Her heart overflowed with praise and wonder at what God had done in Harold's life.

"Thanks, Miss Betsy," he gasped as she finished applying the clean bandages. "You lived your faith in a dark and terrible time, showing us what it means to be a Christian. I finally understand peace and trust in God. I hope my faith will be as strong as yours someday."

"It will," she whispered, bending over him and pulling his blanket up to his shoulders. "God will make you a strong soldier for Him."

Edward said, "Cooper, I know you're wearing a different color uniform, but we're comrades in Christ." He extended his hand, and blue shirt sleeve and gray blanket almost touched as their hands clasped in a hearty brotherly greeting.

"Same feelings here," Thomas spoke up. "Sorry I can't reach that far or come over."

"That's alright. Maybe instead of throwing spitballs at you, I could ask you to help me learn to study the Bible?" Harold asked hopefully. "I'm sorry I was so mean before."

The following afternoon, while a basic theology study proceeded in the dining room, Betsy sat at the kitchen table and wrote a short letter to Philip.

July 20, 1863
My dear brother,

We received your letter and are so glad to know you are safe. I know Mother wrote you a brief note, but I take this pencil in hand to write you some wonderful news!

She wrote about her three soldiers and concluded with an account of Harold's acceptance of salvation.

And so you see, Philip, though the house is still filled with wounded, the tasks are unpleasant as ever, and the graves in the orchard continue to increase, we have a reason to praise the Lord. I understand a little better what Thomas meant when he said war had taught him that God was merciful. It isn't until you're in a dark valley of trial that you find the fullness of God's mercy and His grace and strength for believers.
Keeping the faith,
Your sister,
Betsy Westmore

Chapter 28

Betsy looked up from the uniform she was mending and smiled at the peaceful scene. Harold and James were playing checkers. Rachel unsuccessfully tried to teach Thomas how to play cat's cradle, a game with looped string. Edward was amused by the activities on either side, making helpful comments to Thomas, until the cavalryman threatened to have him play the game; Edward turned his attention to the checkers match. "No, Cooper will get a double jump if you move there, James," Edward instructed.

"Hey, Morten, quit helping him," Harold complained. A few minutes later, James lost the game, but accepted the defeat and thanked his new friend for playing with him.

"So what happens when you get well?" James asked as Harold lay down.

"I'll be sent to prison," he replied simply.

"Oh. But will you escape?"

"I'll make no promises," Harold said, "but I'll admit it'll be harder to escape with only one limb to stand on. I'd be surprised if they give me a wooden leg in prison."

James looked concerned. "But will they treat you nicely? I mean, I don't really like most Confederates, but you're alright now that you got saved."

"Neither side treats their prisoners well," Edward answered regretfully. "And exchange is difficult for enlisted men."

"Exchange?" James asked.

"Yeah, it's like this, James," Harold explained. "If the Yankees capture a couple of colonels, a major, and a few captains, their families, and usually their commanders, want them back. Now maybe the Confederates have a few officers too who need to get back. So under a flag of truce, they arrange an exchange. It doesn't happen real often and very infrequently for enlisted men, like me."

"What about a parole?" Betsy asked as she aimed her thread at the eye of the needle. "I've heard that term, but I don't really know what it means."

"Parole is when the captured soldiers agree not to fight for a certain period of time," Thomas informed them. "Or it can mean they will agree not to try escaping. If a colonel is wounded, his captors may offer him a parole so he can go to a private house to recover. But he'll have to honor his parole and not try to escape. Does that make sense?"

"Kind of," Betsy replied.

"Good." Thomas looked from the tangled string on his fingers to Rachel. "This doesn't make sense to me. I'm really sorry, but I don't understand this game."

"It's alright," Rachel answered, smiling. "Maybe Betsy and I can show you later, and then you'll understand it."

James asked, "So what happened to all the Confederate prisoners who were marched down the pike after the battle?"

"They're probably already in prison," Harold said grimly.

"Fort Delaware and other prisons throughout the northern states likely took them," Thomas remarked.

"When do you think you'll be sent to prison, Harold?" Betsy asked.

"I won't let them send him off until the fever's gone and the leg is sufficiently healed," Dr. Barnes said as he passed through the room and heard the question. "There'd be no excuse for taking care of him, releasing him too soon, and having him bleed to death in a train car."

"There you go," Harold announced. "Now, Miss Betsy, how long can I fake a fever?"

"No, that's not right. But it'll probably be a while longer, I would think, before you'll be moved."

"Oh, good. As much as I'd like to see my regiment comrades and my family, I'm not anxious to exchange my friendly nurses and companionable roommates for a prison." He grinned mischievously.

The injured in the house improved, and, every few days, a couple more were sent to the railroad station and then to their homes or a larger hospital. The tents in the yard were now empty of wounded, some moved into the house, others sent elsewhere. Dr. Barnes, his assistants, and the orderlies established their sleeping quarters in the remaining tents. The cooking, bandaging, supply hauling, wood chopping, and water carrying schedule continued, and the orderlies helped with the chores when they could. The wounded soldiers always looked forward to Father's return from town, hoping to receive letters from their loved ones. Those written words provided encouragement to get better.

Though the children interacted with many injured men, the three soldiers in the dining room were always their favorites. Betsy watched over them, rejoicing in their improved health. Thomas recovered rapidly and was even anxious to be up and moving on crutches, though the doctor forbade him to try yet. Harold was generally pleasant and much more agreeable; he still suffered pain from the healing shoulder and second surgery, but, on the whole, he was better.

Edward concerned Betsy; he was not well. In the previous weeks, the decline was almost imperceptible, but Betsy and the family now noticed the weakness in his voice and motions, and his weariness increased with each passing day. Several times, Betsy asked Edward what the doctors thought, and he skillfully changed the subject. The medical staff gave no information, but did their best to keep him comfortable and minimize the pain. Once Betsy overheard them discussing Edward's wound using undecipherable medical terms, concluding with "it is only a question of time." She had wondered momentarily what that meant.

Betsy thought the three soldiers were almost like older brothers. They could never be exactly like Philip, but they shared some of the same character qualities as the absent brother. She was glad the three men had a friendly truce. Sometimes, they talked amongst themselves for hours.

They often invited the children to join them, and Betsy, Rachel, and James were glad to spend time with their new friends. Bible studies, arithmetic races, story-telling competitions, and frivolous debates occupied the empty hours in the late afternoons and evenings.

On July 22nd, Father brought news that the much-discussed, centralized field hospital had opened that day. It was called Camp Letterman, named after the medical director of the Army of the Potomac. They heard that the wounded who could not be moved to base hospitals or prisons farther east would be transported to this facility to streamline the efforts of care and comfort. The hospital camp was established in the large fields belonging to Mr. Wolf, north of the Westmore farm and near the railroad tracks. From the descriptions they heard, the Westmores believed the location was the same as their favorite picnic place, where they had planned to spend the Fourth of July.

"I expect the ambulances will be here in a day or two to remove the wounded," Dr. Barnes said that evening during supper at the crowded kitchen table.

"This dreadful ordeal is coming to an end," Orderly Lamar remarked.

Dr. Barnes continued. "The supply situation has improved, but it will be even better and more organized in the hospital camp, and the men should receive better care. That," he clarified, "isn't a slight to your work, Westmores. I'll never understand why the medical director left only one hundred and six doctors to care for thousands of wounded."

Betsy tried to imagine what it would be like to have an empty home. She felt relief, thinking of the reduced workload, but she knew she would miss the feeling of accomplishment as the family and medical staff worked together. And she would miss her soldiers.

"Will you go to Camp Letterman?" Father asked.

"I believe they'll have enough doctors now," Dr. Barnes replied. "I'll apply for a furlough to rest and recover my own health and then rejoin my brigade."

"You have done much for the wounded men in your care, especially considering the limited supplies you had at the start," Mother commented sincerely.

"I always wish it could be more," Dr. Barnes said sadly. "But I remind myself what we can do is better than nothing at all. The medical field is still developing. In the next decades, I hope scientists will make discoveries to save countless lives. I'll be pleased to see it, but I'll lament that those advancements will come too late to help these suffering men."

Betsy's throat felt tight. She still regretted her harsh opinion and wanted to make things right with this dedicated surgeon. "I'm sorry, sir," she said very quietly; he turned to look at her. "When you first came here, I thought very unkind things about you. I didn't understand how focused you were and how much stress you worked under. Please forgive me?"

"We all have misperceptions, Miss Westmore. The first time I saw you, I thought you were a helpless girl who would be useless in a field hospital." He cleared his throat. "But I have discovered I was wrong, too. Shall we forgive each other and be more careful in our first opinions?" Betsy smiled and nodded.

It was late afternoon of the next day when the ambulances appeared to transport the wounded to Camp Letterman. Dr. Barnes and his assistants systematically prepared each patient for the short journey in the bumpy wagons. Mother and Father helped the soldiers who could walk or hobble to the wagons outside. The children brought requested supplies or held open doors as the stretchers were carried in and out. Some of the soldiers accepted the move without comment or concern; others expressed worry and didn't want to leave the Westmores' care and the competent attention of the medical staff.

The process was slow; each ambulance carried no more than six men, some less, if the soldiers had to remain lying down. Several hours passed, and sunset came. Betsy was in the yard, spreading a blanket over a soldier waiting on a stretcher. She was trying not to think how hard it would be to send her soldiers away. What sort of care would they receive at Camp Letterman?

Dr. Barnes helped placed a stretcher in the remaining ambulance and surveyed the busy twilight scene. "Don't have room for any more, Doctor, and it'll be too dark to see by the time we get back," an ambulance driver explained, leaning wearily against the wagon. "But you've got more wounded here."

"Come back in the early morning," Dr. Barnes ordered. "We'll stay here tonight."

At dawn, a couple of ambulances returned, and the remaining wounded in the sitting room departed. Betsy hovered in the dining room, unwilling to give up her soldiers, but knowing they had to go. One of the ambulance drivers stepped into the empty sitting room and said to Dr. Barnes, "Um...we've got a problem. You've got three more wounded in that side room, and we're filled up. You want us to come back in an hour?"

"These soldiers can stay unless the doctor objects," Father spoke up. Betsy felt hopeful; maybe she wouldn't have to say good-bye to her soldiers yet.

"It would be best, if you don't mind," Dr. Barnes admitted. "Russell should be moved by stretcher to avoid jostling his healing leg. Cooper's wound might break open, even in a short ambulance ride, and Morten...well..."

"But one's a Confederate," the driver pointed out.

"Yes, but believe me, he's not going anywhere anytime soon," Dr. Barnes replied. "He'll be moved to Camp Letterman as soon as he's sufficiently recovered. I'll make the appropriate arrangements with the surgeons and director for these three to stay for a few days."

The ambulances drove off. Dr. Barnes offered to stay longer. Mother and Father replied they were quite certain they could take care of the soldiers for a few more days and see that they were transported to the general hospital. Betsy stepped into the dining room, reporting triumphantly,

"You don't have to leave. Dr. Barnes says you can stay a few more days!"

Rachel followed and said shyly, "I'm glad you get to stay." Thomas smiled.

Harold sat up and leaned against the wall. "Huzzah," he exclaimed enthusiastically. "Looking miserable and ill must have paid off this time, don't you think Morten?"

Edward kept his hand pressed against his wound as if trying to keep the pain away. "Some of us aren't giving dramatic performances," he said quietly. Realization showed in Harold's eyes, and he looked away.

Again, Betsy felt Edward was hiding something from her, but, before she had time to ask, James bounded into the room. "You get to stay!" he exclaimed. "We can talk and play more games. I wish you could stay forever. I like having you here."

"Forever's a long time," Thomas said teasingly. "You'd get tired of us."

"Oh, no! You could get better and stay here always. And when Philip comes home, we'd have four brothers!"

Thomas and Harold laughed at James's enthusiasm. "What if we want to go home to our families?" Harold asked.

Before James thought of a convincing reply, Dr. Barnes came in. Efficiently, he examined and bandaged the wounds one last time; the soldiers thanked the doctor and his orderlies for their attentive care. The surgeon handed Father a couple of half-empty bottles of medicine and gave directions in a low tone, before saying farewell to the family and thanking them for their generosity, hard work, and responsible actions in the last weeks. Dr. Barnes and his assistants took their horses and rode away.

After the medical staff left, the empty house was silent and very strange. Only the Westmores and the three soldiers remained. Betsy wandered through the deserted rooms. Old, bloody straw mounded on the floors, and there were dark stains on the wood planks. Interior doors had been removed and used as improvised stretchers in the first days. Discarded bandages were heaped in one corner of the parlor. All the curtains were torn from the windows. Abandoned quilts needed to be washed again. The straw ticks and sheets on the beds were ruined beyond repair. Empty medicine bottles and a couple of broken knife blades littered the girls' dressing table. The chairs were scattered through the house, previously used as props or supports. The little tables from the sitting room and parlor were in the hallways, former resting places for boxes of medical supplies.

It was home: battered, chaotic, and filthy, but still home. Father started raking the grimy straw, and Mother and the children swept the littered floors; properly scrubbing the floorboards would have to wait until they had more time. The furniture, scattered all over the house, was replaced to its proper rooms. Until the bedding was washed again, they decided to continue sleeping in the cellar.

While Betsy helped clean, she felt an empty sadness as she looked at the places where so many brave men had lain for the last three weeks. It was a strange feeling. She had thought she couldn't wait for the wounded to be moved, but, now that they were gone, the house seemed empty. And yet it was a relief to know she would not have to clean and bandage wounds every morning, haul water until her arms ached, and cook enough food for a small army. The feelings of sadness were mingled with relief and a prayer for quiet home life.

Chapter 29

That evening, the family sat around the kitchen table, enjoying a peaceful meal for the first time in several weeks. It was wonderful to have everyone seated at the table rather than scattered through the house working at various tasks. When the supper dishes were washed, they found seats on the floor of the dining room, and Father read the Bible.

Betsy listened to the scripture reading and watched her soldiers. Without a doubt, Thomas and Harold were better, but Edward was weak, refusing food and sometimes seeming disoriented. Now, he lay quietly as Father read. At times, Edward opened his eyes, trying to focus; his face was strangely pale. Sometimes, he frowned as if in pain, then he would relax again.

As they said good night, Betsy asked quietly, "Edward, are you alright?"

"I will be," he answered faintly. "Soon." Betsy shivered; something did not seem right in his answer. His physical strength was gone, and, suddenly she realized her strong, stoic soldier looked like he might fade away. Why had she not noticed before?

"Father," she whispered a few minutes later as he was closing the kitchen window. "Edward isn't well. Do you think we should send for a doctor?"

"There's nothing a doctor can do. The wound is too deep…"

Betsy turned and walked away. She knew what Father would have said next. Now, she knew what Edward had been hiding from her. She had seen men die in the last weeks, but they were soldiers she had hardly known. Maybe she knew their names and where they were from, but there had been no close friendship with them. Edward was one of "her soldiers." They had talked seriously. She knew about his family. She had sat with him all night when the pain was so bad. God couldn't let him die! I'll pray for him, she thought. If I have faith and pray all night, maybe God will heal him. If he died, how could I tell his sister?

She went back to Father, trying not to cry. "Can I stay with Edward? I don't want him to feel alone."

"Not tonight," Father replied. "You need to sleep. Edward needs to rest also. I will stay nearby, and, if he asks to see you, I promise I'll come get you."

"Maybe he'll be better in the morning," Betsy whispered hopefully. With a last glance into the dining room, she slipped into the cellar and prayed for his recovery until she fell asleep.

The next morning, she knew her prayers were not answered when she saw the increased pallor on Edward's face. He smiled weakly as she greeted him, asking how he felt. "I'm well," he answered wearily. "The pain is nearly gone."

"Can we get you something to eat or drink?" Mother questioned gently, coming into the room. He shook his head.

When they returned with breakfast for Thomas and Harold, Edward was asleep. Harold laid down a Bible and took the plate of food. "I thought this was Edward's Bible," Betsy commented, picking up the small volume.

"It is," Harold said sadly. "He lent it to me so I could read it. Last night, after you went to bed, he told me I could have it."

Don't cry, Betsy thought desperately, but a single tear ran down her cheek. Harold rested his hand on her shoulder. "Stay strong," he said in an undertone. "He's been unselfish and protective of you... Stay strong now."

"I'll try," she promised, suspecting the day might be one of the hardest of her life. The experiences of the last month had been difficult and overwhelming, but there had been a feeling that hard work and faith could change the situation. There was nothing that could change what would happen next.

Betsy felt frozen as she heard Father answer James and Rachel's questions about Edward. She knew she was failing her promise to Philip when she couldn't think of anything comforting to say to them, couldn't even give Rachel a warmhearted embrace when she cried. She would have spent the whole morning watching Edward, but the house must be cleaned and the noon meal prepared. Betsy went through the motions of working, pausing to see if Edward still slept comfortably.

In the mid-afternoon, Mother sent Betsy downstairs to prepare some soup for supper while she and Rachel scrubbed the upstairs floors, removing the filth and trying to reduce the bloodstains. From the eastern kitchen window, she saw Father and James repairing the garden fences. The vegetables simmered, and Betsy was drying the cooking utensils when Edward said in a natural voice, "Betsy, could you bring me some water and come here?"

She poured the last of the water into a cup and entered the room. "Sit, please," he said as she handed it to him. "Your father tells me you are...distressed about me." Edward looked at her questioningly, and she nodded.

"I've known from the beginning of this ordeal that the wound was mortal. I hope I didn't mislead you into believing I would recover." She shook her head, afraid to speak. "I do not regret dying for my country. When it's all over, it's strange to try to recall a fierce battle. Only flashes of memory remain – perhaps a dying friend, a broken rifle, a clump of odd clover, an officer in the smoke. Our charge into the open meadow was like that. The only thing I can clearly remember is the Union flag upheld in the battle smoke. Flag bearer after flag bearer must have been hit because often the banner wavered or fell toward the ground before someone else caught it. Above all the struggle, pain, and death, the national flag still waved defiantly."

He paused and finished the water. Thomas and Harold were silent, unwilling to intrude in the conversation. Edward went on. "That flag must and will remain the symbol of America. So many have died for it and all that it represents – freedom, justice, safety, hope. Death is not in vain, if those principles are defended."

Edward closed his eyes for a moment, then looked up, and continued. "So you see, I have no regrets, and I am not afraid. There's no fear in death for those who are saved by Christ. Ultimately, He is the One I live for. Like Paul wrote in Philippians, 'For to me, to live is Christ, to die is gain.' "

Betsy felt tears on her cheeks, and the lump in her throat prevented any answer. Edward reached out a shaky hand, and wiped the tears from her face. "No tears for me. If you see my sister, you'll tell her what I've told you?"

"Yes," she promised. "Edward..." she paused, not really sure what to say.

He watched her, his brown eyes steady, calm, and reassuring. "I'd like some more water, please," he said after a long while. Nodding, Betsy picked up the cup and rose to leave the room.

"Betsy," Edward said. She turned in the doorway. "Thank you...for everything." She smiled at him and then went into the kitchen.

The water bucket was empty. She went quickly out to the well and drew fresh water. Father and James had finished their job and were rinsing their dirty hands in the water trough.

"Father, I think you should check Edward. He seems..."

"I'll come at once," he replied uneasily.

Betsy went back to the house ahead of him. She filled the empty cup with water and stepped lightly through the doorway, noticing with surprise that Thomas sat on the floor, leaning over Edward.

"Here, Edward," she said, "I had to get some…No!" She dropped the half-filled cup and knelt at his side. His eyes were closed. His chest was still. "No…" she whispered again, covering her mouth with her hand as her eyes blurred with tears. A moment later, she touched his face and then felt for a pulse. Nothing. He was dead. "Oh, Edward…" she sobbed quietly, picking up his lifeless hand.

Behind her, Harold sniffled. Thomas looked away from her quick glance and wiped his sleeve across his face, turning back toward his bed. She heard Father's footstep, and then he stood in the doorway. Betsy stumbled to him and hid her face on his shoulder, crying for the loss of her friend and for the sister far away. For a long while, Father did not say anything; he held her and let her cry. Finally, he said gently, "Betsy, I know you did all you could for him, but the Lord wanted him to go home to heaven."

James came in the kitchen door, letting it slam loudly. He stopped when he saw Betsy. "What happened? Did Edward die?" He looked into the dining room, knew the answer to his question, sat down on the floor, and started crying.

Betsy knelt down next to him. "Edward's not here. He's in heaven with Jesus. He's home, and he's happy."

"But I'm not," James sobbed.

"Me either," Rachel cried, joining them. After a while, Father and Mother came and they read the Bible for a little while and talked about heaven and a Christian's hope.

In the evening, Father buried Edward in the orchard graveyard, setting his grave a little apart from the others. Betsy's ruined quilt was his shroud. She was comforted by thinking of God's promises and remembering Edward's words to her, but it still did not ease the ache in her heart when she saw the empty place in the dining room.

She sat with her back against the wall, near Thomas. She had watched the burial for a few moments, then retreated to the shadowy dining room. "Betsy," Thomas said quietly, "in the end, he was ready to go to heaven."

Unable to hold back the tears, she hid her face in her hands. She felt Thomas's hand on her shoulder and heard him talking. "Edward and I spoke a long while after you went to bed last night. We talked about his sister. His former hopes for the future. But he told me it was alright. He went peacefully, Betsy. There was no struggle."

She looked up despairingly. "I know he's safe. But I hurt."

"I know," Thomas said simply. "I've lost friends. You have to remember them, but you can't let their deaths destroy your spirit. You have to move forward."

Harold spoke from his corner. "God won't leave you or forsake you. Try to trust Him, even in this hard time." Betsy nodded.

The next morning, on her hands and knees, Betsy fiercely scrubbed the bloodstains on the floor of the sitting room. She contemplated all that had happened and wondered about the purpose of the trials and suffering in the last weeks. It was not anger or even selfish frustration enveloping her; it was a deep and overwhelming sadness. How many men had died within the walls of this single house? Whose blood discolored these floors and stained the hems and sleeves of her dresses? How many would suffer the effects of terrible wounds for the rest of their lives? How many widows, orphans, bereaved mothers, and sisters were mourning for someone who had perished at this place called Gettysburg? The soldiers had died despite the hard work and care. And for what purpose? The war was not over.

Tears ran down her face. She sniffled and scrubbed the floor harder. The stains refused to budge. I give up, she thought, and threw the brush half-way across the room where it clattered against the wall. "Why?" she sobbed aloud. "Why, God? I don't understand the sacrifice that was required. I don't understand the purpose. I'll still trust You, but help me to understand. Why this sacrifice? Why the death of so many good men? Why?"

Chapter 30

"I don't want you to go," James cried a few days later. Outside, Father spoke with a couple of medical personnel who had come to take the two soldiers to Camp Letterman.

"Me either," Rachel sobbed. Betsy did not say anything, trying to avoid crying.

"There now," Thomas comforted, patting James's shoulder. "We're not going to be too far away."

"Maybe you could come visit us," Harold added hopefully.

"We should try to be happy," Betsy commented drearily. "At least Thomas and Harold are better." Her tone left something unsaid, and she was thinking of Edward.

"Betsy," Thomas said, "don't give up." His expression told her that he understood her sorrow. She nodded and tried to smile.

Father and Mother came into the room. Harold looked at them with a mischievous grin, saying, "Now, Mr. and Mrs. Westmore, we're not going to leave unless you promise to come see us at Camp Letterman."

Mother smiled. "Of course, we'll come if we can."

They thanked the family sincerely, but there wasn't time for long conversation since some orderlies entered. Harold was put in an ambulance with five other men from another location. He raised his eyebrows apprehensively, then smiled, and waved goodbye before the vehicle jolted out of the yard. Thomas would make the journey on a stretcher, carried by four men, to prevent a bumpy ride from displacing his healing bones. "Take care of Blaze," he called. "I'll want to trade this stretcher ride for her in a few weeks. No offense, gentlemen," he added to the stretcher-bearers.

Betsy felt lonely as she entered the house and glanced into the empty dining room. She would miss Thomas's quiet smile and confidence and Harold's teasing and friendly arguing. Edward was gone forever; she felt like crying when she thought of his strong faith and never-failing patience. They were gone: two at the hospital, the other in a silent grave.

The floors were scrubbed as clean as possible. The rugs, which had not been damaged, were laid back on the floors. Curtains would have to wait because, aside from some salvaged clothing, there was no extra cloth in the house. The dining room table was so bloodstained that Father split it into wood for the fire. The bedding had been washed, improvised mattress ticks were created, and the beds could be used again. But it will never really be the same, Betsy thought, as she surveyed the interior of the house. Too much has happened here for it to ever be the same.

They sat around the kitchen table which had been temporarily moved into the dining room. Rachel asked to be excused from the table, but Father told her to try to eat. Nobody seemed hungry, even James pushed the food around his plate. Mother dropped her fork, covered her face with her hands, and started crying. Father stood by her in an instant while the children stared. Mother rarely cried and never without reason.

"How long and wretched this month has been," she sobbed. "One month ago today, it all started. Oh, I've tried, but I can't forget all that's happened."

Betsy, with tears running down her face, went to Mother and knelt beside her chair. "But we're safe. Philip is safe. And we're still here." James didn't say anything, but he gave Mother a hug.

Rachel joined her sister. "We've learned that with God's help, we can be strong."

"Yes," Father said comfortingly, "it's not been easy, and the next months will be challenging, but God has taken care of us. He let us be lights for Him. We'll continue to trust Him for each day and let Him guide us through every difficulty."

That night, as she lay in bed, Betsy flopped onto her side and closed her eyes. A moment later, she stared at the darkness again; tonight, every time she tried to sleep, she saw awful images of bloody wounds or dead soldiers' faces and heard cries of pain. Rachel slumbered quietly by her side, increasing Betsy's frustration at her inability to rest.

Finally, she got up and stood by the open window. She could still smell the stench of the battlefield, and it choked her again. The sky was full of stars. She leaned her head against the window frame and gazed at them, her heart asking a thousand questions. There was no voice from heaven, no spoken message in the soft breeze, but as she gazed at the starry heavens a verse of her psalm came to mind. "Be still and know that I am God..." Be still, she thought, lay aside every heartache, every lingering thought, every doubting question. Be still and simply know: God still reigns.

There were no answers to her questions. There was no ultimate resolution. Yet, as she looked toward the dwelling place of God, she resigned herself to wait for answers in His time. When she returned to bed and closed her eyes, she was able to rest, and, though she did not wake with a smile the next morning, she awoke with the resolution to trust God even more.

Although it had been less than a day since the soldiers left, the Westmore children were anxious to see their friends again. Father had heard the hospital always needed fresh produce, and he suggested the family could take some fruit, obtain the proper passes, and visit the general hospital. In the afternoon, the family set out for town, carrying a basket of fruit and a couple of watermelons. The passes were obtained from the provost marshal without much difficulty, and they had no trouble with the sentries on the York Road as they approached.

It was both awesome and saddening to see Camp Letterman. Hundreds of tents stood in neat rows with cooking and storage facilities erected nearby. People moved between the tents or hurried in and out in competent chaos. Sentries directed the Westmores to check the record books at the administration tent to find where their friends were. The tent number was quickly located, and they moved through the canvas city. The flaps were drawn back, and, inside each tent, injured men rested on bedframes and mattresses; both Union and Confederate wounded were together.

In some of the tents, women sat near their husband, father, brother, or son. Sometimes, children clustered around the bedside of their father. There was a feeling of organization and hope at Camp Letterman, but, similar to every other place near Gettysburg, there was still the anchoring reality that most of the men here were badly hurt and might not get better. Some soldiers would recover and journey home or to another hospital while others would rest in the nearby graveyard.

Harold saw the Westmores first and waved excitedly; Thomas grinned from his reclining position. They were in the same large tent with about eight other men who were watching the family curiously. Thomas briefly introduced the Westmores, and the men seemed pleased to meet the family. In answer to the Westmores' anxious questions, Thomas and Harold said they hadn't had much discomfort when they were moved, were surprised and glad to still be together, and were adjusting to their new accommodations. Though, as Thomas said, "It's not as nice as your house."

"But our nurses and doctor seem to be good people, and they give all of us care without partiality. However, it'll take time to figure out the schedule here. It's like military time, except we're stuck in bed," Harold complained.

Thomas smiled wryly. "Yes, it was one thing after another this morning. Breakfast, wash, wounds dressed, chaplain's visit, beef tea to drink, medicine brought for those who needed it… According to one of our tent-mates here, the food, drink, and medicine schedule alone will total to nine visits from the nurse in one day."

While the others questioned Thomas about the routine, Harold quietly asked Betsy, "How are you doing?"

"Alright, I guess."

"I know I'm not an expert on this…but don't let doubt or bitterness overcome your faith. You told me a little about the psalm you memorized. 'God is your refuge and strength.' "

"I know, I've been thinking about that, and it helps."

"Good. Now, Miss Betsy, there was a story I've been meaning to tell you…" He launched into an amusing tale, and, by the end, Betsy was laughing.

The Westmores stayed for almost an hour, talking with their soldiers and meeting the others in the tent. A nurse with a beautiful smile was pleased with the fresh produce and promised the soldiers in this tent would have some.

The camp closed to visitors at four, and it was a quarter to that hour when the Westmores said good-bye and went slowly toward the exit of the hospital camp. Father and

Betsy had walked ahead of the others who had stopped to answer a nurse's polite inquiry. A gentleman in a dark civilian coat approached them and said, "Forgive me for troubling you, but are you citizens of Gettysburg?"

"We don't live in town, but on a farm nearby," Father replied.

"Do you perhaps know a Mr. Henry Westmore?"

"I'm Henry Westmore. May I help you?"

"Perhaps," the gentleman said, looking surprised. "I'm Reverend Fulton, and I have traveled here with the Sanitary Commission from Indiana. My wife came with me. Both of us intend to assist at the hospital here. A young lady traveled under our protection. She's looking for her brother who was wounded and who wrote her a letter from your farm. We thought he had likely been moved to this hospital, but there are no records of him. The young lady's name is Miss Allison Morten, and her brother is Sergeant Edward Morten of the 27th Indiana. Do you know the sergeant?"

Betsy looked away. Miss Morten had come, but she had arrived too late. How could they tell her? Father explained what had happened.

"Miss Morten has been so full of hope," Reverend Fulton said sadly. "She has strong faith, but I believe she has never thought he might be dead."

Two ladies walked toward them. The first was average height and wore a practical dark green hooped dress and a small straw hat to shade her from the sun. She carried a basket and appeared ready to work when assigned a job.

The second lady was tall and slender and almost appeared out of place in this world of dust and blood. Her dress, made of a floral striped calico, had a wide hoop, fitted bodice, and fine undersleeves; her gloved hands held a small parasol, shading her pretty face from the sun while a small fashionable hat tilted forward on her head, covering her dark auburn hair. With the exception of the hat, the clothing was simple, yet contrasted greatly with the surroundings. She almost looked like a gracious princess, but as she came near, her expression betrayed her worry. "Reverend Fulton," she said in a soft voice, "have you heard anything that may be helpful in my search?" He turned and said something to her.

Mother had come, and Father told her the situation briefly. Rachel and James watched curiously. "You're Mr. Westmore?" the beautiful young lady asked, turning toward Father.

"Yes..." Father said slowly, watching Reverend Fulton as if waiting for a cue.

"Where are you staying?" Mother asked gently.

"In a very crowded house in town, but I don't mind. I've come to find my brother." Miss Morten's hands shifted nervously on the handle of her parasol.

"Yes, well, perhaps you and the Fultons could stay at our home," Mother invited. "We live not far from here. It would be quieter."

"You're kind," Miss Morten said, "but I don't think I can rest until I find my brother. He was with the 27th Indiana, and his name is Edward Morten. He said that he was staying at your home. Do you know where he is now?"

Nobody seemed to be able to speak the devastating news. Father and Mother glanced at each other, James looked down and kicked a tuft of grass, and Rachel twisted the ties of her cloth bonnet. Betsy, remembering her promise to Edward, stepped forward. "Miss Morten, I know we're not properly introduced, but I'm Betsy Westmore."

"Oh, you wrote the letter for my brother?" Miss Morten asked eagerly.

"Yes. My family and I and the surgeon did all we could for Edward, but..." Betsy swallowed hard, "in the end, God called him home." Betsy started crying quietly.

Miss Morten's hopeful expression crumpled as the realization settled, and she turned to Mrs. Fulton and embraced her. Reverend Fulton spoke to Father in an undertone, and, a few moments later, he said gently to the weeping girl, "Allison, I think it best for us to accept the Westmores' offer and stay at their quiet home for a few days."

With an effort, she suppressed her sobs, wiped her eyes, and turned to the family. "Thank you. I don't even know you, but Edward...spoke well of you."

They departed and walked silently along a country lane going south toward the farm. Arriving at the house, Miss Morten begged forgiveness for what might seem like bad manners, but requested to be alone. Mother took her and Mrs. Fulton upstairs, and Betsy followed with a basin of water for washing away the dust from traveling.

Mother gave Allison the guest room and the Fultons the boys' room, apologizing for the makeshift mattresses and linens. When Betsy and Mother returned downstairs, Father and Mr. Fulton had decided to go into town to retrieve the trunks and personal belongings. Miss Morten did not come down for supper and told Mrs. Fulton she was not hungry.

Although Betsy was glad they could extend hospitality to Miss Morten and the Fultons, she wished they had not come. It was more responsibility; she wanted to find answers to her questions, to remember Edward, but try to move forward as Thomas suggested. Having Miss Morten here and hearing more about Edward did not seem to bring closure to her grief. Father and Mother gave the Fultons the details of Edward's stay, wound, and death, and they mourned the loss of their young friend. The children sat quietly, listening to the adults' conversation.

"The Mortens attended our church," the pastor said at the end of the story. "I often spoke with Edward and am assured of his Christian character and faith. By his actions and life, I have no doubt that he was a sincere believer."

"Mr. Fulton," said his wife after a while, "do you think perhaps I should stay here with Allison while you go to Camp Letterman tomorrow to assume your duties?"

"That would be best, I think. Miss Morten shouldn't go to the hospital, and she cannot travel home alone."

"You're welcome to stay here at our home as long as you need," Father added.

"Yes, and, perhaps when Miss Morten is better acquainted with us, you could go to Camp Letterman with your husband," Mother said to Mrs. Fulton.

That night, when Betsy went upstairs, she looked at the closed door of the guest room and prayed for the young woman. Later, as she curled up in bed with Rachel close by and James sleeping on the floor, she cried silently for her soldier who had gone home, the sister who had come to find him, and the aching questions in her waiting heart.

Chapter 31

Miss Morten stayed alone in her room the next day; she sent an apologetic message to the family, but preferred solitude. Mrs. Fulton took meals to Miss Morten and, in the afternoon, spent a few hours with her.

"Why does Miss Morten stay by herself?" James asked as he helped Mother and the girls prepare supper.

"She doesn't know us, James, and she received heartbreaking news very unexpectedly. If you think about her situation, you'll understand why she wants to be alone and grieve privately," Mother explained.

"I wish I could stay in my room and cry," Betsy muttered, thinking of how hard it was to move past her grief. With Miss Morten here, Betsy felt like she was reliving her experiences with Edward, and the memories were painful to her already sorrowful heart.

Two days later, at Miss Morten's insistence, Mrs. Fulton walked to Camp Letterman with her husband, prepared for a day of service at the hospital. In the late morning, Betsy was writing a short note to Philip at the desk in the sitting room when she heard the rustle of a hooped skirt. Glancing up, Betsy saw Miss Morten standing in the doorway. She wore a light floral calico dress with ruffles of dark pink on the skirt and wide sleeves with lacy undersleeves. Her hair was twisted back loosely, almost carelessly, and her eyes were red from crying.

Betsy's slight resentment of the young woman was conquered by genuine sympathy. "Miss Morten," she said, standing, "good morning. May I get you something to eat?"

"Don't trouble yourself. I'm not hungry," she answered. "You're Miss Betsy Westmore, if I remember correctly?" Betsy nodded. "You were with my brother while he was here."

"Yes, he was one of my soldiers... I mean one of the soldiers I looked after."

"Walk with me? Show me his grave? I'm ready now," the young woman said bravely.

Compassion overruled Betsy's former feelings about Edward's sister, and she replied kindheartedly, "Yes, Miss Morten."

"Call me Allison." She glanced at her clothing in slight embarrassment. "I never thought he'd be gone when I arrived. I didn't pack any mourning clothes, only pretty dresses that he always liked to see me in. I'll wear mourning for him, but not today. When I say the first good-bye, I want to be wearing a pretty dress. I hope you understand."

They went slowly out the front door and across the grass to the orchard where the headboards marked the graves. Edward had been buried a little apart from the others. They stood near, looking at the dirt mound and wooden board with carved name, regiment, and date. The breeze rustled the leaves of the fruit trees, but, otherwise, it was silent.

Allison went alone and knelt by the grave. After a long while, she turned to Betsy and said, "You were with him all those weeks. Come, sit, and tell me all that he talked about and what he did."

There were more tears as Betsy told about everything from the first time she saw him to the last time he called her name. "Edward was like a brother to me," Betsy said. "He was considerate and protective. He had unshakeable faith. He was strong in a silent, patient way. He wanted you to come so much, and he talked about you often."

"Thank you," Allison said softly then went on, seeing Betsy's puzzled expression. "I'll always regret I wasn't able to be here a week or even two days earlier, but I had no control over the circumstances. I know you didn't take my sisterly place in his heart, but you filled the role I could not because of my absence. You comforted him, loved him with a sisterly affection, and eased his trial of pain. Truly, I am indebted to you."

"But, I –"

"No, no protests, Betsy. I meant everything I said. Truly, I can begin to forgive myself, knowing he was not alone and friendless in his last days of life. Now, I would like to walk alone. Is it safe to do that here?" Betsy suggested she stay within sight of the house, and Allison walked away slowly.

Betsy stayed at the grave and watched her, thinking about what Allison had said. Rachel came from the house and joined her. They watched Allison pacing slowly in the ruined field. Her head was bent. Her hands toyed with a small bunch of tiny flowers which she had plucked. Her ruffled skirt trailed on the ground.

"Her dress is like a fashion plate," Rachel said sadly. "I guess I was wrong in what I once said. A beautiful dress doesn't guarantee an easy life, free of trials. She's a lady in a beautiful dress, but she's lost her brother and is all alone in the world. I'm sure she'd gladly wear the plainest dress, if it meant her parents were still alive and her brother was with her."

Betsy looked at Rachel. How much older she sounded…how the last four weeks had changed her. Part of the older sister rejoiced at the mature thinking, but the greater part ached to have the carefree dreamer return.

"I'll hold fast to my faith," Allison told the Fultons that evening in the sitting room. "My heart's still breaking, but my faith can be strengthened if I cling to God in this time of mourning. Edward's letter is so precious to me. He dictated the words I would need to hear. I can still follow his advice."

The next day, Allison joined the family earlier. She was reserved and quiet. Sometimes, she could not hold back the tears, but she tried to assist the ladies with their work in the kitchen or house. This day, she wore a plain lavender dress and had already asked if she could dye some of her gowns black for mourning. Betsy began to welcome Allison's presence; her conversation with Allison seemed to ease her own grief.

At dinner, James, who was sitting next to Allison, asked, "Miss Allison, what on earth took you so long to get here?"

"James," Mother said quickly. "No."

"It's alright, Mrs. Westmore," Allison replied shakily. "It's a valid question. I had gone to Illinois at the end of June to stay with a cousin who was ill and needed help with her children. She lives on a farm. I did not go into the little town and so didn't even hear the news about the battle until two days after it ended when a neighbor told us. I was a little worried about Edward, of course, but really knew nothing until my uncle – he's a lawyer – arrived at the end of the second week of July to take me home and had a paper with the casualty lists. Edward's name was there. I was anxious to get home, hoping he would be sent back immediately. When I arrived, only his letter was there, and I tried to find a way to travel to Gettysburg. Unfortunately, Uncle had an important court case starting, Grandfather had taken a bad fall and is unfit to travel, and all my other male relatives are with the armies. Finally, Mr. and Mrs. Fulton made plans to go and asked if I wanted to travel with them. We should've arrived in time, except for long travel delays. I regret the slow news and transportation very much, but have to remind myself it wasn't in my control."

"Edward would've understood," Mother remarked.

"I know. He was one of the most caring people I've ever known. Well," she wiped her eyes with the napkin, "I'll see him again in heaven. I can look forward to that day. Now, I really don't understand, why was your home a hospital?"

Father briefly explained the circumstances, but Allison asked probing questions until she had learned almost the entire story of the last month. At the end of the account, Allison said thoughtfully, "You gave nearly all your material possessions to help the wounded…your food supply, the comfort of your home, your time and energy, your beautiful linens. And you did it unselfishly."

"Betsy even gave the fabric for her new dress," James announced.

Betsy kicked him under the table and frowned. She did not want people to know. She did not even want to remember it, blushed as she noticed Allison watching her, and replied simply, "Would it have done any good to have a beautiful dress knowing that its fabric could have been bandages to stop flowing blood? Please, don't say anything more about it."

"When I think about all you have experienced, everything you have given, and your attitudes through it all, I feel humbled," Allison said. "You're civilians, but you have supported the Union as much as the soldiers who fight for it. To me, you are heroes for all the work you have done, the lives you have saved, and the sacrifices you have made."

"Heroes?" Rachel asked, breaking the silence.

James added, "I thought they were only brave soldiers."

"It seems the soldiers will always get the glory, and, rightfully so, I suppose," Allison mused. "But someone should remember the sacrifices of the civilians."

"We're not heroes," Betsy said. "I never felt heroic. Most of the time, I was terrified. There are many things I wish I could forget. We only did what had to be done, and, in the end, nobody will remember that. They'll only think of those who fought here and the ideals they advanced. And perhaps that's the way it should be."

"Perhaps that's the way history will tell the story. Yet for those whose soldiers were comforted or encouraged by your presence and aid...we will never forget what you did, even if it was only little things. What did Christ say? '...And whoever gives one of these...only a cup of cold water...assuredly, I say to you, he shall by no means lose his reward.' You gave so much, perhaps so much you do not even realize it, but I do. The example of the civilians' Christian faith and service may be the only light in the darkness of this war-torn place. It's a silent witness to the power of God's strength, the extension of His mercy, and the limitless boundaries of His love. You lived your faith and showed Christ to a world of hurting soldiers."

Chapter 32

The next morning, at the breakfast table, Reverend Fulton asked Allison when she wished to return home. "I don't know, sir," she replied. "I don't want to inconvenience the Westmores by staying here, but neither do I want you to cut short your time at the hospital."

Mother assured her she could stay as long as she needed. Reverend Fulton expressed his thanks and then said, "The supplies I brought have been helpful, and, though I would be pleased to stay in this mission field all summer, there are many able preachers here now. Mrs. Fulton and I plan to leave next Tuesday, the 11th of August."

"That's the fifth day from now," Allison remarked thoughtfully. "Mr. Westmore, do you think you could help me make the proper arrangements? I…I would like to take Edward's body and bury it properly in the churchyard in our town."

"Yes, I'm sure that can be arranged," Father said.

"Thank you. I know you'll tend the graves here, but I would like my brother buried with the rest of the family, not alone in a faraway place."

On Sunday, they attended church for the first time since the battle. The churches in town had been hospitals and still showed signs of that usage. The Westmores had hoped to see Mrs. Thorn and her family in town, but they were not there. Mother said she would try to visit later in the week. After the services, they walked slowly to Camp Letterman.

Thomas greeted them with a grin as he sat on the edge of his cot, a pair of crutches resting beside him. "Harold and I went to the camp meeting this morning and heard a good sermon. The doctors say I still need to be careful and not put a lot of weight on the limb. But I can get up and use the crutches."

Harold seemed distressed and told his news. "Tomorrow they're moving me to prison. I guess it's good because it means I'm better and stronger, but I'm not excited about getting locked up as though I was a criminal."

"Prisoners aren't criminals," Allison said. "It's really too bad the two governments can't arrange more prisoner exchanges or paroles or something. I know because my fiancé is a prisoner in Richmond. Anyway, Mr. Cooper, don't feel badly about it."

"Thanks. Still, it seems as if I'd do the Confederacy more good as a soldier in the field."

"Hopping on one leg, Harold?" Thomas asked with a teasing glint in his blue eyes.

"Oh, you!" Harold exclaimed, frowning good-naturedly. "Won't you scold him, Miss Betsy? All he does is pester me these days."

"And you tease him, Harold. Come on, don't quarrel like little children," Betsy laughed. It was a bittersweet moment; she was glad to be with her soldiers, but she felt unhappy, thinking of Harold going to prison.

The next day, the family met Harold near the railroad tracks to say good-bye. Allison was with them, but the Fultons were at Camp Letterman. The big smoky engine was noisy, causing them to stand closer together to converse.

"I've had time to think while I've been here," Harold said seriously. "A lot of things that happened to me here at Gettysburg wouldn't qualify as good memories. But I do know one thing: I thank God I was wounded and taken to your house. If that hadn't happened, I might not have become a Christian. I came to Gettysburg a bitter, angry young man. Now, I'm leaving, minus a leg, but with a real understanding of God's mercy and grace. So you see, God's plans are bigger than ours, and He has a purpose even in our pain and suffering."

What a change, and praise God! Betsy thought. The brooding look in Harold's eyes was gone, and his smile was genuine. He was healed, both physically and spiritually. The look of peace on his face, despite his uncertain future, almost made Betsy thankful for the trials they had gone through.

"Well, Miss Betsy, I kept my promise," Harold said, turning to her. "It may be a while before I actually get there, but I'm on my way home. A delay in prison, but going home nonetheless. I'd like to revise that promise I made. I'm going to live for Christ first, and then my family. I hope that's alright with you."

"No objections," Betsy answered, smiling. "We'll miss you."

"I'll miss you. Maybe when this war's all over, I could come back and visit. If I promised not to throw spitballs, send you on countless errands, annoy your friends, cry on your handkerchief, or hold your hand all afternoon, would you want me to come back?"

"Of course. Somehow, even with your pesky actions, you were like an older brother."

He grinned and then said his final good-byes to the rest of the family. "I'm sorry I don't have much to thank you for your kindness, but I couldn't leave without giving you something. Here," he pushed a folded sheet of paper into Mother's hands. "Open it after I leave."

The guards were organizing the prisoners and Harold, using his crutches, hurried away to join the others. The last they saw of him, he was hanging out of a train car, looking back at them and waving one of the crutches.

"I never thought I'd like a Confederate," James remarked. "But he turned out to be a pretty good one."

Mother unfolded the paper. It was a rough pencil sketch of a flickering lantern, like the one hanging in the dining room during the hospital days. At the bottom of the page, it said:

"Let your light so shine before men, that they may see your good works and glorify your Father in heaven," Matthew 5:16. Many thanks for all you did for me.
Your Confederate soldier,
Harold Cooper

They walked slowly into town. "Do you think he'll be alright in prison?" Rachel asked with genuine concern.

"Harold is a strong young man," Father replied. "I think he'll be alright. We should pray that he will have opportunity to share his faith."

"I wish he could've just gone home to his family," Betsy remarked, feeling bad about the lonely life of a prisoner.

"Yes, but remember, although he's your friend, he's still a Confederate soldier, and the Union officers don't want to release more men who could fight against them either on battlefields or by growing food to feed the Confederate armies."

"And remember," Allison said, "to pray for his continued good health. Disease is common in prison, just like in the armies."

"You are concerned about your lieutenant?" Mother asked.

Allison nodded. "I just want him to come home safely. I don't want to find another grave." Betsy reached out and squeezed Allison's hand.

In town, Father went to Mr. Garlach's cabinet shop to obtain a coffin for Edward's body. He came out a few minutes later and said to Allison, "There seems to be a new law from the military guards that, as of today, August 10th, no graves may be opened for removal of the bodies. The provost marshal has issued these orders because there is fear of an epidemic during this hot weather. Mr. Garlach suggests we visit the provost marshal's office and ask for an exception.

Will you go with me?" Allison agreed. They walked through the crowded, busy streets to the Diamond, which was the center of town, and the others waited while Father and Miss Morten stepped inside the headquarters building.

"George, get back here," called a tired woman.

"But, Mama, it's James Westmore."

The Westmores turned and saw Mrs. Thorn and George, coming across the wagon-filled street. She wore a dirt-stained dress and deep sunbonnet and looked exhausted. Mother embraced her, saying, "I'm so glad to see you are safe. We heard you and your family were alright, but there's been no time to visit."

"I know," Mrs. Thorn said sadly. "I came into town today to get some food. I know I'm hardly fit to be seen in these filthy clothes, but I have nothing else left. When we came home, there were no clothes, and everything else was gone or filthy."

"You left?"

"Yes. General Howard and some of his officers had supper at my home on the night of the first day of fighting. I was sorry to only have bread and simple food for them, but they didn't seem to mind. Early the next morning, the general sent us an order to leave. We went south on the Pike and…"

"You should've come to our home," Mother remonstrated gently.

"There were too many troops near, and I wanted to get farther away. Father and I returned in the evening to feed the livestock, but they were gone – a soldier's dinner, I suppose. We stayed away after that and didn't return home until the 7th of July." She looked depressed. "The furniture is gone, the windows are blown out, the floors are as dirty as a pigsty. We've been living in a tent in the yard. Father and I have been digging graves to bury the dead. Sometimes, I think I shall be sick with the horrible stench."

"You shouldn't be doing that hard work. You must think of the baby," Mother reasoned.

"Who else will do it?" Mrs. Thorn countered. "Every man is occupied with the same work or caring for the wounded. The dead must be buried. In such circumstances, if the work is not done, disease may strike the community. I tried to hire some helpers, but they became so ill they had to leave. Father and I manage, and I do try to be careful."

Father and Allison came out of the office, looking dejected. "The provost will make no exceptions," Father explained. "No bodies may be removed until cooler weather in the autumn."

"You will look after his grave for me?" Allison asked the family. "Maybe later I'll be able to return." They assured her they would, and, though not satisfied, she seemed resigned.

To avoid intruding into the young lady's distress, Mrs. Thorn hastily said good-bye and went to get her supplies. The Westmores and Miss Morten walked back through the crowded town and returned home. Allison was very quiet that afternoon, but she informed the Fultons of the situation when they returned in the evening. Since there was nothing more to do, they agreed to continue with their plans to leave the following day. Father made arrangements with Mr. Lightner to borrow a horse to team with Blaze so they could take the large wagon into town.

Allison was up early the next morning. At the breakfast table, she said her trunks were packed and requested to be allowed to wander alone until the time of departure. From the windows, they saw her roaming the fields, gathering a large bouquet of wildflowers. She was a shadowy figure in her black dress and refinished hat, complete with a mourning veil. As they moved the trunks into the wagon and prepared to leave, they saw her kneeling at her brother's grave, saying a private and final farewell. In the wagon, she looked back only once at the lonely grave covered with tears and wildflowers.

Silently, the necessary preparations for travel were accomplished; in a few minutes, they would board the train to return to Indiana. The Fultons came from checking the trunks and thanked the Westmores for their unexpected hospitality.

Allison had been very quiet as though she was afraid to speak, but, in the end, she brushed aside her mourning veil and spoke earnestly. "You said good-bye to that Confederate soldier yesterday, and he told you his life would never be the same because of what he learned at Gettysburg. I don't know why this place has become the turning point of so many destinies and lives. But I know I am grateful for all you did for me and...for my brother. Maybe someday, I can better express my gratitude. When you first met Edward, he was only somebody's brother, but you cared for him as if he had been your family. I'm sure there are sisters like me and other relatives who may never have the opportunity to travel here, but they are grateful for the care that ordinary strangers gave to their loved ones. I only hope I would be as unselfish and courageous as you, if I was in a similar situation…"

The conductor was calling "all aboard." Allison impulsively embraced them, shook hands with Father, and, then, wiping her eyes with her handkerchief and dropping her veil, she glided away to where Mr. Fulton was waiting to assist her into the train car. They saw her sitting at a window, the Fultons near her. She raised her gloved hand in farewell as the train steamed away.

She is courageous, Betsy thought. She faces a life with no family and another dear one still in prison. She weeps, but she is not defeated. She grieves, but she still has faith. She wears black mourning, but remembers the good memories and a future in heaven. She is courageous.

Chapter 33

By mid-August, life at the Westmore home began to balance into a normal routine. House and farm work recommenced. They frequently visited Camp Letterman with fresh fruit or vegetables. Gettysburg and the surrounding battleground began to repair and heal. However, nothing could erase the shallow, eroding graves and the hastily buried dead beginning to resurface in the battle area.

The family was at Camp Letterman one warm summer day, visiting Thomas and some of the other soldiers, when they heard the first rumor. A Gettysburg attorney named David Wills and other prominent men of the community had been discussing the idea of building a national cemetery for the Union soldiers. Supposedly, Mr. Wills had even written to the state governor to discuss the idea, which had been approved, and planning had started for the new cemetery.

"It's probably the best thing that could happen," Thomas said matter-of-factly. "So many families will never be able to remove their dead because they lack the means to travel here or the graves and dead cannot be identified. Rather than have graves destroyed by careless farmers, it'd be much better for this national cemetery to be made. Maybe it will help future generations to understand what happened here. It would honor the sacrifices made by the Americans of this time."

"It's said only Union soldiers will be buried there," Father commented. "What do you think about that?"

"How on earth are they going to guarantee only Union soldiers?" a man, reclining on a nearby cot, wondered.

"I don't know," Thomas shrugged in response to both questions. "We're all Americans. But I guess in some ways, I understand why they only want Union soldiers there. Still, what will happen to the Confederate graves?"

The conversation was permanently interrupted when James entered, carrying a plate of watermelon slices. The recuperating soldiers enjoyed the cool and refreshing fruit, and an amiable seed spitting competition began. A backwoodsman from Wisconsin won when his watermelon seed landed outside the tent in the walkway.

Chuckling, Thomas lay back on his cot and stretched his leg. "How's Miss Blaze?" he asked James.

"She's good. I think she misses you."

"Oh, do you have a sweetheart?" questioned a young soldier who had recently been moved to this tent. "Is she pretty?"

"Yeah, she's beautiful," James announced, not understanding what the soldier asked. "Her coat's a nice chestnut brown. Her eyes are dark brown. Her legs are long, and she has nice white stockings."

"Legs! Stockings!" yelped the young soldier. "What kind of morals do you have?"

Thomas started laughing aloud. "No, no, Blaze is my horse. I'm a courier. James has been taking care of my horse while I've been laid up." Everyone laughed at the mistake, and, after that, Thomas always asked about "Blaze, the horse."

When it was time to leave, Thomas walked a little ways with them. "I can walk the length of three tents and back. I twisted my leg just after Harold left, and those days the doctor made me stay in bed set me back some. But I'm getting stronger every day."

"Do you want to go back to your unit?" James questioned, concerned.

"Yes," Thomas replied.

"When do you think you'll rejoin?" Mother asked, speaking the question in Betsy's mind.

"I'm not sure. From the newspaper accounts, not much is happening. Lee's army got away into Virginia. There've been Union successes in the western region of the war, but I won't be going there. I'll just keep resting and exercising and hope to return as soon as possible."

That evening, Mr. Lightner arrived as the Westmores finished supper. Father invited him to sit down, and Mother poured another cup of tea before taking the stack of dishes into the kitchen and motioning for the children to follow.

"I'm thinking about moving my family," Betsy overheard Mr. Lightner state bluntly. "There's nothing left for us here. We've tried cleaning up the house, but it's so bad that we're sick after a few hours inside. Crops are ruined for this year. Not a stitch of fabric left in the house. Nothing. Don't know if I can start over here, so we're thinking of moving somewhere else."

"Well, we'd be sorry if you left, but I do understand the circumstances," Father replied, setting his cup on the saucer with a clink.

"What about you?"

"We're staying. It's been and will be difficult, but we'll manage."

"Yeah, well…my wife and I think we'll try to stay through the fall and winter and sell the farm in the spring." They talked about other topics for a little while. Then Mr. Lightner asked, "Have you got a new team of horses?"

"No," Father replied, sounding discouraged. "I haven't heard of any for sale."

"I was in town today and heard some news that might interest you. The army horses are government property, but it seems that quite a few of them are unfit for military service. I hear they're going to auction these horses later in the month. I believe August 24th is the sale date."

"Thank you for the information," Father answered; Betsy heard a smile in his tone. "Other damages will simply take time and work to repair, but it is a hardship not having horses for upcoming field-work or hauling. I've been praying we can get a new team."

After Mr. Lightner departed, the family gathered in the sitting room for scripture reading. Father commented, "We've lost many material things, but we've been fortunate. The house is still habitable. We can make do with what is left."

Looking at the bloodstained floor, Betsy felt conflicted. It was as though she was caught between three thoughts, all pulling in separate directions: grief over the past, hope for the future, and passive resignation.

Eight days later, the feeling of hope was slowly conquering. They had attended church services in town, using Blaze and a horse borrowed from the Lightners to pull the wagon. Thomas had received a pass, came into town, and met them at the church. Though he walked with a limp and sometimes had to stop and rest, he said the journey had not been difficult.

After the service, they went back to the farm. Mother and the girls worked together in the kitchen while James set the table. Father and Thomas talked quietly in the sitting room. Betsy enjoyed working in the kitchen, and it was fun to have a visitor.

During the last week, Father had built a new dining table. For now, it was still without a tablecloth, but the worn napkins and neat place settings did not seem out of place on the clean wood. As she glanced around the table at her family and new friend, Betsy believed that though there would always be unpleasant memories surrounding the summer months of 1863, she could move forward. If Philip had been there, she would have been almost perfectly content.

At the dinner table, James chattered about the new team he hoped they would get, and, the next day, when he came home from the sale, he was not disappointed. Father had purchased two strong horses. Both were dark brown with black manes and almost looked like a matched team, except for slightly different heights.

"This one," James informed the girls, pointing to one of the horses, "got a saber cut on the leg which didn't heal up properly. But she can still walk, and Father thinks some poultices will help her get even better. And this one has a few bullet wounds that are mostly healed up, but she's not strong enough to be a cavalry horse anymore. Oh, and Father said I should ask you for ideas of names."

"Queen and Princess," Rachel suggested, though James wrinkled his nose.

"I don't know," Betsy said as James looked at her. "Did you have anything in mind?"

"Don't laugh, now, but I thought 'Hope' and 'Faith' would be good names, seeing how we had a lot of hope and faith that God would take care of us and get us some new horses."

"Well, those are different names for animals, but I like them," Betsy admitted.

Rachel smiled. "They're nice names."

Hope and Faith settled into their barnyard and stalls. The next day, Father started harvesting the east field. He worked the horses carefully, making sure they would not be injured again, but the team did well, and the following days were busy with the grain harvest. The grain in the west field had been lost; it was an early crop and should have been harvested in July, but the heavy rain and the medical staff's horses left nothing worth gathering.

"What are you doing, Father?" Rachel asked one

evening as he sat at the desk, looking through the account book and writing on a scrap of paper.

"Trying to estimate our financial situation this year," Father replied, frowning at the paper.

"Are we out of money? We could be beggars," James suggested excitedly.

Father glanced up with a tense smile. "We won't become beggars."

"How bad is it?" Mother asked quietly.

Anxious silence filled the room, and Betsy stopped knitting, worried by this situation she had not expected. "I don't think we'll have extra crops to sell this year. The west field is the largest, and we usually sold those crops. Our harvest this year will have to be for our own food."

"At least we'll have food," Mother said. "What about the damages needing repair?"

"We have savings in the bank," Father reassured. "There are things that won't be replaced or repaired immediately. We'll have to avoid all extra expenses, but we should praise the Lord that we sold good crops the last few years."

On the first day of September, two months after the battle, Father was unhitching the horses near the well, James was pumping water, Rachel was catching the young chickens, and Mother and Betsy were returning from the garden. The late afternoon air was cool and pleasant.

"Greetings, Westmores," Thomas said, coming around the corner of the house. "I got a pass and decided to take a little walk." He looked healthy, but a little tired.

"Oh, you came to see the horses," James exclaimed.

"No, actually I came to see my human friends. But your new team looks good. Exactly the way you described them, James."

"Join us for an early supper?" Mother invited.

"It'd be my pleasure," Thomas replied, straightening his blue vest and the cuff of his long-sleeve plaid shirt. He sat down on an upside-down bucket and rubbed his leg.

"Are you alright?" Betsy asked.

"Oh, yeah, but it still feels like a long walk. At least I'm cavalry, not infantry."

"When you're ready to go, I'll take you back in the wagon," Father offered.

"That's kind," Thomas replied, "but I want to try a different mode of transportation."

"What?" Rachel questioned, petting the chicken in her arms.

"I'm not telling yet," Thomas answered with a mysterious grin. He reached into his pocket and pulled out a cloth bag. "James, did you ever get up to Culp's Hill to collect bullets?"

James shook his head sadly.

"I thought so. But I suppose every little boy who lives this close to a battlefield ought to have a bullet collection." Thomas handed him the cloth bag.

James dumped the contents on a board and squealed. "Ooh, thank you! These are nice. Look Father! Look Betsy! I got ten bullets and two pieces of shrapnel. Where'd you find these?"

"Found two while walking here, but traded some stuff to other soldiers for the rest."

"I'm so excited. Wait 'til I show George…and Philip, when he comes home!"

At the supper table, Thomas announced, "I got some good news yesterday. My commander wrote to me. I've been promoted to sergeant for my actions – or what I call attempted actions – during the battle."

"Congratulations," Father said.

"When do you have to report back?" Betsy inquired. "Will you have time to visit your family?"

"I don't think I'll be able to see my family this autumn, but I can probably get leave in the winter. The doctors believe I'll be ready for duty in about a week. If I can prove one thing to them."

"What's that?" Rachel questioned.

"Ride back."

"Is it a wise thing to do?" Mother asked cautiously.

"Well, the break's healed. I can walk a good distance unassisted. I'm fairly strong. I've sat on a chair in the riding position with no discomfort. I'm planning to ride bareback tonight to prove the point and avoid the stirrups which might cause some discomfort."

"So you're going to keep being a courier?" James asked apprehensively.

"I hope so. But I won't try jumping tall fences for a while, alright?"

Thomas insisted on helping with the supper dishes and, afterward, went out to the paddock and whistled for

Blaze. She trotted over willingly and hung her head over Thomas's shoulder with a nicker of welcome. "Hey, old girl. Good to see you again. Ready to get back out there and carry some more orders?"

The children leaned on the fence and watched as Thomas stepped into the paddock and slipped a bridle onto his horse, talking quietly to her and checking the scars of the bullet graze. A few minutes later, Thomas sat securely on the horse, but laughingly told the family their farm was the setting of his worst dismount and remount.

Slowly, he walked Blaze around the fence. "I can ride back to Letterman," he announced. "Mr. Westmore, if it's not too much trouble, could you ride one of your horses and bring Blaze back here for me? I can't keep her at the hospital camp."

Father went into the barn to saddle Faith. Thomas halted Blaze by the fence and chatted with the girls. James was too busy petting Blaze and having a one-sided conversation with her to talk with anyone else.

"Have you heard from your brother?" Thomas asked.

Rachel shook her head, and Betsy replied, "Not recently. Father read a newspaper, and there hasn't been a lot of military action. We assume he's alright. I just hope he's not sick. He wrote that he was ill in June."

"He's probably alright," Thomas reassured. "I've learned Westmores aren't easily defeated."

Betsy sighed. "I wish he was here. I think he'd have answers to some of my questions."

"Betsy, you'll find your answers someday. For now, don't let your questions steal your trust in God." He looked at her meaningfully, then changed the topic. "What will you do this autumn?"

"Harvest the garden and orchard, preserve the food, and probably keep visiting the soldiers at Camp Letterman," Rachel said.

"And school will start again," Betsy added. "Mother started us on lessons at home a couple weeks ago, so hopefully we won't be behind in the classes."

"I don't want to go to school," Rachel stated in a timid voice.

"Why not? You used to like to go." Betsy wondered what was bothering her sister.

"It doesn't matter," Rachel mumbled.

"It does," Thomas said quietly. "Why wouldn't you want to go to school?"

"Because…" Rachel tried not to cry, "I saw the country school filled with wounded. One time, Father let me go with him into town to get supplies. We had to take a couple of boxes to the country schoolhouse. It was worse than the hospital here at our home. And I just know I won't be able to go near that building without thinking of all the awful things I saw there."

"I see," Thomas replied supportively. "Maybe you should talk with your parents. I'm sure they'd understand. Maybe you could attend a different school, at least for a little while." Betsy reached out and held her sister's hand.

"I guess so. Now you probably think I'm a coward," Rachel muttered.

"No, I couldn't think that of you or your family, Rachel."

Chapter 34

A week later, Thomas arrived in the morning, startling Mother and the girls by knocking at the front door as though making a formal visit. He seemed to have taken extra care with his uniform, his hair was trimmed, and he had shaved carefully.

"Thank you for inviting me to have dinner before I leave," he said as they entered the sitting room. "It was kind of you, and I will appreciate a good noon meal before the afternoon riding."

Mother smiled. "Well, we couldn't let you leave hungry. You need some good food to make that uniform fit properly again."

Thomas smiled and pulled at his coat. "I guess I did lose some weight. Hospital diet isn't exactly the most filling food. Is there anything I could help with? I was rather lazy when I was staying here."

"No, we'll have dinner in about an hour, and there isn't a lot to finish."

"Come outside, come outside," James called. "We can do something."

Thomas winked at the girls and told James, "Oh, we'll do something alright. You can help me clean and check my riding tack."

Later, at the dinner table, they enjoyed companionable fellowship. They talked about the good memories of the summer. James asked a hundred questions; the girls mostly listened. They lingered at the table until Thomas pushed back his chair and said he'd best get saddled up and ready to start. He tried to insist on helping with the dishes, but Mother waved him out the door. "Not this time, Sergeant Russell. You've got to get ready to ride. Go on."

When Mother and the girls went out to the barn, Thomas had saddled and bridled Blaze and was fastening his saddlebags and bedroll. "You sure have a good horse, Thomas," James said, watching with a dreamy look.

"Want to ride?" Thomas asked casually as he secured the last strap.

"Oh, yes!"

Thomas boosted James onto Blaze and helped him settle in the cavalry saddle. "Here, borrow my new hat, so you'll feel like a real cavalryman."

James put on the hat, and his grin was like a thousand candles. He waited expectantly. "Um, Thomas, are you going to lead Blaze?"

Thomas handed him the reins. "Blaze is a good horse. She knows you're a young rider. I'll think you'll do just fine. Walk her out of the barn and all the way around the house."

"Yes, sir," James called, saluting.

"You've greatly pleased him," Father commented as they watched James ride.

"Aw, he's a good boy. I'm glad I can make him happy," Thomas answered.

"He'll talk about nothing else for the next five months," Betsy said, smiling.

After James returned and made an ungraceful dismount, Thomas said, "Well, I've got to head out. But I couldn't leave without thanking you properly for everything. I'm not good with fancy words. Thank you for all your care and encouragement. It's hard to believe that I'm actually going to ride away from here." He looked down for a couple of seconds, and then said cheerfully, "I've got a few things for you." He pulled a little bag from his pocket and gave Mother and Father a small card. "I had one made for my parents, but they gave me two copies, so I thought you might want the other." It was a photograph of Thomas.

"Thank you. It's very special," Mother said gently.

"Now, for James…" He unfastened the pin on the front of his hat. "Here you are. Something from the cavalry."

James was so surprised he could not speak; he gave Thomas a quick hug.

"Miss Rachel, Camp Letterman was boring, so I started whittling. I hope you like it." Thomas handed her a delicately carved wooden horse.

"Oh, I do. It's very pretty. Thank you."

"Betsy, this is small, but I thought you might like to wear it with a pretty dress someday." He placed a gold button with the United States eagle emblem in her hand, and she examined it.

"It's a pin?"

"Yes, made from a broken button."

"Thank you. That is very thoughtful of you. I'll wear it on a special day."

"Well, thank you again. I'll miss you all," Thomas told them.

"We will miss you, too," Mother said with a slight tremble in her voice. She gave him a hug.

Father shook Thomas's hand. "Take care of yourself."

"I'll try, sir. Thank you."

"I want you to stay forever," James wailed, wrapping his arms around Thomas's waist.

"There now, James," Thomas reasoned, bending down. "I can't desert. I've got to be a good soldier."

"But sometimes good soldiers die," James stated solemnly. Betsy swallowed hard.

"I'll be careful," he replied awkwardly.

"Promise?" James questioned. Thomas nodded, and then James smiled. "Alright."

"I'll pray for you," Rachel said. Thomas gave her a hug, and tugged her braids, making her smile.

Betsy was last, and she felt tears in her eyes. "Thank you, Thomas. You were always encouraging in those hard days. You were like an older brother with all your knowledge and confidence. I'll miss you."

"Don't cry," Thomas warned, his own voice quiet. He gave her a quick embrace. "You were a sweet and patient little sister. You never retreated from a challenge. If you were in the military, I'd say you deserve a promotion." Betsy laughed.

He swung into the saddle with practiced ease. "Tell your cousin we keep our promises. You're riding back," she called happily.

Thomas gave a quick nod and a sloppy salute. Then he was off, starting at a trot. The children ran to the pike and stood on the fence to wave. He cantered northwest toward town and looked back one last time.

Though part of her wanted to cry, Betsy smiled. This is not a time for tears, she thought. This is a success. It is answered prayer. One of our soldiers has fully recovered and is returning to duty.

During the next weeks, the children settled into a routine of studying their schoolbooks at home and reciting their lessons to Mother in the afternoon. They visited Camp Letterman several times a week. The soldiers were happy to see the children, who reminded them of their own loved ones at home. Sometimes, Father, Mother, or Betsy would write letters for the men or read to them. James enjoyed talking to the soldiers, and Rachel was a good listener or story reader.

One day in mid-September, as the family prepared to leave, one of the friendly nurses approached them and said, "We're planning a picnic and entertainment for the invalids on the afternoon of the 23rd of this month. Would you perhaps like to attend and bring some home-cooked food for them to enjoy?"

Father nodded to Mother, and she said, "Yes, that sounds very nice. Is there anything particular I should bring?"

"Maybe some pies or cakes if you have the ingredients."

"We can now purchase most food items through the stores or from the commissions," Mother replied.

"Oh, good," the nurse said with a smile. "It will be a very patriotic day, and I've noticed some of the convalescing soldiers really enjoy visiting with your family. They'll be glad if you attend."

The day before the event, Mother and the girls prepared a variety of special foods. A pound cake cooled by the open window, filling the house with a sweet aroma. Two fruit pies were in the oven. Betsy and Mother took turns beating egg whites for a light cake while Rachel prepared berries for a sauce. When the soldiers left the house, the Christian Commission had stopped providing food for the family, though they could still purchase supplies inexpensively from the organization.

"I'm so glad we were able to trade for the eggs in town," Mother commented. "We've made do without them so long, but it's nice to be able to really bake again."

"Yes, but I wish there were an easier way to beat them," Betsy complained, rubbing her sore arm. "Beating egg whites on a platter with a fork isn't fun."

"I know it's selfish of me," Rachel began, "but I wish I had a new dress to wear tomorrow."

"At least your Sunday dress survived," Betsy murmured. "Mine became bandages since it wasn't removed from our room quickly enough. The only clothes I have left are the burgundy dress and this one which, after repeated washings, is still blood stained at the hem and sleeves."

"Do you think we can get fabric for pretty dresses?" Rachel asked hopefully.

"I think there are some dresses in a trunk in the attic that were mine or your grandmother's. We'll get them down and see if they can be made into new clothes for you girls. I know you need new dresses, but we're simply going to be content with made-over clothes this year. Purchasing new fabric would be an unnecessary expense, and we must be careful with our resources at this time."

"Yes, and I suppose hardly anyone will be thinking about new dresses this fall, so perhaps we'll still be respectable," Rachel admitted with her fashion-conscious air. "Do you think we could get the dresses down today and sew all night so I could have a new one to wear tomorrow?"

"No, Daughter. We'll get the dresses down soon, but not tonight." Rachel sighed when she heard Mother's answer, but she accepted the decision.

Even without new dresses, Betsy felt excited as they started in the wagon for Camp Letterman with baskets of sweets and fruit in the back. Rachel's Sunday dress had grown a little shorter on her, but it still fit tolerably well. Betsy wore her bonnet trimmed with dried spring flowers and hoped no one would mind her faded dress.

An air of festivity brightened the atmosphere at Camp Letterman. The day was beautiful, and most of the soldiers smiled as they lounged in the tents, waiting to be called to the picnic. Medical staff and civilians from town were finishing some preparations at long tables set up in the shade of canvas flies. The Westmores took their food baskets to the kitchen house which was filled with nurses and hospital matrons bustling around and completing the last-minute details.

"Oh, those desserts look delicious," said Mrs. Holstein, who was in charge of food preparations for the camp. "Thank you, Mrs. Westmore. Oh, Mr. Westmore, perhaps you could help the orderlies carve the meat. You cannot believe the amount of food that has been donated for this happy day. About five hundred chickens, twenty-five hams, oysters, all kinds of baked goods from the local ladies, and ice cream!"

When the soldiers had come to their places at the long tables, the volunteers – nurses, kitchen helpers, and local civilians – carried out the platters of food and served the men. The Westmore children were assigned to help pour water or hot coffee into the tin cups.

It was wonderful to see the recovering soldiers smiling, joking, and laughing. Faces, that months before had been tense and drawn with suffering, were now filled with pleasure and hope. Everyone was grateful for the fancy picnic. Only a few of the Confederates acted rudely and greedily stuffed their mouths with all the food they could reach; some orderlies saw what was happening and sent those ungentlemanly Southerners back to their tents.

When the feast was over, the ladies attacked the mountain of dishes with soapy water. The Westmore children helped to dry and put away the dishes, and, with so many volunteers working together, the job was accomplished quickly. "Go enjoy the entertainment," Mrs. Holstein ordered. "We've nearly finished here. And thank you for your help this afternoon."

In the dusky evening light, Mother and the children found Father who had been helping some of the soldiers move to an open area where a makeshift stage had been set up. "They've had games and a minstrel performance already. I believe the band will play next." Lanterns had been hung on thick cord and lit the stage area. Band members came with their brass instruments and set up quietly. "I understand it's a local band from the town of York," Father said.

The conductor came and started the little concert with a lively march. The soldiers were enthusiastic about the music and sometimes sang along when they recognized a tune. Later, some of the popular sentimental songs were performed. Most of the soldiers had tears in their eyes when the last song was played. The words were not sung, but rather whispered by hundreds of homesick voices:

"To thee, I'll return, overburdened with care,
The heart's dearest solace will smile on me there.
No more from that cottage again will I roam,
Be it ever so humble, there's no place like home.

Home, home, sweet, sweet home!
There's no place like home...
There's no place like home..."

Chapter 35

A week later, Betsy and Rachel sat on the sunlit porch, tying bunches of fragrant wildflowers to dry. "Betsy, are you unhappy?" Rachel asked, breaking the peaceful silence.

"No," Betsy replied quickly. "Well, sometimes...I don't know...I don't understand the purpose of everything that's happened. I wish our soldiers were still here. I want the war to end. I want Philip to come home." She knotted the string tightly around the flower stems and blinked away the tears in her eyes.

"I think you are very brave, Betsy." Rachel hugged her. "I hope I can be as brave as you when we have to go back to school."

Betsy looked up in surprise, then remembered their conversation with Thomas. How do I help her? she wondered. "I think Thomas had a good idea," she finally said. "Maybe we could go to a different school for a while. Could you talk to Father and Mother about it?"

Rachel nodded. "I'll try."

Father came toward them, looking warm and dusty from his walk to town. "We received some letters. Here, Betsy, there's one addressed to you." She took it eagerly.

"Enjoy your letter. I'll take the flowers inside," Rachel said, laying the floral bundles in a basket.

Alone, Betsy opened the envelope and pulled out a single page, recognizing her brother's handwriting. Did I keep my promise? she wondered, evaluating her actions in the last weeks. Betsy refocused on the letter. Philip wrote encouragingly; he had received her letter about Harold's repentance and had heard from Mother about Edward and Miss Morten. The next section was uplifting:

Mother says you've been very brave and that you were responsible in all the challenging situations. I'm proud of you. When I asked you to be brave, responsible, and to look after Rachel and James, I only imagined giving you goals for a peaceful setting. You fulfilled those goals in a terrifying and certainly unforeseen situation. I know there are probably many things you don't understand, but don't let doubt hinder your helpfulness. God is your refuge and strength. Trust Him and continue to keep your promise.

Betsy sighed contentedly. She had kept her promise, and Philip was pleased. His words were encouraging. "I can't let sad memories or unanswered questions hinder me. Please help me to understand why this battle and destruction had to happen, Lord," she whispered, "and help me to keep assisting my family and those around us."

Mother called from inside the house, and Betsy slipped the letter into her apron pocket and hurried inside to help with supper preparations. Later, after the meal, Father handed two letters to Mother as they sat around the dining table.

"If those letters in your hand aren't from Philip, I wonder who they're from," Rachel said to Mother.

Mother opened one, scanned the page, and said with a smile, "This one's from Thomas."

"Oh, read it aloud," James requested excitedly.

September 16, 1863
Greetings Westmores,

It has been a week since I left, and I'm writing to say that I'm back with my company. All is well. I'm adjusting to my new duties as sergeant. The army is in Virginia, but I understand the regular cavalry is raiding deep into the state. General Buford is recognized as a brilliant commander and will probably go far.

James, you'll be pleased to hear Blaze is well. Seems happy to be back on the picket line with her other friends.

Cousin Will was glad to see me. He sends his thanks to Miss Betsy and family for sending me back.

Miss you all. I will always be grateful for your care and the chance to be part of your family for a couple of months. It was encouraging to see your faith and Christian love. It's to keep America safe and united for God-fearing families that I'm fighting. Maybe someday I'll be fortunate to have a family of my own. I guess I'm fighting for the future.

Well, I'm out of paper.
Your soldier and friend,
Sergeant Thomas Russell

"That's a nice letter," Rachel commented. "I miss seeing him these days."

"I'm glad we heard from Thomas," Betsy said. "I've been hoping he's alright. I wonder where Harold is now and how he's doing. Do you think we could get a letter from him, Father?"

"I'd be surprised if we received news of Harold from prison. They wouldn't want him to send or receive information that could aid in his or others' escapes."

"Who's the next letter from?" James wanted to know.

Mother opened it and squinted at the fine text. "Betsy, could you read this for us?"

Betsy picked up the pretty stationary covered with elegant penmanship and leaned closer to the lamp.

September 18, 1863

Dear Westmore Family,

Please excuse this tardy letter. You have been often in my thoughts, but I struggled to find the words to write.

Please accept my gratitude for your hospitality when I was at Gettysburg. You went beyond common kindness in your actions to me. You really cared and were comforting and reassuring. Since I know of your thoughtfulness to me, I also know what a blessing you were to the injured soldiers in your home. Edward was well cared for and never in want, if you could provide what he needed, and I am forever thankful for your compassion toward him.

I am doing as well as can be expected. I wear mourning,

but I am learning to rejoice that my brother is safe in our eternal home. There is no more suffering there.

I have heard nothing from my fiancé, Lieutenant Carver. But military authorities in Washington have written to me. They are attempting to exchange him. I pray I will see him soon. Losing my brother and the man I hope to marry would almost be too much to bear.

My friends and extended family in town have been very good to me.

Forgive me for not writing more at this time. Sorrow and gratitude leave me wondering if words can ever adequately express my feelings.

Sincerely,

Miss Allison Morten

"Isn't it surprising how strangers so quickly became friends?" Betsy remarked after slowly refolding the letter and slipping it into the envelope.

"We cannot predict or understand how God will use us to encourage or influence others," Father said.

"But we didn't do anything extraordinary," Betsy reasoned. "Nearly everyone in Gettysburg did the same thing. It wasn't like working in a faraway mission field."

"No, it was life," Mother answered. "By simply living our faith no matter what the circumstance, we were able to be shining lights for Christ."

"We never know the effects of our actions," Father concluded.

The letters were laid in a wooden box along with Thomas's photograph, Harold's sketch, old family letters, and marriage certificates. They are part of our family history, Betsy thought.

The warm September days slipped away, and the cooler weather came. The Westmores harvested the late fruit – peaches and apples – in the orchard and the blackberries from the brambles at the edge of the east field. Father said some of the farmers whose orchards had been battlegrounds had little, if anything, to harvest; the family shared some of their extra fruit with their neighbors.

One Sunday, as they rode in the wagon past the location of the new national cemetery on Cemetery Hill, the children asked Father about it, and he explained what had been happening. "Since the weather is cooler, the process of disinterring the dead has begun. Mr. Samuel Weaver, a drayman in town, is overseeing the opening of the graves. He has told people he is certain not one Confederate soldier will be buried in the cemetery."

"So they're digging up bodies?" James asked, wrinkling his nose.

"Yes, and trying to identify if the soldier is Union or Confederate. If you children should ever happen to be in the area where this is happening, I want you to leave. It is a gruesome process."

"What happens if the dead are Union soldiers?" Betsy questioned.

"The bodies are placed in proper coffins and hauled by wagon to the cemetery where other crews are digging deep graves arranged in a pattern by an architect named Mr. William Saunders," Father said. "If a body was identified, the original headboard remained, or someone kept burial records, then the deceased's name is re-marked on a temporary wooden headboard at the new grave. I've heard they are arranging the cemetery graves by state, and unidentified soldiers are buried with their comrades of the same state, but their headboards say 'Unknown.' "

"What about Confederate soldiers' graves?" Mother wondered aloud.

"Someone told me the Confederate graves are left untouched," Father admitted. "If a Confederate soldier is exhumed by mistake, they rebury him there, not in the new cemetery. I don't know what will happen to their graves."

Later in the week, Father returned from town and came into the sitting room where Mother and the girls were mending. "I got the tool repaired at the blacksmith's," he said. "There's a notice in town that any family members wishing to reclaim the body of their Union soldier must do so at this time, or the soldier will be buried in the National Cemetery. I think we should write to Miss Morten." Mother agreed and promised to write the note that evening to ensure it would be sent as soon as possible.

"Also," Father continued, "the school in town will reopen on October 19th, just over a week away. I didn't hear if the country school would open, but I believe it would be best for the children to attend in town, at least for part of this school year."

"Now I can look forward to going to school," Rachel said. "Thank you, Father."

"You're welcome. I'm glad you talked with Mother and me about your fears. I think you will enjoy school in town. Some of the other parents say the teachers are very kind."

"It will also be a nice walk into town during the autumn," Betsy remarked, looking forward to the new experience.

After supper, Mother sat at the desk and wrote the letter. She had been writing for a little while when she laid down the pen and turned to look at Father. "Henry, there's the dedication ceremony for the new cemetery. I know Allison intends to have Edward reburied in Indiana, but she might appreciate the service honoring the soldiers. Do you think it would be appropriate to invite Allison to come and attend with us?"

"Yes," Father replied, "but I understand the dedication date has been changed from October 23rd to November 19th. I think it was because a famous speaker they're inviting needed more time to work on his address."

"Oh? Do you remember who it was?" Betsy was surprised by the excitement in Mother's voice.

"A Mr. Edward Everett, if I recall," Father remarked. "I think I've heard of him before."

"Mr. Everett!" Mother exclaimed. "Why, he's one of the most famous orators in America. People pay to attend his lectures. He's quite famous and has toured the country giving speeches to raise money for good causes. I remember that he formerly served in the government and was also the United States' ambassador to England. Mr. Everett in Gettysburg?"

"What will he talk about?" James wondered.

"Well, it will be a speech to dedicate the cemetery and honor the soldiers," Mother explained. "But since he's such an educated man and a very gifted speaker, it will be an excellent experience for you children to hear him and at such a historic event, too."

A couple of days later, Mother and Betsy went to town to get the notebooks, chalk, and pencils the children would need when school started next week. The ladies who stopped to greet them and talk for a few minutes were full of news about the upcoming dedication ceremonies. They explained that a committee had been established and hospitable ladies were volunteering to host important visitors who would be attending. "I've even heard that Mr. Wills has invited President Lincoln," one lady said.

"Do you think the president will come to Gettysburg?" Betsy asked after the friend had walked on.

"I don't know," Mother responded. "It'd be exciting if he came, but I think I'm most interested to hear what Mr. Everett says. I remember reading some of his speeches when I was a teacher and wishing I could hear him speak someday."

"Mrs. Westmore," Mr. Buehler, the postmaster, called from the porch of the post office where he stood watching his children playing on the sidewalk. "Good day. A large parcel has arrived for your family. It isn't heavy. Would you like to take it with you?"

"I wonder who it's from," Betsy said as they stepped outside again after receiving the brown paper package.

"It looks like Miss Morten's penmanship, but why would she send us a package?" Mother said.

At home, the others gathered quickly and the parcel was opened. Mother picked up the note and read aloud:

Dear Westmore Family,

You accepted the situation with self-less grace, but I know it must have been a trial. You didn't complain or tell me specifically, but I thought these items might be appreciated.

Mrs. Westmore, I know they cannot replace your family heirlooms, but they were made with care by the ladies of my sewing society.

Betsy, the other item is for you. I thought perhaps red would not be your choice color anymore, so I have taken the liberty of choosing something else. I hope the other fabrics will be useful in replacing lost clothing items.

Please accept these as a token of my continued gratitude and respect for your family.

Sincerely,

Miss Allison Morten

Mother lifted the last paper wrapping and picked up two sets of beautifully embroidered white table linens and an everyday tablecloth and napkins. Beneath, there were a few yards of muslin and plaid cotton. At the bottom was a dark blue fabric with a scattered pattern of tiny wheat stalks; resting on top of this fabric was a fashionable black belt, black buttons, and a dainty collar.

"Oh, Betsy, now you'll have a new dress," Rachel breathed. "It will be lovely, and maybe you'll have it in time for the ceremony."

"Allison is too kind," Betsy stammered, amazed that the young woman she had known only for a couple of weeks could be so thoughtful.

"To think she noticed the missing linens and considered how much they had meant to me," Mother said, closely examining her new treasures.

Edward was right, Betsy thought. Allison is a beautiful young lady in appearance and fashionable clothing, but, more importantly, she has a beautiful spirit.

The new linens went on the table immediately, replacing a mended scrap of calico and the faded napkins they had been using. Betsy put aside her new fabric for a little while; there was so much to be finished with the harvest before school started.

The fruit had been gathered, and Mother and the girls made jam and canned. None of the summer vegetables had been preserved; most had been used in soups to feed the wounded or given to Camp Letterman. However, the autumn garden harvest of pumpkins, squash, potatoes, and carrots was stored in the corners of the cellar. One field of grain had been reaped and ground into flour, but, as Father had estimated, there was no extra to sell this year. They purchased some provisions and planned carefully to make the food supply last until the next summer.

Chapter 36

School started in town on the 19th of October. Betsy, Rachel, and James enjoyed the quiet walks into town in the crisp autumn air and their studies in the large two-story school building. James liked being with his friends, and Rachel smiled more as she interacted with girls her own age. During recess times, Betsy talked with other young ladies. Sometimes, they talked about their older brothers in the army, and, occasionally, they wondered about the soldiers they had cared for during the summer. Mostly, they talked about lighthearted topics – new dresses or bonnets, cooking, and ideas for Christmas gifts for their mothers. It was nice to interact with other girls and to forget about the summer's experiences and the war for a little while.

When Betsy knew her lessons, she sometimes helped the teachers with the younger children. Reading, writing, arithmetic, natural science, and history were the main subjects. In her history class, Betsy had started studying the great events of the past – the siege of Troy, the conquests of Caesar, the fall of Rome, the Crusades, the Reformation, the wars in England, and the founding of America. She wondered what people living in those eras thought as the great events took place around them. Did they realize something extraordinary was happening? Or did they even know these events were history-making?

Outside the schoolhouse, rumors swirled with the falling leaves as the Westmore children heard the townspeople talking about the famous people who would supposedly attend the dedication ceremony. Betsy wondered if this coming event would someday be history or if it would simply fade into the local annals.

Every day, as they walked past the cemetery, more and more graves had been made and headboards erected. Still, it was said the officials estimated the work of bringing the dead to the cemetery would not be completed until next spring or summer because the work could not continue during the winter. Somehow, the enormity of the battle was not fully realized until the children saw how many of those headboards stood in the growing cemetery and thought about how many more would be added to that final resting place.

One day Betsy carried home two letters, finding it difficult not to open them since one was in Allison's handwriting and the other in Philip's. At home, though, she read Allison's to the family. After the usual letter greetings, there was important news.

After much consideration, I have decided I will not bring Edward's body home to be buried at our church. It seems much more fitting that he should be buried with his comrades in this new and honorable cemetery. It is not that I don't care or can't afford to bring him here, but it seems better that his final grave should be with those who fought for the same ideals he cherished. It is right that the flag he died to protect should fly forever over his army grave. Please be certain his grave is marked with name, dates, and regiment. Someday, I will come back and remind my children of their uncle's sacrifice.

The letter went on, and Allison expressed her appreciation for the invitation to come for the ceremony, but declined, saying:

My reason for the long delay of this reply and inability to come in November is that my Lieutenant Carver is home. He stays at his mother's house, but I see him every day. He is so weak, so thin, so tired. He does not get out of bed yet, but we are trusting rest, good food, and encouraging family will help him recover. I do not wish to leave him, and I think Edward wouldn't have wanted me to attend a funeral instead of a wedding. I only wish my brother was here...but we have decided to follow his advice, and, as soon as Lieutenant Carver is strong enough, we will have a quiet ceremony at home and be married.

I hope you will understand. Betsy, wear a beautiful dress, and, if you can, leave flowers at Edward's grave for me on the day of the cemetery dedication.

Sincerely,

Miss Allison Morten

"I'm glad Lieutenant Carver is safe," Betsy said, refolding the letter.

"Yes," Mother replied. "She won't forget her brother, but I'm thankful she is moving forward and fulfilling Edward's wishes."

Father opened Philip's letter. He wrote he was in good health and that, yet again, his regiment had been guarding supply wagons during the Battle of Bristoe Station in mid-October. Betsy hoped the regiment would have to stay on guard duty for the remainder of the war; James and Rachel agreed.

At the end of October, Mother and the girls started on Betsy's dress. Betsy had chosen a simple tailored pattern. Miss Pierce had heard about the new dress when the girls had met in town, and she insisted on lending Betsy a corded petticoat which would make the skirt stand out, similar to a hoop, but not as cumbersome.

While Mother began cutting and basting the new dress, the girls finished the hems on Rachel's altered frock. Her dress had been made over from one of the lavender-scented dresses from the trunk in the attic. The fabric was dark rose pink, and, since Rachel's birthday was in January, they decided to make her skirts longer, brushing the top of her shoes.

The girls had worried about what Mother would wear, but she reminded them that her Sunday winter dress had been stored safely in the attic and would be fine for the upcoming event. Thankfully, Father and James's good clothes had not become bandages.

On Sunday, November 1ˢᵗ, the family had gone to church in town, heard the latest news from their friends, and was driving home in the wagon. The cemetery gatehouse, sentinel on the hill, had been repaired, and the Thorns were back in their home. As they drove slowly past, Frederick Thorn ran to the fence and greeted them. Father stopped the horses.

"Good day, Frederick," Mother called. "Is your family well? We didn't see you in town after church services this morning."

"We're good. I have a new little sister!" Frederick exclaimed. Betsy smiled at Rachel. A little girl to watch over and spoil when they visited, how fun!

"Is your mama well?" Mother asked.

"I guess so. She's sleeping upstairs, and Grandmother won't let us see her. Do you want to see the baby?"

"Well, we wouldn't want to disturb…" Father began, but then Mrs. Masser stepped out and beckoned them to come in.

As they entered the warm parlor, Frederick took them to the wooden cradle where George kept watch like a guard. John played nearby, unconcerned about his new sibling. Mrs. Masser picked up the tiny baby wrapped in a bundle of blankets. The little one slept peacefully, her mouth half-open, and a small hand resting on her chin as if contemplating this new world she had entered.

"Do you want to hold her, Miss Westmore? I was taking some tea up to my daughter, and perhaps Mrs. Westmore would like to come with me?"

Betsy nodded, sitting down in a nearby chair, and the baby squirmed before settling in her arms. Rachel leaned over and watched the infant. As the ladies went upstairs, the little boys chatted quietly, and Mr. Masser came in and talked with Father.

"She's so sweet," Rachel breathed, watching the sleeping baby.

"Yes," Betsy agreed. So much has happened here, baby girl, Betsy thought. You remind us to hope for the future: a future when this war will be over and your father will come home.

Ten days later, in the very early morning, Mr. Weaver, his crew, and a wagonload of coffins arrived at the Westmore farm. "Do you know anything about the soldiers buried on your property?" Mr. Weaver asked Father as they stood in the downstairs hallway. Half-hidden by the wooden partition, the children sat on the stairs and watched.

"These are the records I kept," Father replied, handing him the small notebook. "It's all that we know."

Mr. Weaver thumbed through the pages. "This is good." He glanced out the open door. "And I see that the graves are still marked. We'll exhume the Union soldiers for removal to the cemetery. The Confederates will stay here. I'd advise your family to remain in the house. The sights are unsettling."

Later, Betsy went to get water at the well to wash the breakfast dishes. Mr. Weaver was standing there. "Do you know where your father is?"

"No, sir, but I can look for him."

"Perhaps you'll be able to confirm for us? You see, one of my workers accidently tripped on a grave marker and it splintered. The grave isn't listed in the notebook. If we showed you, could you identify it?"

"Maybe…" she answered, and he asked her to come.

"This one," Mr. Weaver said, pointing to the grave a little away from the others.

"It's a Union soldier," Betsy responded quietly. "His name is Edward Morten, and he was a sergeant in the 27th Indiana Regiment."

"You're certain?"

"Yes. I took care of him before he died." Betsy looked away, wanting to cry.

"Betsy, hurry up, or we're going to be late for school," James shouted from an upstairs window, obviously unaware of what was happening. "Rachel can't find her spelling book, and she says you were using it. Come help her find it." She hurried to the house, blinking away the threatening tears and trying to forget her heartache.

By the time the children were ready to leave for school, Edward's body had been removed, placed in a coffin, and set in a wagon. Though it had not been their original intent, they followed the wagon up the pike to the cemetery. They went silently, like mourners for the men transported to their final graves. Forgetting school, they followed the caskets to the new cemetery. There, the coffins were unloaded and moved to the appropriate areas. "Indiana, 27ᵗʰ," one of the workers called, reading the tag.

"Here, with the others of the regiment," another answered. A deep hole was already dug. The coffin was lowered slowly. The children had inched their way closer, and now the workmen noticed them. "Are ye relatives?"

"No," Betsy answered. "But he was our friend, and we know his sister."

"I'm sorry, miss. His grave will be marked. You'll be able to find it later. There's nothing more to see here."

Outside the new cemetery, the children cried. "We're going to be late for school," Betsy finally sobbed.

"I don't care," James whimpered. "I wish Edward was still alive. I wish all those soldiers were still alive."

"But Edward is with Jesus," Rachel whispered. "We shouldn't cry for him."

"I know," Betsy said, trying to wipe her eyes. "But think of how many sisters' brothers are in that cemetery. And I just don't understand why…"

"None of us do," Rachel admitted wisely. "Come on, we have to go. School's about to start." They dried their tears, but their hearts were still sad as they descended into town.

"Maybe all those famous men who are coming here will have an idea about why all this happened?" James suggested.

"Maybe…" Betsy answered.

Chapter 37

Later that afternoon, Betsy left the school building and met her siblings in the yard. They walked slowly through town. "I'm unhappy," James moaned. "I was too sad to study, and my teacher scolded me for not paying attention. I'll bet her friend wasn't buried today."

"I have a headache," Rachel complained.

Betsy wished she could encourage her siblings, but her own renewed grief and questions made her feel unqualified to comfort. She was glad they were going home at last. It had been a long day at school, and, like James, she had not focused on her schoolwork.

"Miss Westmore, Miss Westmore," a girl's voice exclaimed. Betsy saw Miss Tillie Pierce and waited for her friend to join them. "Oh, I'd been hoping I'd see you today," she said, when she caught up. "We have some fabric that somebody gave us. It's all pastel calico, mostly pink, yellow, and light green, and Mother says it would make the most impractical soldier's quilt in the world. Would you like the fabric to make a new quilt?"

Betsy's throat was tight, remembering what had happened to her quilt. It had been Edward's quilt, and, in the end, it had been his shroud. She swallowed hard, and

Rachel squeezed her hand. "Yes. I'd appreciate it, if you can spare the fabric." Betsy smiled faintly.

"Of course. As I said, we can't use it for the soldiers, and I don't need a new quilt. Won't you stop at the house and take it?"

They stepped in at the Pierce home, and the girls were pleased with the fabrics. Tillie wrapped the material in brown paper, and the children started off again. Betsy felt relieved to have something new and exciting to think about on the walk home. Edward would not want us to be sad, she thought.

"We can always make a new start," Betsy said with confident hope. "We don't have to understand everything, but we can't give up."

"Are you talking about life or a quilt?" James wanted to know.

"Both," Betsy answered.

At home, Mother smiled when she saw the fabrics and heard the girls' plans for a new quilt. "I like your ideas," she said as they explained the quilt patterns they were thinking about. "Are you alright?" she asked, looking closely at her children.

Rachel explained the silent funeral at the cemetery and the sad memories it had prompted. Mother talked with the children, comforting and encouraging them. "Now," Mother said, seeing the hope reflecting in the children's faces after they had prayed, "I have a surprise for Betsy. Go in the parlor, Daughter, and you will see it."

"Did you finish it?" Betsy exclaimed, feeling a tingle of excitement as she went into the hallway and pushed open the parlor door. "Oh, thank you, Mother!" she said, seeing the long-sleeve, blue calico dress hanging on a peg by the sewing table.

"You're welcome," Mother replied, hugging Betsy. "I know I said you were going to finish the hem, but I had some time today and was able to do it myself. Now, it's ready for you to wear in a couple of days."

"I think I should write to Allison and tell her thank you again," Betsy said, holding up the dress and admiring the pretty and fashionable design. Later, Betsy re-read the short note she had penned.

November 11, 1863
Dear Allison,

Thank you again for the beautiful blue fabric. Mother surprised me today and finished hemming the dress while I was at school. I will wear the dress for the dedication ceremony.

Today, Edward's body was taken to its final grave in the national cemetery. He rests with his regiment comrades now. I will leave dried flowers at his grave on the day of the dedication as you requested.

I know Mother has written to you, but I wanted to say I hope you and Lieutenant Carver will be happy in your new life together. Come and visit us someday.

Your friend,
Betsy Westmore

The next Monday, strangers began arriving in town, and the school-children saw them walking on the streets. As Betsy waited for James and Rachel, she watched the people passing on the sidewalk.

"Do you know a good place to stay?" inquired one young man in a blue uniform. "I'm on leave, and I've come back to this place of victory."

"Maybe one of the hotels?" Betsy suggested, shrugging.

"Do you think we could find some bullets?" asked an excited young woman in the next strolling group. Flirtatiously, she was hanging on the arm of her handsome companion and looking around as if expecting a county fair atmosphere.

"Oh, I'm sure," he responded carelessly. "We'll traipse around the fields and see the sights. We came early to have a good time..."

A good time, Betsy thought, shaking her head sadly. They have no idea what happened here, and they will never understand.

Next, came an elderly couple. The woman's black dress and the black band around the man's sleeve and hat indicated mourning. They did not speak, but moved slowly along the sidewalk as though searching for answers and a loved one. When the children passed the military cemetery a few minutes later, Betsy saw the mourning couple had found the grave of their family member.

From the schoolhouse on the following day, the children heard whistle blasts from the trains and knew hundreds of people were arriving. They saw the strangers wandering on the streets as they looked from the school windows. "It's another invasion," Betsy murmured to herself. This time it was not armies or wounded; it was a mixed crowd of curious, pleasure-seeking, or sincere people coming to attend the ceremony on Thursday.

"No school till next week," James said jubilantly as they met outside to walk home. "I don't think we'd even be able to get into town. Look at all these people!"

"Rachel, don't forget. Papa says there's letters for you at the post office," one of the Buehler children called.

"Oh, yes," Rachel answered. "Betsy, can't we stop and get the letters? Maybe one is from Philip."

"Of course," Betsy replied. "But then we must hurry home. Mother and Father will need our help to get ready for the event. Clothes need to be ironed, shoes polished, food prepared, the wagon cleaned, harness shined…"

Later, as they ate supper after finishing the chores, Rachel asked, "Can we open the letters?"

"In a moment, Rachel," Mother replied. "I'm anxious, too, but let's finish eating first, so the food doesn't get cold."

"President Lincoln is supposed to arrive tomorrow evening," James announced while stirring his soup.

"Yes, I heard that," Father remarked. "I went up to Camp Letterman to see if they needed any help, and they were correct in their previous estimation. The wounded have all been moved to base hospitals farther east. The tents are being packed, and they expect the camp will officially close on November 20th. Anyway, one of the doctors told me about the schedule of events."

"Is anything happening tomorrow other than the president arriving?" Rachel asked. "We've heard so many rumors, and I don't know what's true."

"Well, the president and other dignitaries are supposed to arrive in the afternoon and evening along with more spectators," Father explained. "I believe there'll be a patriotic concert in the Diamond and maybe some speeches. We'll go into town in the late afternoon and take supper with us."

"We wouldn't want to miss the important events happening in our town," Mother said, then glanced at her son. "James, stop picking the onion out of the soup. It won't hurt you."

James grimaced at the vegetable, then asked, "What do you think the president looks like?"

"You've seen his likeness in the paper," Betsy commented before taking a bite of bread.

"Yeah, but that was a woodcut sketch. What do you think he looks like in real life? Do you think we'll get to meet him?"

"I think it'd be scary to meet the president," Rachel said, laying down the butter knife.

"Why'd it be scary?" James wanted to know.

"Well, he's very important," Rachel reasoned.

James shrugged and raised his eyebrows. "So?"

"President Lincoln will have many prominent people

to meet," Father remarked. "I'm sure we'll see him, but I'd be surprised if you actually meet him."

After dinner, they opened the letters. Mother read Philip's aloud.

November 10, 1863
Dear Family,

I am well. You have more excitement in Gettysburg than I have here. I have read in the papers that President Lincoln, Mr. Everett, and other famous folks are coming for the cemetery dedication. I wonder what they will say. In some ways, I think it would be better for an army chaplain to read the burial service than for politicians to make speeches. But, if they can stay focused and not mix in their political beliefs, perhaps it will be appropriate. You will have to send me an accurate report.

Rachel, thank you for the information about the new dresses. I'm sure you will look very pretty, and I wish I could be there with you all.

James, I liked your note and am glad you are doing well in school. No, I don't think pulling girls' braids is very nice. Don't do it. I think your next memory verse should be Matthew 7:12 – "Therefore, whatever you want men to do you, do also to them, for this is the Law and the Prophets." I'm impressed that you learned fifteen verses last month.

Betsy, no, I haven't seen Sergeant Russell. He's in a different corps, and lowly sergeants don't have time to go looking for lowly privates in this army.

Mother, I received your note today. Was very glad to hear about Mrs. Thorn's little girl. Mr. Thorn had received a letter and shared his news a day or two before. Everyone in the company thinks it's nice that her middle name is the Gettysburg general's name: Meade. Rosa Meade Thorn is a pretty name.

Father: glad to hear the crops were alright and that you will have enough to get through the winter. I'll try to convince the generals around here that next summer they should battle somewhere else.

Not much is happening here right now. I suppose we will start building huts for the winter soon. Maybe I can apply for leave and come home for a few weeks, but don't set your hopes too high. After all, I'm only your son and brother,

Private Philip Westmore

"I wish Philip could be here to attend the ceremony with us," Betsy commented, "but I'm glad he's doing alright."

"That would be nice," Mother sighed. Father nodded.

Rachel said, "I'm glad he hasn't been in a battle."

"Yes," James said. "Guarding supplies might be very interesting." He glanced at the other letter on the table. "Who's that one from?"

"Let's open it and find out," Father suggested.

November 11, 1863
Dear Westmores,

Thanks for the recent letters. You are kind to write.

I'm missing all the excitement of cavalry raiding with this headquarters courier duty. General Buford has certainly distinguished himself this autumn. Saw him a couple days ago. Seems to be in bad health, but as determined as ever. Lucky the man who rides with Buford or gets a chance to chase down the troublesome Confederate partisans.

Heard about the dedication of Gettysburg cemetery. Wish I could be there.

I am well, and my family is well from what I hear.

Blaze likes her new military-issued blanket.

Am hoping to get leave for Christmas to see my family and will make a quick trip to New York for Cousin Will's wedding on New Year's Day. Do you hear anything about Miss Morten? What about Harold?

I've got to close if this is to be sent off today. Still remember you all and am grateful for your care and friendship.

Sincerely,

Sergeant Thomas Russell

"He sounds busy," Mother remarked.

"He probably is," Father replied, refolding the letters and going into the sitting room to put them on the desk.

"I'm glad Blaze is doing well, aren't you, Betsy?" James asked.

"Yes, and I'm happy Thomas is safe."

"You miss him, don't you?" Rachel said quietly.

Betsy nodded. The soft glow of the lamps illuminated the small room like during the long nights in the summer, but how different the room looked now. Betsy sighed. Part of her longed to see her soldiers again…Thomas's quiet confidence, Edward's patient expression, Harold's teasing grin. For a few weeks, they had been like older brothers, and now, she missed them almost as much as she missed Philip. They were gone and would probably never come back.

"Is everything alright?" Mother asked, touching Betsy's shoulder.

"Yes…just thinking," Betsy answered.

"There are so many memories, good and bad, aren't there?"

Betsy nodded. "And still so many questions…" She whispered, then smiled. "But now I'm thinking of the good memories and about our soldiers."

Chapter 38

"There's not a chance you'll be able to get your wagon into town," Mrs. Thorn called to the Westmores from her doorstep as they slowed to a stop outside the gatehouse. The sunlight had broken through the overcast sky, and the morning's rain had cleared in time for the evening's events. Looking at the jam of wagons, carriages, and people on the roads leading into town, Betsy thought every resident near Gettysburg and half the people in the Union had decided to attend. "Leave your wagon and team here," Mrs. Thorn suggested. "You'd better walk, if you intend to go to town this afternoon."

They took her advice, and, carrying their basket of food, coats, and shawls, they started toward the crowded town. Rachel shrank from the milling people, but Betsy held her hand, and they pressed on, following Father's hat and Mother's bonnet through the crowd and keeping an eye on James.

The crowd was excited and boisterous. Townsfolk and strangers rushed around, exclaiming about rumors concerning the famous people arriving and acting as though they had something grand to celebrate. Father managed to get to the Diamond, and they found a place to stand where the crowd was not so dense.

"Why are they happy?" Rachel asked, motioning to the people.

"I don't know. What's there to be happy about?" Betsy answered. "I guess we're glad the Union won the battle, but I didn't think there was going to be a noisy celebration."

People wandered around talking about politics, asking questions, speculating on what really happened, and waiting for the presidential train to arrive. Betsy surveyed the scene: the excited people, the banners, and patriotic festoons. It was like pouring stinging medicine on her aching heart wound.

"Why such a sad face, missy?" asked a portly man in a fine suit, probably a local politician from a prosperous district. "Glorious victory happened here, you know. You're not some secession supporter, are you?"

Betsy shook her head, glancing to where Father and Mother were talking with Mr. and Mrs. Broadhead nearby. Wishing the man would go away, she answered, "I know about the military victory. I live here, sir." He seemed polite, but his cheerfulness annoyed her.

"You were here? What was it like?" the man questioned eagerly, toying with his watch chain.

"You don't want to know," Betsy responded, turning away.

"No, really, I do."

"Tell him what happened," Rachel whispered.

"He thinks war is glorious," James stated. "Tell him."

"Please, miss, what was it like?" the man persisted.

Betsy turned and faced him, looking him calmly in the eye. "At the start, our horses were stolen by raiders. During the battle, the ground shook with cannon fire. Artillery shells shrieked through the air, exploding in our fields until a signal was put up to warn them that our house was a hospital. There were so many wounded at our home I could hardly walk across a room without stepping on them. I cooked food and tore our linens into bandages. The surgeons worked to the point of exhaustion, and there were still more wounded to help. A seventeen-year-old boy died in my mother's arms. An officer died while my sister sat near him, reciting a psalm. I stood by an operating table holding a light. I dressed wounds so horrible that I became sick. I sat with men who endured intense suffering. I wrote letters for the wounded. I visited them at Camp Letterman. We still have bloodstains on our floors. I know a sister whose brother will never come home because he is buried in the military cemetery." She took a steadying breath, then concluded forcefully. "What happened here? Blue fought gray, and the aftermath was crimson. Death was destructive, hearts were broken, and tears were shed. That's what happened here."

The man had stared at her in shock as she recounted the events. By the end, his head was bowed, and, when he looked up, there were tears in his eyes. "I'm sorry."

"It's not your fault," Betsy said quickly. "But you should know and understand what happened here. The Union won, but it wasn't glorious."

"I see why this," and he motioned to the bustling crowd, "bothers you. Forgive my inconsideration. May I do anything to make amends for my comments?"

"Just don't forget the sacrifices made here," Betsy answered softly as Rachel squeezed her hand. He nodded and turned away. Betsy wiped away the tears in her eyes with her handkerchief.

The blast of a train whistle startled her. People rushed toward the railroad station and the street became jammed. "The president must be arriving," Mrs. Broadhead said to Mother. They stepped out of the way of the hurrying people. "I believe he is staying at Mr. Wills's house, and, if we stay here, we'll surely see him pass."

"Those are the law marshals who have come as some sort of guard or security force for the president," Mr. Broadhead mentioned as some tall men in dark suits and hats walked past clearing a way through the crowd.

President Lincoln came next, walking slowly and with dignity in the evening shadows. Betsy stood on her toes to see over the lady in front of her while Rachel and James peered through the space made by a gentleman who had his hand on his hip. The president was very tall, and his hat made him seem even taller. He smiled to the cheering people, stopped once to shake hands with a young soldier in the crowd, and waved in a common, friendly way. Even though he smiled, an air of solemnity cloaked him as though he could not and would not forget the reason he had come to this small, formerly insignificant town.

Betsy watched him and sensed that he understood what had happened here, even though he had never seen the place before. Had his Gettysburg experience been somewhat like theirs? One of desperate hope and uncertainty? He hadn't seen the dead on the fields, but he must have seen the stark casualty numbers on paper. Had he thought of how many families were weeping? He hadn't dressed wounds in a field hospital, but perhaps he had visited injured Gettysburg soldiers in the Washington hospitals; Betsy had heard the president did that occasionally. This was his first and likely only visit to Gettysburg, but Betsy thought he would never forget the sacrifices his soldiers had made here. Yet what did he think was the purpose of those sacrifices? She wondered what he would say tomorrow in his speech.

The president entered the Wills' house, and now people began talking about the others who had walked into town with him. Mr. David Wills, the event planner, had been there. Mr. Edward Everett had come to greet the president. Then there were a number of dignitaries who had accompanied the president from Washington City: foreign ministers of state, military commanders and soldiers, the Marine Corps Band, the secretary of state – Mr. Seward – and a couple of other cabinet members.

A band played patriotic tunes in the Diamond. The Westmores found seats on a bench and sat down to listen to the music and eat their supper. The rousing tunes kept James marching in place as he munched his sandwich, and the others enjoyed the well-played songs.

The evening became a blur of people, torch light, music, and cheering. At one point, they saw the president walk to the house where the secretary of state was staying. The crowd begged for a speech and then waited expectantly. Betsy almost laughed when she heard the president say he could not make a speech tonight because he had nothing to say. Elsewhere in town, though, other politicians made lengthy speeches.

"It's late," Father said finally. "I think we should go. Between the calling for speeches and the drinking, it's going to be a loud night in town, and we don't need to stay."

Betsy was glad when they started the ascent up Cemetery Hill, leaving behind the boisterous people. She had enjoyed the music and was still thinking about President Lincoln and wondering what he would say. Yet the rest of the atmosphere convinced her that many of the people, like the gentleman who had spoken to her, had no real idea what had happened.

The cemetery was quiet, and, in some places, lanterns hung along the pathways, illuminating the wooden headboards standing in neat rows. The battle had been won, and that was a reason for quiet thanksgiving, but, as she looked at the graves, Betsy found no reason to celebrate. She wondered what the attitude of the crowd would be tomorrow. She thought Philip was right; maybe they should have just read a military burial service and avoided this event that was turning into a wild celebration of things which happened only in the imagination.

Chapter 39

The notes of a solemn bugle call resounded over the Gettysburg hills. Betsy opened her eyes and lay still in bed, listening to the bugles softly echoing each other in the stillness of breaking dawn. She recalled the words to a patriotic song the crowds had chanted so blithely last evening.

"He has sounded forth the trumpet that shall never call retreat;
He is sifting out the hearts of men before His judgment seat.
Oh, be swift, my soul, to answer Him…"

That's what happened here at Gettysburg, Betsy thought sadly. Many of the soldiers were called from these fields and hills into eternity and the presence of God.

She lay there thinking, and Rachel was dressed before Betsy sat up. When Rachel teased her about lounging in bed, Betsy got up to assist her braiding her hair. "Do you need any help?" Rachel asked, before slipping out the door.

"No," Betsy replied. She sat down at the dressing table to brush, plait, coil, and pin her hair. When her hairstyle was completed, she started dressing in the day clothes, and, a few minutes later, she checked in the mirror to make certain the dress was fastened properly. The dark blue calico made Betsy's blue eyes seem especially bright. The bodice fit comfortably and was embellished with a tiny ruffle at the dropped shoulder seam. With the corded petticoat beneath, the long skirt flared prettily out from the black belt at the waist. Betsy leaned closer to the mirror and picked up the brooch Sergeant Russell had made. Carefully, she pinned it between the edges of the linen collar which was hemmed with a tiny bit of thread lace. "There," she breathed. "Thomas would be pleased. I think Allison would also be satisfied." She thought of Harold, smiled, and said, "He wouldn't like the color and would say something teasing." Smoothing the skirt one last time, she went downstairs to help with breakfast preparations.

When they started toward town a little while later, the autumn sunshine lit the hills, meadows, and fields. The leaves that had not been stripped from the trees during the summer conflict drifted softly to the ground as a little breeze touched the landscape. The scars of battle on the Gettysburg land could still be seen. It would be decades, perhaps even centuries, before they wore away. Yet it was still a beautiful day, and Betsy marveled at the seasonal changes as they walked along the pike. They had decided not to take the wagon since they could not drive into town anyway. Mrs. Thorn had promised to save them places near the speakers' platform at the cemetery, and they would join her after the procession in town.

They went into the soldiers' cemetery where Betsy silently laid a bouquet of dried summer flowers on the grave of Sergeant Edward Morten. No one said anything, and, after standing at his grave for a few moments, they departed silently and continued toward town.

There, the scene was completely changed from the previous evening. People were solemn and subdued. The celebration of victory was over. It was time to honor the dead at this large-scale funeral. Even the half-masted flags waved slowly in the soft breeze, trying to whisper a final farewell to their defenders.

The Westmores found places to stand under a shade tree along Baltimore Street. Around them people talked quietly. Some complained about the noise of the previous night, others fussed about their crowded accommodations. Supposedly, there were close to forty people staying at the Wills family's house alone, and many other homes were even more crowded. Other people speculated what the orators would say. Betsy noticed many people had come to Gettysburg searching for answers to questions similar to hers.

It was after ten in the morning when the procession began coming down the street. The Marine Band marched first, mournfully playing a dirge, and they were followed by soldiers of the 2nd U.S. Cavalry, moving slowly and solemnly along the street. Union generals and their staff officers, more cavalry, and some artillery units went by; their blue uniforms and the solemn flags were a quiet reminder of the Union victory. In their dark suits and with white bands around their hats to identify them, the marshals came next, guarding President Lincoln.

Today, the president did not smile. Occasionally, he glanced at someone in the crowd, but he seemed focused in thought. He wore a black suit, and the hat he held at his side had a mourning band around the crown; he appeared to be grieving with and for the nation. His face looked careworn and weary as though he carried a burden of grief. He did not seem to recognize or hear the people who quietly cheered as he passed. When Betsy could no longer see him, she turned her attention to what was passing in front of them: political dignitaries, delegations from Union cities, another band puffing a wailing dirge, faculty and students of the local colleges, private citizens, and finally, the honorable Mr. Edward Everett, riding in a carriage.

"I understand he has to ride in the carriage because of his poor health," a man, standing nearby, remarked to his friend. "They also had to set up a tent near the speakers' platform so that Mr. Everett could rest before his speech."

The spectators of the procession followed, going up Cemetery Hill and toward the speakers' platform. Again, Betsy and Rachel waded through the crowd, keeping their parents' hats in sight while James held onto Father's coattails in an attempt to stay with them. After many polite "excuse me" and "pardon us," they reached the place where the Thorns and Massers waited; it was close to the platform, and the Marine Band was nearby. James and the Thorn boys were immediately interested in the fine uniform of the drum major and began discussing the merits of wearing so much gold braid.

After a while, the bands ceased their somber music, and a tall man who was introduced as Marshal Ward Lamon, master of ceremonies, stood and read messages sent by dignitaries unable to attend the dedication service, including General Meade. The crowd inched closer together. Betsy thought they might be crushed in this mass of people. She was glad she was standing close to the platform and could hear quite well. Then more music was performed, followed by the arrival of Mr. Everett and a minister.

The minister, introduced as Reverend Stockton, prayed a long prayer which included reminders of God's providence during the battle and a plea for comfort. As he concluded, he led the assembled crowd in reciting The Lord's Prayer. Betsy felt tears on her face as she whispered the sacred words, and, glancing around, she noticed others were affected also; even President Lincoln and Mr. Everett were wiping their eyes with their handkerchiefs.

The Marine Band slowly played the hymn "The Old Hundredth." As the final notes of the song faded, Marshal Lamon introduced Mr. Edward Everett. There was a ripple of expectation in the crowd. What would the famous orator say? Betsy waited anxiously. Could Mr. Everett answer her questions regarding the reason for the battle?

Mr. Everett stood and gazed toward the west for a few moments. When he spoke, his powerful voice was filled with emotion, and he gestured grandly. "Standing beneath this serene sky, overlooking these broad fields now reposing from the labors of the waning year, the mighty Alleghenies dimly towering before us, the graves of our brethren beneath our feet, it is with hesitation that I raise my poor voice to break the eloquent silence of God and Nature. But the duty to which you have called me must be performed..."

He spoke in eloquent words that sometimes puzzled Betsy and challenged her to unravel his train of thought. Mr. Everett spoke about the honorable burial of warriors in Ancient Greek Athens and compared it to the honor given to the American soldiers that day. "...I feel, as never before, how truly it was said of old that it is sweet...to die for one's country...that their fellowmen may live in safety and honor." Betsy swallowed hard; his words sounded similar to Edward Morten's when he had tried to comfort and prepare her before his death.

She watched a large flag, slowly fluttering near the platform, and remembered Edward's story of seeing the flag in the battle smoke. Mr. Everett's loud voice interrupted her thoughts as he spoke toward a climactic point. "... Let a nation's fervent thanks make some amends for the toils and sufferings of those who survive. Would that the heartfelt tribute could penetrate these honored graves!"

The speech then detailed the history of the summer military campaign and the Battle of Gettysburg. The orator spoke in grand terms, making what happened here sound like it belonged in the annals of history alongside famous battles. He mentioned the Confederate cavalry raid: "You need not, fellow-citizens of Gettysburg, that I should recall to you those moments of alarm and distress, precursors as they were of the more trying scenes to follow…" The campfires on the western hills, the arrival of General Buford, and details of the first day of fighting concluded with insightful words, remembering what the civilians had experienced. "To you, fellow-citizens of Gettysburg, I need not attempt to portray the anxieties of the ensuing night…you passed the weary hours of the night in painful expectation." Betsy shivered, recalling the fear she had felt when Thomas had explained how large the armies were.

Mr. Everett continued and gave a full account of the next two days of military actions, concluding his history with an acknowledgement of the providence of God. Then he spoke about the aftermath. "The tremendous losses on both sides…attest the courage and obstinacy with which the three days' battle was waged. Few of the great conflicts of modern times have cost victors and vanquished so great a sacrifice…" He told about dying soldiers and the civilians who were near them. "…But I will say, that, since this terrible war has been waged, the women of the loyal States, if never before, have entitled themselves to our highest admiration and gratitude… Yes, brothers, sisters of charity, while you bind up the wounds of poor sufferers, – the humblest, perhaps, that have shed their blood for the country, – forget not Who it is that will hereafter say to you, 'Inasmuch as ye have done it unto one of the least of these my brethren, ye have done it to me.' " Betsy thought about when she had sat with Harold when he was suffering, and how she had done it to obey God's principle. She tried to appreciate Mr. Everett's description of the past events, but she hoped he would try to explain, not just tell what she already knew.

The next part of the speech was difficult for Betsy to understand since Mr. Everett tried to define rebellion, secession, and the war politics, using grandiose examples from history. He also encouraged the reunification of the divided country.

James was bored and attempted to stand on one foot without pitching forward into the fine lady standing in front of him. Betsy tapped his shoulder, frowned, and shook her head.

"What's he talking about?" James whispered.

"I'm not exactly sure," Betsy admitted and sighed.

"He's sure been talking an awful long time…"

"Shhh…"

The orator slowed his speech and seemed to be coming to the end. "And now, friends, fellow-citizens of Gettysburg and Pennsylvania, and you from remoter states, let me again, as we part, invoke your benediction on these honored graves. You feel, though the occasion is mournful, that it is good to be here. You feel that it was greatly auspicious for the cause of the country, that the men of the East and the men of the West, the men of nineteen sister states, stood side by side, on the perilous ridges of battle. You now feel it a new bond of union, that they shall lie side by side, till a clarion, louder than that which marshaled them to the combat, shall awaken their slumbers. God bless the Union; it is dearer to us for the blood of brave men which has been shed in its defense. The spots on which they stood and fell; these pleasant heights; the fertile plain beneath them; the thriving village whose streets so lately rang with the strange din of war...the little streams which wind through the hills... Seminary Ridge, the Peach Orchard, Cemetery, Culp, and Wolf Hill, Round Top, Little Round Top, humble names, henceforward dear and famous – no lapse of time, no distance of space, shall cause you to be forgotten." He mentioned again the Ancient Greeks and a quote from one of their funeral orations, before raising his voice toward a mighty ending. "But they, I am sure, will join us in saying, as we bid farewell to the dust of these martyr-heroes, that wheresoever throughout the civilized world the accounts of this great warfare are read, and down to the last period of recorded time, in the glorious annals of our common country there will be no brighter page than that which relates The Battles of Gettysburg."

As the crowd stood in silent awe of Mr. Everett's oration, Betsy wondered about his conclusion. Did we make history? Are we part of history just because we did what we had to do? Can anyone really find glory and brightness in what happened here? Dissatisfied, she looked down, defeat sweeping over her. Mr. Everett's speech had only prompted more questions for her searching mind.

Chapter 40

Betsy did not have time to consider her uncertainties and questions. The ceremony proceeded. A Maryland singing group sang a consecration chant. Then Mr. Lamon stood and said simply, "Ladies and Gentlemen, the President of the United States."

Mr. Lincoln stood, put on his reading spectacles, and unfolded a couple sheets of paper. His voice was not fine like Mr. Everett's, but he spoke with deep sincerity.

"Four score and seven years ago our fathers brought forth on this continent, a new nation, conceived in Liberty, and dedicated to the proposition that all men are created equal.

"Now we are engaged in a great civil war, testing whether that nation, or any nation so conceived and so dedicated, can long endure. We are met on a great battle-field of that war. We have come to dedicate a portion of that field, as a final resting place for those who here gave their lives that that nation might live. It is altogether fitting and proper that we should do this.

"But, in a larger sense, we cannot dedicate – we cannot consecrate – we cannot hallow – this ground. The brave men, living and dead, who struggled here, have consecrated it, far above our poor power to add or detract. The world will little note, nor long remember what we say here, but it can never forget what they did here. It is for us the living, rather, to be dedicated here to the unfinished work which they who fought here have thus far so nobly advanced. It is rather for us to be here dedicated to the great task remaining before us – that from these honored dead we take increased devotion to that cause for which they gave the last full measure of devotion – that we here highly resolve that these dead shall not have died in vain – that this nation, under God, shall have a new birth of freedom – and that government of the people, by the people, for the people, shall not perish from the earth."

The president's speech was over, and Betsy had found the answers to her questions. In the small and narrow view, there was no purpose. Yet, looking up and to the future beyond, the dead would not have died in vain because the liberties and freedoms cherished by Americans would pass to the next generation. Edward's hope could be reality.

Freedom and blessing could not come without sacrifice and trial. Was God using this war – this Battle of Gettysburg – to prepare America for something far-reaching? "Be still and know that I am God; I will be exalted among the nations, I will be exalted in the earth."

Betsy smiled as she watched the president return quietly to his seat while the crowd cheered and applauded. She still had to trust God for the future, but she was inspired by the reminder that His ways are higher and more powerful than ours. She had her answer: the sacrifice was for the future. Betsy stood straighter, the weight of her searching questions slid away. Doubt and questions were replaced with better understanding, strengthened trust in God, and real hope.

With these new realizations, thoughts of the past were not as painful when another dirge was sung and Reverend Baugher pronounced a short benediction. The eight-gun artillery salute shattering the stillness did not seem fearsome; it was honoring the fallen heroes. As the ceremony concluded, the dignitaries left the platform slowly and prepared for the processional return to town.

It was strange. Betsy thought she should have been sad, but, for the first time in months, she felt almost carefree and could have spun around with open arms if she'd been alone. She still didn't like the war, missed Philip, and wished Edward was alive, but there was a purpose in the sorrow. She, like the soldiers buried nearby and others still in faraway camps, was willing to make sacrifices for the future...for tomorrow. There was a purpose, a reason, and she saw with clarity that God still reigned.

Caught up in the excitement around them, Frederick pulled on James's arm. "Come on, let's go see the band conductor!" They darted across the cleared aisle way.

George Thorn started to follow and then stopped as his mother gasped. He had cut in front of President Lincoln, causing him to stop and glance down at the little boy. Mrs. Thorn began to apologize.

Mr. Lincoln smiled at her, showing he was not offended. He patted George's head and gently directed him back toward his mother.

"Oh, George, do you not have any manners?" Mrs. Thorn scolded after the president departed. "You ran in front of Mr. Lincoln."

"Sorry, Mama. But he seems very nice and wasn't angry."

Mrs. Thorn smiled ruefully and said to Mother, "Well, perhaps someday he'll boast that President Lincoln patted him on the head…"

When the Westmores arrived in town, the procession had just ended. The president was holding his hat and talking with a few people while the ever-present marshals tried to escort him into Mr. Wills's house.

"Look!" Rachel exclaimed. A couple pieces of paper had tumbled from the inside of the president's hat and fluttered along the street. James and Rachel ran to collect the farther ones, and Betsy picked up the one at her feet. It looked like an old campaign speech and was dated several years previous.

"Here, you take them back to him, Betsy," Rachel directed, pushing the papers into her sister's hand.

"Um, Father…" Betsy started.

"I'll go with you, if you like." Together, they explained to one of the stern marshals what had happened, and he let them step inside Mr. Wills's house.

Mr. Lincoln was standing in the dimly lit hallway talking with Mr. Everett, but he turned when the marshal got his attention. "Yes?"

"These people have something for you."

"Mr. President, these papers fell out of your hat. My brother, sister, and I got them before they blew too far away. Here they are." She held them out, looking up at him nervously.

"Well, I'm much obliged," Mr. Lincoln said, taking the papers and tucking them in his coat pocket. "Do you live here in Gettysburg?"

"Yes, sir," Betsy replied respectfully. "We live on a farm about a mile from town." She felt a little surprised by his question and a little awed that he would take time to talk with her.

"And what's your name?" he asked in his slow, kind voice.

"Miss Betsy Westmore, and this is my father, Mr. Henry Westmore."

President Lincoln shook hands with Father, saying, "I hope your farm wasn't damaged too badly in the battle?"

"We were fortunate, sir," Father replied. "There was a field hospital at our home, but, on the whole, not as many damages as at other places."

Mr. Lincoln nodded solemnly. "Do you have a son in the army?"

"Yes, Mr. President. My son, Philip Westmore, is serving in the 138th Pennsylvania Infantry."

"I hope he will come home safely to you, Mr. Westmore."

Betsy felt a little shy, but she wanted to tell the president that his address was encouraging. When he turned back toward her, she said, "Sir, I liked your speech. It helped to answer some questions I've had for a long time about the reason for the sacrifices made by so many soldiers here."

"I'm glad, Miss Westmore," the president said, shaking her hand. "Please greet the rest of your family for me. And now, I have to go," he turned and walked toward Mr. Wills who was beckoning to him from the dining room.

"Did you really meet the president?" James asked when Father and Betsy rejoined the family. Betsy nodded excitedly.

"Oh, I'm so happy for you," Rachel exclaimed, giving her sister a quick hug.

"What a special experience!" Mother said. "Did he seem nice?"

"Yes," Betsy said, feeling a little dazed. She had really met the president of the United States, talked casually with him, and returned his missing papers.

"He seems like a kindhearted person," Father remarked. "He asked if I had a son with the army and hoped the farm hadn't been destroyed."

Mother looked surprised. "That was considerate. I would not have supposed the president would have taken time to ask such questions."

They stayed in town for several hours, enjoyed a couple of band performances, and saw President Lincoln walk to a patriotic meeting with Mr. John Burns, the old man who had gone out to fight the Rebels.

It was late afternoon when the Westmores walked down the Baltimore Pike toward their home. Cannons and soldiers were gone; questions were answered. The Gettysburg world seemed peaceful once again. Warm light held back the shadows in the quiet setting. Birds warbled in the trees. The harvested fields rested, waiting for winter and coming spring. The house stood, sturdy and welcoming. Some fences still needed repair, yet home looked normal and comfortable once again.

Mother and the girls prepared a simple meal. Rachel set the table with the new embroidered linens from Allison. Betsy sliced the fresh bread, baked the previous morning. Placing the bread basket on the table, Betsy glanced out the west window, thinking of how she had fearfully watched for Confederates so many months before. The clock's ticking echoed in the peaceful silence.

"The horses are good," James announced, coming in from helping with the barn chores. "But, they're disappointed they didn't get to see their friends."

"What friends?" Rachel asked, confused.

"Oh, the other cavalry horses," he replied matter-of-factly. "Those cavalrymen in town looked pretty fine, don't you think? I just hope they stay safe in battles."

"Go wash up for supper, James," Mother directed, smiling at her son's enthusiasm. "Betsy, why don't you pour water to drink? We'll be ready to eat soon."

The water pitcher and the bucket were empty. "I'll have to get some, Mother," Betsy explained, going outside. She pumped the water at the well and started back, walking carefully to avoid spilling it on her new dress.

Betsy glanced at the now peaceful yard, barn, and house. The new horses stood in the paddock, and the young chickens scratched in the pen near the henhouse. The Confederate raiders were no longer feared, the operating tables and wounded were gone, and even some of the graves in the orchard had been removed.

She shook her head, thinking about all that had happened in the last five months. Fragments of scenes and colors swirled: blue coats, gray blankets, crimson streams. Who could have thought so much heartache, suffering, sincere prayers, good memories, and precious smiles could be twisted into their lives in so short an amount of time? But that was the past. A past of sacrifice paving the way for a future of continuing liberty and national unity.

Betsy smiled as she looked at the heavens. The remnants of the sunset glowed in the western sky with the faintest hint of blue and crimson. "We've seen His strength and providence," Betsy whispered. "In all those times, it was true," she said with a smile. " 'The Lord of Hosts is with us, The God of Jacob is our refuge.' "

Author's Historical Notes

Though the Westmores are a fictional family, many of their experiences are based on those of real historical families who lived in the Gettysburg area. Their farm is also fictional; to the best of my knowledge, the real location of the Westmore farm would have been on part of James McAllister's land.

I have done my best to ensure the historical authenticity of the story and spent many months researching the Battle of Gettysburg, the military commanders and regiments, the aftermath of the fighting, and the civilians' accounts. Some parts of the story have been told carefully to keep the content suitable for young readers.

Sometimes, I included or mentioned real historical people who lived in Gettysburg or who were with the armies. I have researched these people and worked to portray them accurately and respectfully in the pages of this story. At the end of this section, there is a list containing the names of the real historical characters and military units mentioned in the story in the order of their appearance.

For additional historical information about the people and setting of this story, please visit my website and blog:
www.Gazette665.com

Governor Andrew Curtain

General Robert E. Lee

President Abraham Lincoln

General Jubal Early

138th Pennsylvania Infantry

Mr. Spangler

Mr. Wolfe

Eliza Thorn

Peter Thorn

Frederick Thorn

George Thorn

John Thorn

Gates Fahnestock

Charles McCurdy

Nathaniel Lightner

James McAllister

George Sandoe

Tillie Pierce

Mr. Pierce

Mrs. Pierce

Miss Eyster

Mr. Winter

Mr. Buehler

Mrs. Buehler

Hugh Scott

Joseph Broadhead

Mr. Masser

Mrs. Masser

87th Pennsylvania Infantry

Skelly boys

Shield boys

5th Michigan Cavalry

6th Michigan Cavalry

Dan Skelly

Albertus McCreary

Mr. Schick

Captain John Myers

John Burns

Sheriff Samuel Wolfe

Deputy Zachariah Myers

Colonel William Gamble

General John Buford

Grey Eagle (John Buford's horse)

17th Pennsylvania Cavalry

General Winfield S. Hancock

General John F. Reynolds

General Oliver O. Howard

General George Meade

First Corps, USA

Second Corps, USA

Third Corps, USA

Fifth Corps, USA

Sixth Corps, USA

Eleventh Corps, USA

Twelfth Corps, USA

First Corps, CSA

Second Corps, CSA

Third Corps, CSA

27th Indiana Infantry

10th Virginia Infantry

2nd Massachusetts Infantry

US Christian Commission

US Sanitary Commission

Virginia Wade

Mrs. Shriver

1st Minnesota Infantry

Colonel Colvill

Laura Bergstresser

Anna Garlach

Mrs. Garlach

Sarah Broadhead

Georgeana Woolsey

Mr. Olmstead

Jane Eliza Newton Woolsey

Colonel Blood

Jonathan Letterman

Mr. Garlach

Provost Marshall M. Patrick

David Wills

Mrs. Anna Holstein

Samuel Weaver

Edward Everett

Rosa Meade Thorn

The Marine Corps Band

Mr. Seward

2nd US Cavalry

Reverend Stockton

Ward Lamon

Reverend Baugher

Acknowledgements

As I've worked on this exciting project of writing and publishing a book, I've been blessed to have many encouraging people around me. I'd like to personally thank and acknowledge the people who have helped make the completion of this project possible.

A huge "Thank You" to my editing and proof-reading team: Susan Bierle, Beth Esposito, Nathan Bierle, Shawn Bierle, Emily Rascon, Robert Rasband, and Josiah Bierle. You're awesome! I appreciated the feedback (and suggestions for improvements).

Cheryl Schoenberger – thank you for catching the vision of the book and bringing it to life on canvas for the original cover artwork.

Ted McCord – I'm grateful for your friendship with my family and how you've encouraged me to always study and love history. It's so special that you wrote the foreword for my first book!

Stephanie Huffman – I appreciate your advice and wisdom as I've been learning about the publishing process. Thanks for taking time to answer my questions and recommend helpful resources.

Gettysburg National Military Park Library – many thanks to the library staff for sending me copies of the primary and secondary sources about the area near Rock Creek, the local churches, and town civilians. The information in those documents was very helpful.

I'd like to thank my friends and acquaintances in the Civil War Re-enacting/Living History community. You kept me inspired, and you have no idea how my experiences in the field with y'all have contributed to this story.

About the Author

Sarah Kay Bierle, a historian, writer, and living history enthusiast, has wanted to write books ever since she penned a first sketch of this novel when she was nine years old. Eleven years later, after much planning and prayer, she began to completely re-write the original story, drawing on months of research to achieve historical accuracy.

Sarah was homeschooled K-12, completed an accelerated distance learning program for college, and graduated from Thomas Edison State College with a BA in History. Sarah believes in reading good literature and participating in hands-on learning to supplement traditional studying; she is grateful to her parents for allowing her to explore and learn. Her love of knowledge and teaching has prompted her to become involved in living history and blogging, where she shares her belief that "history is about real people, real actions, and real effects, and it should inspire us today."

When not researching or writing, Sarah enjoys spending time with her parents and siblings, volunteering, playing music, quilting, or visiting with close friends. She desires to share a message of hope in Christ through her daily life and her writing.

To order books,
find historical resources,
or contact the author,
please visit:

www.Gazette665.com

CPSIA information can be obtained
at www.ICGtesting.com
Printed in the USA
FSOW04n0354271015
12551FS